GALENA HOUSE

Still, by Design.

a novel

AVERY LANE MAXWELL

Publisher: Galena House Publishing Frisco, Colorado

First Edition Printed in the United States of America

ISBN: 979-8-9937250-2-4

For more information, visit: averylanemaxwell.com friscoinnongalena.com

GH (Galena House) and the Galena House Publishing imprint are trademarks used by Avery Lane Maxwell.

For Me. For the version of myself who kept going, even when he didn't know where home was.

xoxo

ACKNOWLEDGMENTS

This book is for those who have walked beside me, in ways both seen and unseen.

To my Mama, whose love and strength still echo in everything I do — I carry you with me always, the very heart of who I am. To Bruce, for sharing your beautiful creation with me and welcoming me into your world of possibility. To Mandy & Jeremy, for grounding me at the end of each day — your steadfastness is the soil I stand on. To Jon, whose heart knows no limits, and whose quiet generosity touches everything he does. And to Grandmama, whose wisdom still guides me — I carry it with me, always, and I feel you with every step.

Minnie: Thank you for believing in me, when I couldn't believe in myself.

CHAPTER ONE
THE CARETAKER

———

HE MOVED THROUGH THE INN THE WAY SOME PEOPLE MOVE through prayer—slow, deliberate, attentive. The hour held its breath, as if even the walls knew not to interrupt.

At dawn, the light came soft and diffused through the east windows, turning the air into floating threads of gold. Elias never turned on the overheads this early; he liked the way the day revealed itself gradually, like it was learning to trust him again. The floors glowed where a century of footsteps had burnished them smooth. The scent of roasted beans lingered in the air—his own careful handiwork from the night before— earthy, bitter, alive.

The old wood of the banister was warm to the touch even before sunrise, as if it remembered every hand that had steadied itself there. The building had that kind of memory: quiet, loyal, forgiving. Sometimes, when he was alone like this, Elias felt it breathe with him—wood expanding, pipes humming, radiators whispering warmth. It was an intimacy that existed only before the first knock at the counter, before footsteps disturbed the rhythm.

He liked this hour best: before the guests stirred, before the kitchen clattered awake. The silence belonged to him alone.

He began his ritual—checking the espresso machine, wiping down the marble, setting two demitasse cups on the tray though he only ever used one. Routine had become devotion, and in devotion, he found order. Each gesture meant something. The rag smoothing the counter was forgiveness. The second cup was hope. The hiss of the first pull rose like incense, curling through the half-light. The scent reminded him that something beautiful could still be coaxed from the burnt, the crushed, the ground-down.

He leaned on the counter, waiting for the first pour to steady. Steam rose and caught the morning light like breath turning visible. The coffee settled, rich and dark, its surface trembling before stilling completely. Elias liked that moment—the exact second between movement and rest.

Outside, the world began to wake: the stream rushing behind the building, the faint echo of boots on icy sidewalks, a gull's lonely cry slicing through the mountain air. A thin line of smoke rose from the bakery chimney across Galena Street, carrying the first scent of sugar and heat.

He took a sip—hot, bitter, grounding. The kind of bitterness that made sense.

Some mornings, he thought of his old life—the blur of faces and endless motion he once mistook for purpose. The cities where silence felt dangerous, where he couldn't hear his own thoughts over the noise. A decade ago, mornings had meant survival, not stillness. Now, purpose meant care.

The grinder stopped. He poured a second shot, though he didn't need it. August would tease him later for drinking both, but Elias liked the symmetry of it—the quiet satisfaction of two small cups facing one another across the tray. Maybe it was preparedness. Maybe it was waiting.

He crossed the lobby, his footsteps echoing softly against the cedar floors. The Inn seemed to breathe with him—the faint hum of the baseboards, the steady pulse of the heater, the scent of wood oil rising from the polished railings. The chandeliers above flickered in slow rhythm, their imperfect glow somehow truer than any steady light.

On the bookshelf near the piano, a copy of The Alchemist lay facedown, a guest's late-night read left open like an offering. Elias smiled faintly. Everything is written, he thought. He'd read that line years ago, before he believed in signs.

Now, he wasn't so sure.

He knew every creak, every flicker, every imperfection of this place. The stair that moaned like an old violin. The key that never fit the office door quite right. Even the slightly off-pitch piano—it was all part of the Inn's rhythm, its music of wear.

He reached the front windows just as the first light spilled over Mount Royal. The peaks were pale and unguarded, dusted in early snow. The town below still looked half-asleep —chimneys breathing smoke, bakery lights flickering on, a dog trotting beside a bundled jogger. Beyond that, the mountain held its calm authority, silent but impossibly alive.

He pressed his palm to the cold glass. The mountain's air seeped through faint cracks, and it felt almost like touch—the mountain reminding him: You are here. You are still here.

"I know," he whispered.

The words left no mark, but he felt them settle anyway.

By seven, the Inn began to stir. Lavender oil drifted from the spa below, carried upward through the vents, mixing with the smell of butter and baking scones. Doors thudded upstairs, voices murmured, a faucet turned. A kettle sang softly in the distance.

Elias smiled. The quiet hour had ended, and with it, his solitude—but he didn't mind. The silence had done its work.

He returned to the kitchen, tying his apron. The espresso cups clinked gently on the tray. The morning light reached deeper into the room now, turning the marble counter to a muted river of gold. His heart felt both heavy and light—that strange ache that came from caring for something that wasn't entirely his but depended on him all the same.

On the front desk, the ledger lay open to a fresh page. In the corner, August's handwriting waited for him:

Remember: beauty's in the doing.

Elias touched the edge of the page, tracing the curve of each letter with his fingertip. He didn't know if August wrote that for him or for himself. But either way, he needed it.

———

B Y THE TIME THE CLOCK IN THE LIBRARY CHIMED HALF-PAST SEVEN, the Inn had slipped into motion — slow, organic, inevitable.

The first door opened upstairs, followed by another. A shower hissed to life, water striking tile like applause. From the kitchen, the faint clatter of metal joined the morning symphony — spoons against porcelain, the hum of the refrigerator, the patient heartbeat of the espresso machine reawakening.

Elias moved among it all without hurry. He refilled the cream pitcher, folded napkins into neat thirds, checked the pastry tray even though he'd already checked it twice. The scones were perfect: golden edges, soft centers, sugar crystals glinting in the light.

He loved the transition between stillness and life — the way sound returned to the building like blood returning to a limb.

Outside, a delivery truck idled near the curb, the driver hauling a crate of milk up the back stairs. Elias met him halfway, offered a nod, exchanged a few words about the weather. It had snowed higher on the pass overnight; the peaks were brighter, their edges sharpened by cold.

"Going to be a good day for skiers," the driver said.

Elias smiled. "Good day for coffee too."

When he came back inside, warmth met him like an embrace. He paused a moment, letting his body readjust to the softer air. The Inn's wooden bones creaked quietly in approval.

From the hall came the light tread of footsteps — deliberate, unhurried.

"Morning," August said.

He appeared in the doorway with his sleeves rolled, the faintest trace of flour dusted along one wrist. His hair was still damp from the shower, curling slightly at the edges. He carried a kind of calm that didn't come from rest but from acceptance.

"Morning," Elias said. "You beat the sunrise again."

August smiled. "You left it no choice. Coffee?"

"Already waiting."

Elias handed him the second cup — the one he always poured but never expected anyone to claim. August accepted it without ceremony, took a slow sip, and exhaled like someone greeting an old friend.

"Good pull," he said.

Elias leaned on the counter, watching the light crawl up the wall. "It's better when it's quiet."

August nodded. "Everything is."

For a while, they didn't speak. The Inn didn't need them to. The heater ticked softly; the aroma of baked sugar filled the air. Outside, a jay shrieked from the aspens, breaking the stillness for just a heartbeat before silence reclaimed it.

August set his cup down. "You ever think about how much faith it takes to run a place like this?"

Elias looked up, surprised. "Faith?"

"Every day, people walk through those doors expecting warmth, comfort, beauty — and we give it. Even on the days we don't have much to give ourselves."

Elias smiled faintly. "That's not faith. That's work."

August chuckled. "Same thing, if you do it long enough."

He crossed the room to open the side window, letting in a draft of pine-scented air. The morning light widened, gold and forgiving.

Elias glanced at the counter — the ledger open, cups waiting, pastries aligned — and felt that small flicker of satisfaction that came from readiness.

A bell chimed at the front door.

"First one," August said, brushing his hands on his apron.

Elias nodded. "Let's open the day."

The first guest was a young woman with a red scarf and a camera slung across her chest. She smelled faintly of cold air and curiosity.

"Good morning!" she said brightly, eyes scanning the shelves, the fireplace, the walls crowded with framed maps. "This place is unreal."

Elias smiled — the soft, professional kind that made people feel seen without being spotlighted. "Welcome to the Inn on Galena. Breakfast's just through there."

She looked around again, as if the air itself was worth photographing. "You must love it here."

Elias paused. "I do," he said, and it was true in a way that surprised him.

When she disappeared toward the dining room, August raised an eyebrow. "You handled that like a sermon."

"Habit," Elias said, but he was smiling now.

More guests arrived — a couple from Denver who always stayed in Room 205, an older man who greeted August by name, two friends still laughing from the drive up. The space filled with warmth and the gentle chaos of plates and greetings.

Through it all, Elias kept his rhythm. Refill. Wipe. Pour. Listen.

He noticed the small things: the way the morning light shifted from pale amber to honey as it climbed; the way the mountain wind rattled the chimney flue; the way people leaned in closer to one another when the world outside was cold.

It wasn't loud, but it was alive.

He glanced up once and caught his reflection in the glass of the pastry case — sleeves rolled, jaw set, eyes clear. For the first time in years, the man looking back at him didn't seem like a stranger.

Around nine, when the first rush had thinned, August leaned against the counter beside him. "You ever miss it?" he asked.

"Miss what?"

"Whatever came before all this."

Elias took a slow breath. "Sometimes. But only the parts that didn't survive."

August studied him. "That's a good answer."

"It's an honest one."

The clock ticked quietly in the background.

Outside, Frisco was waking in full. Ski shuttles passed, children laughed, and the sun had climbed high enough to lay a soft brightness over the Inn's porch. A jogger ran by, breath clouding the air. Elias recognized the rhythm in his stride — that familiar persistence that used to drive him, too.

He wondered, briefly, if he'd run later — maybe up toward Rainbow Lake, just far enough to remember what distance feels like.

For now, though, there was work. And warmth. And the soft ache of belonging to a place that gave more than it asked.

— · —

BY MIDMORNING, THE INN HAD FOUND ITS TEMPO.
The dining room was a low hum of conversation and clinking cutlery, sunlight filtering through gauzy curtains that swayed with each sigh of mountain air. The scent of scones,

citrus, and coffee blended into something wordless but complete.

Elias moved through it like current — quiet, steady, invisible until you looked for him. A refill here, a folded napkin there, a soft greeting murmured just before it was needed. He'd learned that most hospitality was about timing: not presence, but permission.

"Can we get a little more cream?" a guest asked, her voice gentle but tired.

Elias was already at her elbow with the pitcher. "Of course."

She blinked in surprise, then smiled, as if she'd been remembered by the universe. He liked that reaction — not the gratitude, but the ease that followed.

The Traveler sat in the corner by the bookshelf, their notebook open, pen hovering above the page. They'd been here three mornings now, always alone, always observant. Sometimes they wrote; other times they simply watched, as if the world might offer an answer if they were still enough.

"Can I top that off for you?" Elias asked.

They looked up, eyes bright but tired. "Thank you. I was hoping you'd ask."

He poured slowly, careful not to spill. "You working on something?"

"A story, maybe," they said. "Or a prayer disguised as one."

Elias smiled faintly. "This is a good place for either."

They nodded, glancing toward the windows. "It feels designed for remembering."

He didn't know what to say to that, so he just refilled the sugar jar and moved on.

In the kitchen, August was kneading dough, the steady rhythm of his hands matching the beat of the Inn's pulse. The flour dust hung in sunlight like morning fog.

"Full house tonight," he said without looking up.

"Good," Elias replied. "The energy feels right."

"Energy," August repeated, amused. "You sound like my sister. She used to say houses have moods."

"They do," Elias said. "This one forgives easily."

August laughed, the sound low and honest. "Maybe it just likes you better."

Elias wiped his hands on a towel and leaned against the counter. "I think it likes being cared for."

"Same thing," August said, glancing up with that half-smile that always meant he was about to say something true. "Everything alive responds to attention. Even us."

Elias looked toward the dining room, where sunlight dappled over the wood floor and guests laughed softly into their cups. "Then we're in the right line of work."

By noon, the guests had dispersed into town — boots crunching on snow, jackets rustling, doors clicking shut behind them. The silence that followed was the best kind: earned.

Elias exhaled, stretching his shoulders. He opened the back door, letting in a rush of cold air that carried pine sap and woodsmoke. The mountains stood sharp and blue under a sky so clear it hurt to look at.

He stepped outside for a moment, coffee cup in hand, and leaned against the railing. The street below was quiet. Across the way, the bakery owner waved from her doorway, flour up to her elbows. Elias lifted his cup in salute.

For a heartbeat, the world felt suspended — perfect, ordinary, whole.

He thought of how long it had taken to feel this kind of peace again — the quiet that wasn't empty, the stillness that didn't demand escape.

He had run for years — from cities, from noise, from himself. But here, standing in the crisp mountain air, he felt no urge to move.

The Inn, the town, the morning — all of it breathed with him.

Inside, he gathered dishes from the last table, wiping away crumbs that glittered like sugar in the sunlight. The Traveler had left a page of their notebook open, a single line written neatly across it:

Some places heal you by watching you live.

He smiled, tucking the note back where it had been.

From the back of the kitchen came August's voice: "You heading out for your run?"

Elias shook his head. "Not yet. I think I'll just breathe for a while."

August appeared in the doorway, holding a mug of tea. "That's a kind of running too."

They shared a look — the kind born of quiet understanding rather than words — and then the day continued, unfolding the way only good days do: without hurry, without demand, each moment small and deliberate as breath.

—∼—

Afternoon into Evening

—∼—

B Y EARLY AFTERNOON, THE LIGHT HAD CHANGED. IT FELL THROUGH the lobby windows in long, honeyed shafts, painting the air in warm geometry. The Inn always looked softer at this hour—like a living thing turning its face toward rest.

Elias had opened the front doors to let the scent of the mountain in: pine and snowmelt, the faint tang of cold stone. The heater hummed less now, replaced by the distant hush of wind coming down from the ridge.

On the piano, a record spun lazily through Malibu Nights— low enough to be almost imagined. He liked it that way, music as texture rather than event. The room seemed to pulse with it, a slow vibration under everything.

He polished the glasses behind the counter, one at a time, not because they needed it but because stillness demanded its own small tasks. Each reflection bent the light differently: prisms of movement, small proofs of care.

He reached for one of the champagne flutes from the top shelf—the pair reserved for Room 205's anniversary guests. They'd be checking in later that afternoon, the couple who returned every winter, always requesting the same corner room with the mountain view. He didn't know their names by heart, but he knew their laughter, their way of holding hands without thinking about it.

He breathed on the glass and buffed it to a perfect shine. Outside, the snow had begun to melt on the edges of the porch, water glinting like spilled mercury.

The music shifted—LANY again, the chorus humming softly: "I hope it's okay for me to say it..."

The lyric landed in him like a pulse. There were days when he could feel every word between the lines—what was said, what stayed quiet, what forgiveness sounded like when no one was listening.

He smiled faintly. "It's okay," he murmured to no one.

The afternoon drifted. Guests came and went; the rhythm of the Inn expanded and contracted like breath.

A young couple returned from the slopes, faces flushed with cold and laughter. Elias met them at the door with towels warmed by the radiator. "Hot cocoa in five," he said, and the woman's grateful nod felt like sunlight itself.

The Traveler was still in the corner, notebook open, pen resting motionless between their fingers. They'd been sitting there long enough for the light to move across their pages, from gold to rose to amber. Elias noticed that sometimes they wrote, and other times they just listened—to footsteps, to the wind pressing at the windows, to the sound of August's quiet whistle from the kitchen.

"Do you ever get tired of the quiet?" the Traveler asked when he passed by with the tray.

Elias shook his head. "No. It's what gives the noise its meaning."

The Traveler smiled as if that answer would end up in their notebook later.

By late afternoon, the Inn settled into that half-silence before dinner: the hush between the day's fullness and the evening's soft undoing.

Elias stepped outside again. The air had cooled, the mountain shadow stretching long across town. Down the hill,

Frisco stirred gently—shop doors closing, someone tuning a guitar on the corner near the lake path, the scent of bread from the bakery mingling with woodsmoke.

He leaned on the porch railing, coffee cup in hand, and let the breeze move through him. Somewhere in the distance, the creek caught a slant of fading light, turning the water to fire for a brief moment.

He closed his eyes and listened. The sound of wind through pine needles, the faint rustle of a flag somewhere near Main Street, the steady rhythm of his own heartbeat—all of it folded into a kind of music that needed no melody.

When he opened his eyes, the town had softened under the dusk. The lights along Galena flickered on, one by one, like slow confessions.

He turned to go inside.

The evening returned him to warmth. The fireplace was lit now, the air thick with the scent of cedar smoke and baking sugar. August moved behind the bar, pouring tea for an older couple, his voice low and kind. The chandelier light flickered gold against the wine glasses.

"Room 205's ready," August said when Elias passed by. "You set the tray?"

Elias nodded. "Two flutes. Local sparkling cider. I polished them twice."

August smiled. "You always do."

He leaned against the counter, drying his hands on a towel. "You know," he said after a moment, "there's something about this hour. When the guests start to settle and the air gets heavy with stories."

Elias glanced at him. "You think houses can listen?"

August tilted his head, amused. "I think the good ones never stop."

He looked around the room, at the guests laughing softly, the flicker of candles, the steady hum of conversation blending with the wind outside. "Maybe that's why this one's lasted. It remembers the quiet."

Elias smiled. "Then we're in the right place."

Later, when the guests had drifted upstairs and the record player clicked off, Elias returned to the window. The moon had risen behind Mount Royal, throwing a pale shimmer across the snow. The town was still, the kind of stillness that feels like holding your breath.

He leaned his forehead against the glass. His reflection layered itself over the night—the outline of a man who had run too far and finally stopped.

Somewhere behind him, August hummed a tune under his breath, the same one Elias had caught himself humming days before. The sound wove through the quiet like a thread of light.

He closed his eyes. The Inn breathed with him.

Evening Close

NIGHT ARRIVED GENTLY, LIKE A GUEST WHO'D STAYED BEFORE AND knew where everything belonged.

The last of the twilight pooled in the corners of the lobby, where the shadows deepened to a soft blue. Elias dimmed the sconces, one by one, until the firelight became the only pulse in the room. The crackle was steady, content. Outside, snow had begun to fall again—fine, weightless flakes tumbling through the halo of the porch light.

He stood near the hearth, sleeves rolled, apron hung neatly on its hook. The glow brushed against his skin, catching the faint sheen of exertion that lingered from the day. He was lean in the way mountain air makes a person—defined not by vanity but by rhythm: early mornings, steady labor, breath that came honest. His arms bore the quiet shape of strength rebuilt from care rather than pride.

His features softened in the firelight. The sharp line of his jaw, the freckle near his temple, the kind of smile that didn't appear often but lingered when it did. His hair, still damp from a late shower, curled slightly beneath the brim of a gray cap. There was something unassuming about him—like he was always on the verge of disappearing into the work he loved.

Yet, the Inn saw him. The light seemed to settle differently when he was near, as though the place recognized its keeper.

He leaned over the counter, writing the final notes of the day into the ledger: Fireplace logs restocked. Room 205— anniversary tray delivered. Guests content.

He paused, pen hovering. Beneath it, he wrote one last line: Still here.

The words looked small but steady on the page.

From somewhere above, a floorboard creaked—a guest turning over in their sleep. The sound felt tender, proof of life continuing.

Elias walked to the window. The street was nearly empty now, the bakery dark, the snow laying itself down in slow, patient layers. He could see his reflection in the glass—firelight behind him, winter beyond. His eyes caught the faintest trace of wonder, the kind that comes from realizing how much can still be rebuilt.

Behind him, the fire sighed and settled lower.

He touched the glass lightly, as if testing the line between two worlds. "Progress," he whispered, "not perfection."

And for the first time in a long while, he believed it.

—— ~ ——

Nightfall

—— ~ ——

THE INN SLEPT, BUT ELIAS DID NOT.

He moved softly through the hallways, the floorboards murmuring under his steps, a lullaby the house seemed to hum only for him. Outside, snow whispered against the windows — small, rhythmic, patient. The fire in the hearth had gone to embers, but their glow still held warmth enough to paint the walls in trembling gold.

He carried a mug of tea through the empty lounge, past the piano, past the framed photograph of the Inn from fifty years ago. The image always made him pause — the building the same, but the people changed. Smiling faces frozen in a moment that had already passed. He wondered what they had dreamed of, what they'd run from, and whether they ever found the stillness he was chasing.

He sat by the window. The night outside was so clear that the stars seemed close enough to touch. Each breath clouded faintly against the glass before fading back into transparency.

For a long while, he said nothing, thought nothing — he simply existed in the hum between heartbeats.

It had taken years to find peace in quiet moments like this. To stop fearing silence. To understand that it didn't mean absence — it meant presence. That kind of learning didn't come easily. It was a lesson taught by sobriety, by solitude, by the ritual of beginning again each day.

He looked down at his hands — steady now, strong in their small imperfections. The faint mark from an old burn on his wrist. The callus from polishing glassware. The healed scar near his thumb. All proof of what staying looked like.

The tea had cooled, but he drank it anyway.

When he rose, the moonlight caught him in motion — shoulders still lean, posture still sure, the quiet strength of someone who'd learned to live inside the moment rather than outrun it.

Upstairs, the guest rooms were silent except for a faint murmur — someone talking in their sleep, a laugh caught in a dream. He smiled at the sound, as if the Inn itself were whispering secrets back to him.

He passed Room 205, the faint scent of lavender still curling from beneath the door, and paused at the top of the stairs. The air was cool, the mountain breathing faintly through the old wooden frame of the building.

He closed his eyes and listened:

The ticking of the grandfather clock. The faint hum of the pipes. The world turning quietly beyond the walls.

He felt it all — the weight of the night, the grace of his small survival, the soft promise of morning already gathering beyond the ridge.

Just before dawn, he finally returned to his own room.

The bed was neatly made, as if waiting for him to admit he was tired. He placed his watch and bracelet on the nightstand, both glinting faintly in the dim light, and sat at the edge of the bed. For a moment, he rubbed the back of his neck — that familiar ache that never fully went away, the echo of days spent lifting, running, caring, repeating.

He smiled to himself. Progress, not perfection.

Through the window, the first faint blush of morning began to bloom — pale rose spilling into silver, the sky shifting like a living breath.

He thought of the guests who would wake soon, of the smell of espresso waiting, of the small world he'd built through attention and care.

He thought, too, of the boy he used to be — the one who had run from everything that hurt, who thought healing meant escape.

And then, quietly, he whispered into the fading dark:

"You're home."

CHAPTER TWO

THE AFTERNOON

———

G

BY MIDDAY, THE INN SHIFTED ITS WEIGHT. THE HUM OF MORNING gave way to the loosened rhythm of lived-in hours. Guests lingered over scones and fruit, laughter soft and easy, the smell of espresso and brown sugar thick in the air.

The stereo near the kitchen window hummed faintly— LANY's Malibu Nights threading through the room like sunlight through gauze. Elias always played it low, so you had to lean in to hear the words.

I'm lonely, I'm lonely, I'm lonely too.

The song wove through the dining room, brushing against the hush of conversation. A couple swayed slightly in their seats; a teenager by the fire traced patterns in her glass. Elias stood behind the counter, polishing cups that didn't need polishing, the melody tugging something soft from under his ribs.

He'd once told August that some songs didn't heal wounds —they kept them open just long enough to let the light in.

A timer chimed from the kitchen, breaking the spell. Cinnamon and butter unfurled through the air, folding into lemon polish and faint lavender from the spa. He smiled, thinking of the guests who'd wander down later, soothed by the same scent he'd mixed by hand—trial and tenderness, equal parts.

The phone rang. Elias answered with that easy hospitality that lived in his bones. "Good afternoon, Frisco Inn," he said. "This is Elias."

"You sound exactly like the website promised," said a woman's voice—lilting, amused.

He laughed, genuine. "That's the nicest thing anyone's said to me today."

They spoke briefly—directions, reservations, small talk that mattered more than it seemed. When he hung up, August passed by balancing a tray of pastries, raising an eyebrow that said don't get too comfortable. Elias answered with a quiet grin. They moved in rhythm—no need for words, the kind of familiarity that feels like music.

By one, the lunch crowd thinned. A guest sketched the mountain in the corner; the Traveler wrote quietly in Plato's nook. The Inn pulsed with its own heartbeat—the tick of pipes, the scrape of chair legs, the slow fade of another LANY song, Thick and Thin.

August reappeared with two cups of tea. "Drink," he said. "You look like you're trying to outrun your pulse."

Elias smiled. "Green jasmine. You always know."

"It's a gift," August said dryly. "How's our guest?"

"Quiet. But not in the lonely way. In the listening way."

August's eyes softened. "The best kind."

They stood in that easy quiet—the kind that makes space for breath. Another song drifted in, softer now. I Don't Wanna Love You Anymore.

Elias caught his reflection in the espresso machine. There was someone steadier in that mirror, someone who belonged to a place but not yet to himself.

"You've found your rhythm," August said.

"Or it's found me."

"That's usually how it happens."

Elias didn't answer, but what he thought was this: Every afternoon at the Inn feels like a heartbeat I don't have to remember to keep.

---~---

Evening Close

---~---

BY DUSK, THE INN HAD GROWN REVERENT—THE WAY A CATHEDRAL grows quiet after the last hymn fades. Cinnamon lingered in the corners, lavender in the vents. The last notes of Malibu Nights trembled before surrendering to silence.

Elias stood at the bar, watching the amber light bend across polished wood. Guests had gone upstairs; a half-eaten scone sat abandoned on a plate. He collected it gently, the way one handles memory.

August appeared in the doorway, towel over his shoulder, sleeves rolled. His expression was the same as always—half-tired, half-content.

"You're still here," he said.

Elias smiled. "Where else would I go?"

"That's not what I meant."

"I know."

They fell into rhythm—August washing, Elias drying. The water ran warm; the house hummed around them like a familiar instrument.

"You've done well today," August said. "Feels balanced."

"It's the guests," Elias said. "They bring symmetry when they settle in. Like the building exhales through them."

"Maybe that's what a good day is," August said. "When everything exhales at once."

Elias paused, drying a glass. "Do you ever think it's too perfect?"

August laughed. "You sound like someone who's never cleaned a drain."

"I mean it. This place... it's designed too well. Like it knows what we need before we do."

"Maybe that's not design, Elias. Maybe that's grace."

The word settled in him—quiet, weighted, understood without knowing why.

Outside, twilight rolled down the mountain, painting the street indigo. The lamps along Galena flickered alive, their glow stretching across the path like little invitations to rest.

"Remember when I told you I faked it well?" Elias asked.

"I remember. I didn't believe you then either."

"I think I meant it. But maybe now I don't have to."

"No one stays the same here," August said. "The Inn doesn't allow it."

Rain began to patter against the windows. Upstairs, the Traveler's footsteps paced a soft rhythm. The Inn breathed with them all.

"Come on," August said. "Let's lock up before the mountain starts singing again."

Elias smiled. "You think it does that?"

"I think everything alive makes music when it's listened to long enough."

He turned off the last light. For a moment, the room went still. Then—from the stereo, faint and ghostlike—a single piano note. Elias couldn't tell if it was real or something the house had remembered.

He let it linger.

And the house breathed out the rest of the note, slow, the way it let go of everything—gently, and in its own time.

And the day folded itself perfectly into night.

The Quiet Unraveling

THE MORNING BEGAN AS THEY ALL DID: LIGHT SIFTING THROUGH THE lace of frost on the window, steam rising from the first cup, the low hum of the espresso machine filling the air like a prelude. Elias stood behind the counter, watching the crema bloom — golden, slow — and felt something faint shift inside him. The silence, once his favorite companion, carried a new weight today.

The Inn was immaculate. Too immaculate. Every cup aligned, every towel folded, every scent of cedar and citrus perfectly in tune — and yet something in him faltered.

He exhaled through his nose, steady, practiced, but the rhythm caught.

Routine had been his salvation once. Now, it began to hum like a song he'd played too many times.

He carried the tray to the lounge, the mountain's light stretching long through the windows. The first guests would soon descend — cheerful, chattering, full of the ease he'd once wanted for himself. But today, he felt the distance between their laughter and his stillness.

He picked up a glass cloth, started polishing the champagne flutes for Room 205 — a couple celebrating their tenth anniversary. They'd ordered sparkling cider, not wine, after Elias had told them he didn't drink. "Still celebratory," he'd said with a grin. The woman smiled in quiet understanding.

He could still hear the echo of her voice now: "Then here's to staying awake in the world."

The glass caught the light, scattering small fragments of morning across the bar. LANY's "Malibu Nights" hummed faintly from the old stereo, just the line he always heard differently: "I hope it's okay for me to say it..."

The lyric seemed to linger, unfinished.

He stopped, glass in hand, listening. For a moment, it felt like the world had tilted slightly — like something in the rhythm of the Inn was off. A pulse missing.

Alyssa's voice floated through his memory: "When it starts feeling too quiet, Eli, that's usually when something's waiting to speak."

He closed his eyes, steadying himself with the slow, grounding breath that had become his ritual. Inhale. Exhale. Count to four.

When he opened them, the glass had left a faint ring of light on the counter — circular, perfect, temporary.

Outside, the sky had turned that particular shade of gray that meant snow was coming. Guests left for the slopes wrapped in scarves and hope. Elias tidied, counted keys, adjusted the vase on the check-in desk for no reason other than to move something.

He wasn't sad — not exactly. It was more like a hunger without shape.

The Inn, for all its warmth, could turn too quiet after everyone left. It was the kind of silence that asked questions. The kind that reminded you of your own pulse.

He made himself a second espresso. It didn't help.

He opened The Alchemist to the page where he kept Alyssa's letter, the one written on linen paper, creased at the corners from too many readings. He didn't even have to unfold it — he knew the words by heart.

"You don't owe the world joy every day, Eli. Just truth. Joy will come find you when it's ready."

He closed the book, but the ache stayed.

By afternoon, the storm had rolled in — a white curtain descending over Frisco. The streets vanished into snow. The mountain disappeared. Guests returned early, cheeks flushed, boots dripping.

One of them — a teenage girl named Ava, maybe sixteen — lingered at the counter, her gloves soaked and smile unsure.

"Hot cocoa?" Elias asked.

She nodded. "Please."

He steamed the milk, added cocoa powder, a pinch of cinnamon. She watched the foam rise like something magical.

"This place," she said softly, "it feels... alive."

Elias smiled faintly. "It is. It breathes differently every day."

She nodded, thoughtful, then said, "My mom says when you love something enough, it starts to recognize you."

He froze for half a second, the words landing like snow on glass — quiet, and yet shattering.

"That's a good mom," he said.

"She's gone," the girl replied, matter-of-fact but small. "But I think she'd like this place."

Elias poured the cocoa, topped it with cream. "Then she's already here."

The girl smiled weakly, took the cup, and walked toward the fireplace.

When she left the next morning, she tucked a small note under her saucer: "Thank you for listening."

Elias folded it, placed it in the drawer beside Alyssa's letter. He didn't know why, except that it felt like the right kind of company.

That night, after the storm cleared, Elias stood by the window, watching the town glow beneath a moon washed silver. The Inn was quiet again, but not empty. The kind of quiet that watches over rather than presses in.

He traced the condensation on the glass with his finger — a small circle, the same shape as the light ring from that morning. He thought of Alyssa, of Ava, of all the people who'd passed through this place needing something they couldn't name.

Maybe he was one of them too.

He whispered, "I'm still here," and for once, the mountain didn't echo back. It simply listened.

CHAPTER THREE

THE ECHO OF CONNECTION

———

G

S NOW HELD THE TOWN LIKE A LONG INHALE. BY MORNING, THE plows had carved soft channels down Galena, leaving drifts piled like sleeping animals along the curb. The Inn woke gently: pipe tick, kettle hiss, the first two guests whispering their plans while zipping jackets with mittened hands. Elias moved through it all, steady as breath.

He placed a tray at the front desk—two bowls of citrus, a small vase with three stems of eucalyptus, the mail he'd grabbed from the post box on his dawn walk. Bills, a glossy brochure, a postcard with a watercolor of a blue house and a live oak.

His hand paused.

Elias, the card began in Alyssa's handwriting—round, confident, slightly slanted like it wanted to keep moving. She always used his full name when she wanted him to really listen. Look what I drove by yesterday. They painted it the color of late summer. Porch swing's still crooked. I heard the cicadas even though it's off-season. I swear places keep a soundtrack. Thought you'd like to know she's still humming.

He let the postcard warm in his palm. The ink had smudged once, right where the word humming curved back on itself, like her hand had rested there—like she'd considered another word and then decided this one mattered.

He set it gently on the ledger and slipped a finger beneath the flap of a thicker envelope—linen paper, familiar weight. A letter.

Eli, I dreamed you were lacing your shoes on the back steps and laughing at me for tying mine in double knots like I'm still ten. In the dream I said, "Some of us like to be sure," and you rolled your eyes and said, "Some of us like to feel the wind."

Woke up missing you in the kind of way that isn't sad—just real.

Dad's been quieter on the phone. He pretends the garden is a full-time job. You know how he is: "Tomatoes don't judge." I think he wants to visit Colorado in the spring. He won't say it, so I will.

I walked past the blue house. Sat on the curb like an eavesdropper and listened. There's a sound the live oak makes when wind moves through it. I think it's the same sound your Inn makes when people sleep.

I'm proud of you. Not because it's perfect. Because you stayed long enough to hear the song.

—Aly

He read it once, again, then once more the way he read the steam rising from the first pull—slow, trusting the shape of what revealed itself. He slipped the letter into The Alchemist, back where all his most tender things lived, and returned to the morning like someone re-entering a room where music had been playing low all along.

Guests filtered out into the newly plowed day, boots squeaking on clean snow. The Traveler stayed, writing in neat lines, a cup of orange tea sending up narrow blue ribbons of steam. August hummed as he leaned over the menu insert—Thursday: Still, by Design—inking a tiny flourish on the corner like a secret signature.

By late morning, light flooded the front windows, bouncing off the snowbanks in brilliant shards. The phone rang.

Number withheld, tone familiar.

"Frisco Inn on Galena, this is Elias."

"Hi, stranger." Alyssa's voice sent warmth through the receiver, the kind that started in the throat and worked outward. "Did the world gift you a snow day?"

"Half a one," he said. "It's glittering. The mountain looks scrubbed."

She breathed a laugh. "I can hear it. You sound... lighter."

He leaned against the oak counter and let the moment be ordinary. "Got your postcard. And the letter."

"I figured you'd read the letter last," she said. "You always did. You like to hold weighty things for later."

He smiled at the truth of it. "You wrote: I'm proud of you."

"Yeah," she said. "I'll write it again, if you want."

"Say it," he said, softer than he meant to.

"I'm proud of you," she repeated, slower, like she was laying the words on a shelf for him to find again. "Not for being fixed. For being here."

He stared past the ledger to the window where a boy dragged a red sled uphill, falling twice and laughing both times. "I had a day yesterday," he admitted. "Nothing dramatic. Just... the song got repetitive. I started wanting a new instrument before I finished learning this one."

"Restlessness is still a kind of listening," she said. "You taught me that."

He rubbed the bridge of his nose. "Sometimes I want to run until my lungs empty out all the old smoke."

"Run," she said. "But let yourself come home winded."

A pause. The kind with love inside it.

"You mentioned Dad," he said.

"He wants to come in spring," she answered. "He'll pretend it's the tomatoes, but we both know it's you."

Elias pictured their father's work-rough hands, the way they hovered over seedlings like apologies. "I'm not the worst thing that happened to him," he said, voice flat, practiced.

"And you're not the best thing that never could," she countered, easy. "You're his son. That's messy. That's allowed."

He let out a breath he didn't know he was holding. "Will you come with him?"

"Try and stop me," she said. "I want to see the way light lands on your coffee. Everyone keeps telling me it's 'church, but caffeinated.'"

He laughed, sudden and free. "Tell them it's a small prayer you can drink."

"Done. Hey—before I go—do you remember the porch swing?"

He closed his eyes. "The crooked one."

"You always said it creaked like it was telling secrets. I got on it yesterday. It still does."

"What did it say?"

"That you owe me a run," she said. "And a morning where we don't talk about the past at all."

"I can do that," he said.

"I know," she answered. "That's why I called."

The line hummed in the soft way lines hum when two people decide not to treat distance like a country. "I'll text you a photo at first light tomorrow," he said.

"If you forget," she teased, "I'll call the front desk and leave an embarrassing message with your boss."

"He's not my boss," Elias said, reflexively amused.

"You know what I mean," she said. "The man who knows where you keep the spare keys."

"Fair," he said.

"Okay. Go back to your chorus of mugs," she murmured. "I love you."

"I love you too."

They hung up, and the world came back—the kettle, the low thrum of the baseboards, the small clank of August setting a stack of plates with the care of a man arranging stones in a river.

"Your sister?" August asked, not nosy—just neighborly.

Elias nodded. "She dreams in porch swings."

"Good," August said. "Porch swings are honest. They never pretend to be still."

The storm's aftermath left town luminous and slightly stunned. Guests returned with cheeks chapped ruddy and eyes bright, trailing snow and stories. A boy with a red scarf told Elias he'd seen a fox step into his boot prints and follow them like a game. A couple from New Mexico argued, gently, about whether to eat early or late; they compromised on now, and August added a spoonful of sugared citrus to their plates in celebration of compromise itself.

Midafternoon thinned. The light blued. Elias stacked clean saucers, aligned the handles, and felt the quiet deepen the way lakes deepen at the center—less visible, more profound.

A soft knock at the side door. Mail again. Not much—just a small padded envelope with Alyssa's handwriting on the label. For the Thursday Salon (Open when courage is low).

He didn't open it. He set it upright behind the register the way people set photographs facing the room, as if the image can look after the living. The sight of her letters felt protective. Even unopened, they held.

He drifted to the window. The mountain wore its winter with ceremony. Below, Frisco exhaled steady plumes of human heat—furnaces, laughter, the bakery's oven sighing out another tray of sugar. The Inn, catching all of it, seemed to settle a fraction deeper into its foundation.

Something tightened in his chest—not pain; more a reminder. Love could feel like this: a pressure that didn't crush, a weight that told you which way was down.

He wiped the counter. He wiped it again.

"Walk?" August asked, materializing at his shoulder as if summoned by repetition. "Ten minutes. I'll watch the lobby when we're back."

Elias glanced at the clock. "We?"

"We," August said, already shrugging into a jacket. "We're allowed to leave things beautiful for ten minutes."

The cold met them clean and bright. Galena's snowbanks sparkled, each crystal a quiet vote for wonder. They crunched past the bakery (waved), the gear shop (nodded), and the tiny post office where the clerk had taped a paper snowflake to the window with a piece of string and hope.

"You looked far away this morning," August said without preamble.

"I was remembering and... not," Elias answered. "Alyssa called. I didn't know how much I needed her voice until I heard it."

August's mouth tipped. "That's how mercy sneaks in."

They turned toward the lake path. Ice chuckled under a veneer of melt. A child, mittened to the elbows, tried to catch a snowflake on their tongue and declared failure with dignity.

"Do you ever wonder," Elias said, "if the quiet is hiding something from you?"

"No," August said. "I wonder if I'm hiding something from the quiet."

They walked without talking then, letting the town continue its low conversation with the day. On the way back, they passed the bench where older locals came to talk weather and the price of firewood. It sat empty, a small stage awaiting its troupe.

At the Inn's steps, August touched the railing as if checking a pulse. "You're planning to open Thursday's salon with the Vietnamese coffee?"

Elias nodded. "And with a line."

"Which one?" August asked.

"To pay attention is our endless and proper work," Elias said, and felt the sentence fit his mouth like it lived there.

August smiled. "Then your work is showing."

Inside, warmth received them. The lobby smelled of lemon oil and a day well-lived. Elias glanced at the padded envelope from Alyssa and felt, absurdly, brave.

Evening drew its amber curtains. The dining room softened into murmurs, clinks, the little silences couples make when they're content to eat and listen to one another chew. LANY drifted out like memory: not the ache-song tonight, but something tender that tried to put stars back where they belonged. The lamp near Plato's Corner haloed the Traveler's notebook, pages filling in an even hand.

A guest at the counter—mid-forties, gentle face, nerves showing. "I—uh—this is silly," he said, laying a folded napkin on the wood like a confession. "My daughter sent me here. Said I needed to learn to like mornings again."

"Not silly," Elias said. "Brave."

The man chuffed a tiny laugh. "She said there's a place in the world where coffee is a love language."

"Right here," Elias said lightly, and meant it. He set to work: tamp, pull, pour. The crema offered up its small galaxy before settling into earth. He slid the cup forward. "Sip while it's singing."

The man took a cautious taste. He closed his eyes. When he opened them, they looked almost relieved. "I think I forgot it could be like this."

"Most things can," Elias said. "Given attention."

After the man moved away, August leaned in. "You just wrote your own sermon again."

"I'm out of practice," Elias said.

"You're not," August murmured. "You're just telling the truth on purpose."

Later—after the last plate was washed, after the fireplace whispered itself lower, after the chandelier hum quieted to a moth's dream—Elias stood in the doorway of the empty dining room and fingered the padded envelope. Open when courage is low.

He didn't feel low. He felt... near. Like the edge of something kind.

He opened it anyway.

Inside: a small stack of index cards tied with baker's twine, each card in Alyssa's hand. On top, a title: Cards for When You Forget.

He slid the first card free.

You are not late.

Second card:

Water finds the shape of anything patient. Be patient with yourself.

Third:

Remember: no one hears your heartbeat like the house you love.

His throat went warm and tight at the same time. He wanted to laugh, or run, or sleep for eight hours under a heavy quilt. Instead he tucked the cards into his apron, feeling them sit there like matched stones.

He turned off the last lamp. The room leaned into darkness with relief. Snow tapped once at the window as if to say still here.

At the stair, he paused and pulled out one more card, not looking, just trusting.

Text me the first light.

He smiled, fished for his phone, typed to Alyssa 🩶:

First light tomorrow. Wish you were here to boss me into a longer run.

Three dots appeared almost instantly.

I'll boss you across state lines, she wrote. Sleep. The mountain wants to show off.

He slipped the phone into his pocket and climbed. Halfway up, he turned back and listened. The Inn made its nighttime music—pipes, wind, wood remembering how to hold. He breathed along with it, slow, deliberate, attentive.

"Still," he said softly to the dark, "by design."

The banister, warm from many hands, seemed to agree.

The Small Grace

By the next morning, the world smelled like forgiveness.

Snow had stopped in the night, leaving Frisco swaddled under a quilt of clean white. The roofs were soft mounds, the trees a lacework of frost. The Inn, still humming with the low heat of its pipes, felt alive again—content, as if it had been waiting for this quiet.

Elias woke before dawn. The air in his room was cold enough to see his breath, but the first light made the frost on the windowpane shimmer like dusted sugar. He dressed in silence, every motion measured—shirt, apron, breath, thought. Downstairs, he could already hear August in the kitchen, humming low, the scrape of a pan, the small clatter of knives.

He followed the sound.

The kitchen was wrapped in the soft gold of early light, everything warm and slow. Steam rose from the kettle in ribbons. The scent of cinnamon curled through the air, sweetened by cream warming on the stove. August stood at the counter, stirring with a rhythm that felt ancient and familiar.

"You're early," August said, without looking up.

"Couldn't sleep."

"Storms do that. Shake the dreams loose."

Elias smiled faintly. "The boy from 204—he's alright?"

"Hand's fine," August said. "Came down a few minutes ago to shovel the steps. Said he owed you a coffee."

Elias chuckled softly, pouring beans into the grinder. "I'll take it."

The burrs whirred—a slow roar that filled the small space. He measured by instinct now, by sound and scent. The first pull hissed, releasing that bitter bloom that always grounded him. He poured two cups, set one beside August.

"Peace offering," he said.

August took it, inhaled deeply, and sighed like a man receiving absolution. "You know," he said, "it's always the morning after the storm that makes me remember why I love this place."

Elias leaned against the counter, watching the snow outside blush under the sun. "Because it feels new again?"

August shook his head. "Because it feels earned."

By seven, the Inn began to wake in earnest. Boots thudded on the stairs, laughter floated down the hall. Someone sneezed, and someone else called "Bless you" through the door. The smell of fresh scones and cinnamon cream wove through the air like a melody you didn't need to hum to know.

Elias moved through the motions: trays, mugs, napkins folded in careful thirds. But it didn't feel like repetition today.

It felt like prayer.

When he reached the dining room, the scene before him made him pause. Guests gathered at the long table—hands wrapped around steaming mugs, cheeks pink from cold. The Traveler sat near the fire, sketching. The boy from 204, sleeve rolled up, was showing his brother the bandage as if it were a medal. Someone laughed—bright, full, honest. It echoed against the beams and made the chandeliers tremble.

Elias felt something shift inside him. It was small, but real. A warmth that didn't ask permission.

"Morning, everyone," he said, voice gentle but sure. "Breakfast will be worth the wait."

A cheer went up. August bowed dramatically from behind the counter, earning another round of laughter.

Elias served first—plates warm, scones dusted with sugar, cinnamon folded into the cream like memory. Each cup he poured felt intentional. Not just caffeine. Communion.

The Traveler raised their mug. "To the small graces," they said.

Elias tilted his head. "Which ones?"

"All of them," they replied. "The kind you don't notice until they're gone."

He smiled. "Then we're surrounded."

By midmorning, the storm had melted into soft streams along the road. The sound of dripping gutters mixed with the hush of the mountain's thaw. Elias stepped outside for the first time in hours. The air bit at his face, sharp but forgiving. He drew it in deep—the scent of pine, smoke, and cold iron.

His phone buzzed in his pocket.

Alyssa 🤍: Got your photo. The light is ridiculous. It looks like the mountain's pretending to be a saint.

He smiled, turned the phone toward the ridge, and took another picture. The peaks glowed gold now, sunlight cutting through the mist like an answered prayer.

Elias: You'd love it. Smells like cinnamon and redemption.

Alyssa: Good combo. You sound happy.

He hesitated. Then wrote: Not happy. Just here. But that feels enough.

Three dots appeared. Then: That's all joy ever is.

That afternoon, the Inn stayed half-empty—the kind of lull that begged for stillness. Elias refilled the cream, restocked the shelves, then wandered into the library. A record spun quietly—LANY again, low enough to feel rather than hear.

He sank into the armchair by the fire. The flames whispered. He let his mind drift—not backward, not forward, just through.

He thought of Alyssa sitting on that crooked porch swing, listening to the oak whisper. He thought of August humming over lemon zest. Of guests who laughed loud enough to shake the rafters. Of the boy who'd bled a little and healed a little more.

He thought of the Inn—not as a place, but as a pulse. The kind that could outlast even its keepers.

He closed his eyes.

The song's chorus rose just enough for him to hear the words: "I'm trying my best to let you in."

He smiled, faint and full.

"Me too," he whispered.

By evening, the snow reflected the sunset like fire caught in ice. The guests gathered again—this time for warmth, not need. Elias moved among them with quiet grace, refilling cups, listening, laughing when the stories grew wild. August played a game of chess with a hiker who didn't know the rules. The Traveler read aloud a poem about belonging, the kind that made people silent without knowing why.

Outside, the porch lights glowed amber. Inside, the air shimmered with the scent of coffee and cinnamon, and something underneath it that was just warmth remembering its own name.

And for the first time in a long while, Elias didn't feel like he was mending. He felt made.

CHAPTER FOUR

WINTER LIGHT

——

G

— ~ —

Christmas at the Inn

— ~ —

T HE SNOW STARTED IN WHISPERS — SMALL, SILVER THINGS THAT didn't seem sure of themselves. By nightfall, it was a curtain. Thick, slow, forgiving.

Elias stood by the lobby window, watching the world turn white. Each flake caught in the porch light, drifting like ash and memory. Inside, the fire hummed softly in the hearth, and the scent of clove, orange peel, and freshly-baked gingerbread filled the air. The Inn glowed against the storm — a warm lantern in a valley of silence.

He'd strung the garlands himself that afternoon, pine and juniper twined with ribbon, a few gold ornaments from the thrift store shining like small moons. The record player murmured "I'll Be Home for Christmas." It wasn't nostalgia, not really — just a quiet promise that for some people, home could still exist.

August had been in the kitchen since noon, humming along as he prepared the Christmas Eve dinner — roasted root vegetables, herbed chicken, a bread pudding that made the whole house smell like caramel. Every few minutes, he'd call out, "Taste this, will you?" and Elias would appear, spoon in hand, smiling.

By dusk, the guests had gathered — travelers who hadn't planned to end up here, couples escaping city noise, a family with two children who spent an hour naming the snowflakes on the window.

Elias moved among them with the practiced ease of someone who found peace in motion — topping off coffee, refilling cider, adjusting the fire. His apron was dusted with flour, his hair messy from steam. And yet, he glowed.

A small boy handed him a folded note. Inside, written in uneven pencil:

"Thank you for making it smell like home."

Elias kept it in his pocket for the rest of the night.

Later, after the guests had drifted upstairs, he and August sat in the quiet dining room. The candles were down to their final inch. Snow pressed against the windows in soft waves.

August raised his mug of hot chocolate — thick with cream, dusted with cinnamon. "To stillness," he said.

Elias clinked his cup against it. "To doing the next right thing."

"Same thing," August said.

They drank.

From the corner, the tree lights flickered — the gold ones he'd found at the hardware store, the kind that never blinked, only glowed. Beneath them, wrapped in plain brown paper, were small gifts for the staff and guests — wool socks, postcards of the mountain, chocolate bars from the shop down the street.

Elias had written a note to go with each one. None of them signed. Just:

"You are part of the story now."

When the fire finally burned low, Elias stepped outside. The snow had stopped. The town was quiet — not empty, just full of hush. The moon hung over Mount Royal, clean and patient.

He could see the reflection of the Inn in the snow — the soft amber glow in every window. He whispered, "Thank you," though he wasn't sure to whom — maybe to the mountain, maybe to himself, maybe to whatever had led him back here.

The wind answered with a long, low sigh through the pines.

— ∼ —

Christmas Morning

— ∼ —

T HE SMELL OF COFFEE WAS THE FIRST THING HE NOTICED — NOT HIS own, but August's, rich and dark, filling the air. When he came downstairs, the fire was already roaring, and carols were playing softly from the record player.

On the front desk, a single envelope waited. His name, in a looping, familiar hand. Inside, a note.

"Merry Christmas, Elias. The house remembers joy — it just needed you to remind it how to listen."

No signature. But he didn't need one.

He looked around. The guests were beginning to trickle down in slippers and sweaters, laughter spilling into the room. Alyssa was helping the children build a snowman outside, her scarf trailing bright red against the white.

For the first time in years, Elias realized — the ache had turned into something else. Not absence. Not longing. Just warmth.

He took a deep breath, the air cold and pure. The world smelled like pine and coffee and something very close to grace.

He whispered, "Merry Christmas," and the Inn, as always, seemed to answer.

The First Week of January

T HE FIRST MONDAY OF JANUARY DAWNED SOFT AND BLUE, THE KIND of light that made the frost glitter like lace. The holiday crowd had thinned, but the Inn still hummed — quieter now, slower, like it was exhaling after a long held breath.

Elias stood at the front desk, coffee in hand, reading the messages guests had left in the ledger. "Best sleep of my life." "You can feel the love in the walls." "We came for the snow, stayed for the calm."

He smiled. He didn't need reviews; this was enough.

—— ❧ ——

The Staff

—— ❧ ——

L ENA, THE MORNING COOK, ARRIVED FIRST — BUNDLED IN HER PARKA, cheeks red from the cold. She was from Leadville, and she swore the thin air made her biscuits rise better. She moved around the kitchen with quiet rhythm, humming gospel under her breath, the smell of butter and sage trailing behind her.

"Morning, Eli," she said, handing him a plate before he even asked. "You look like you slept for once."

"New year," he said. "New habits."

She gave him a look that said we'll see.

Then came Marco, the night attendant — young, sweet, with an energy that refused to dim even after double shifts. He was studying at CMC, saving money for his architecture degree. He had a sketchpad tucked into his apron pocket and often disappeared to draw by the fire between check-ins.

He waved a muffin in greeting. "I fixed the upstairs heater."

Elias blinked. "Already?"

Marco grinned. "It was either that or listen to Room 3 complain again."

"Efficient and diplomatic," Elias said. "We'll keep you."

"Temporarily," Marco said, winking. "Until I design your new spa."

Elias chuckled. "Deal."

Alyssa had come up after the holidays. Just for a while, she'd said—though the bag by the back stairs sat there the way things do when they've decided to stay. The blue house was still hers, the porch swing still crooked; only the distance had changed, twenty minutes of mountain road now instead of a postcard's width. All those letters had been her way of standing in the same room as him. Now she just stood in it. She'd wanted, he understood, to hear the place humming for herself.

By ten, Alyssa had joined them — scarf trailing, hair caught in a clip, cheeks kissed pink from the cold. She came in with a burst of air and laughter, balancing a tray of folded linens.

"Laundry's done," she said. "And you're welcome."

"Angel," Elias said.

"Don't push it," she teased, then leaned in. "Jacob's outside with the salt. You know — the man who apparently lives here now?"

He shot her a look, but she just grinned, disappearing toward the back hallway.

Through the window, Elias could see him — shovel in hand, sleeves rolled, salt bag slung over one shoulder. The kind of simple grace in movement that used to make Elias look away. Now he didn't.

He stepped out into the cold. "You don't have to do that."

Jacob glanced up. "You'd rather I sit inside looking at you while you do it?"

Elias laughed despite himself. "Fair."

"I like the quiet," Jacob said. "Snow listens better than people."

"Not always," Elias said. "Sometimes people surprise you."

Jacob's smile lingered, small and real. "You've gotten poetic."

"I've gotten practiced."

The Guests

I NSIDE, THE REMAINING GUESTS DRIFTED THROUGH THE MORNING LIKE scenes in a snow globe. There was the older couple in Room 2, who played Scrabble every day at the same table by the fire, their laughter soft as flannel. The woman always ordered peppermint tea; the man always pretended he didn't need glasses. There was Ava, the teenage girl from Christmas, back for one last night before school. She sat near the window sketching, earbuds in, her cocoa cooling beside her. And a writer — name unreadable on the registry — who spent each day in the library scribbling in a weathered notebook, sometimes pausing to listen when the espresso machine hissed.

Every face in the room felt known now. Every presence softened the edges of what had once been solitude.

Elias moved among them with the rhythm of someone who finally trusted his place in the world — pouring coffee, lighting candles, adjusting the record needle when the song skipped. From the kitchen, Lena called out, "Cinnamon rolls or scones for the late risers?"

"Scones," he said. "The lemon kind. Let's give them a little brightness."

"Like boss, like breakfast," she teased.

At noon, when the guests headed out to town, Elias leaned against the counter beside Jacob, watching the snow fall in slow spirals outside.

"Feels different this year," Jacob said. "The quiet doesn't hurt."

Elias nodded. "It's supposed to feel lighter after the weight lifts."

Jacob tilted his head. "And what about you? Still waiting for something?"

Elias thought about it. "Not waiting. Just... listening."

"To what?"

He smiled faintly. "The sound of things staying."

That evening, after dinner, Alyssa coaxed everyone into a makeshift New Year's coda — candles, cookies, one last toast to the season. Marco played guitar softly in the corner; Lena danced with the old couple; Ava read aloud a poem she'd written about the Inn.

"It smells like forgiveness and coffee," she said, cheeks pink. "And when you breathe too deeply, you remember who you were supposed to be."

Applause filled the room — not polite, but genuine.

Elias stood in the back, hand around his cup, eyes damp with pride. He caught Jacob's gaze across the room — no words, just warmth.

For the first time, it didn't feel like something beginning or ending. It just was.

And that, he realized, was enough.

—— ~ ——

Reflection

—— ~ ——

The Spring Thaw Run

T HE SNOW HAD STARTED TO PULL AWAY FROM THE CURBS IN SLOW, shy streaks — thin ribbons of melt tracing the shape of the town. You could hear it before you saw it: the drip from rooftops, the quiet music of runoff, the earth waking up underfoot.

Elias stepped outside just after dawn, laces tight, breath clouding in the cold. The air still carried the sharp edge of winter, but beneath it there was something sweeter — the faint scent of pine sap, thawing soil, and woodsmoke drifting from a nearby chimney.

He jogged toward Main Street, his stride finding rhythm with the heartbeat of Frisco itself. The town was half asleep — bakery lights flickering on, a single plow brushing aside the night's last dusting of snow. His shoes splashed through shallow puddles where ice used to be, each step a small proof of motion.

He'd run these streets before — last summer, last relapse, last return — but this morning felt different. The air wasn't punishment; it was invitation.

He passed the lake's edge, where mist hovered low and the mountains mirrored themselves in gray-blue stillness. Breath in, breath out. The world expanding, contracting. Every exhale felt like something leaving his chest that had been waiting all winter to go.

At the halfway point, he slowed near the trailhead — the one that curved behind the Inn, tracing the line of the creek. Meltwater tumbled over the rocks, quick and alive, sunlight catching the ripples like shards of gold. He stopped, bent slightly, hands on his knees, smiling through the sting of cold air.

Behind him, the town bell rang seven.

He looked up toward the ridge, where the first light touched the peak of Mount Royal, soft as breath. The color was that impossible gold — the one that made him believe again in beginnings.

When he returned, the Inn was waking.

Lena's laughter spilled from the kitchen, mingled with the smell of cinnamon and yeast. The front door stood propped open to let in the air, and somewhere upstairs, Alyssa was humming while changing linens. The record player crackled alive — not LANY this time, but something acoustic and gentle, a song about staying.

Jacob was on the porch steps, sanding the new handrail he'd built the week before. He looked up when Elias appeared, cheeks flushed from the cold. "You're up early," Jacob said.

"Had to see what the world looked like after the melt."

"And?"

"Still beautiful," Elias said. "Maybe more so for the cracks."

Jacob smiled — the kind of smile that didn't need finishing. "Coffee's inside. I saved you the last of the house roast."

Elias wiped a hand across his brow. "You're learning."

"I watch the master," Jacob said, standing to follow him in.

Inside, the Inn breathed warmth. Sunlight cut through the windows, laying gold bars across the floorboards. The scent of espresso mingled with lemon zest — Lena's muffins rising in the oven.

Elias poured two mugs, steam curling like handwriting between them. "To spring," Jacob said.

Elias clinked his cup lightly. "To returns."

They stood by the window in comfortable silence, watching the last flakes slide off the eaves and disappear into the wet earth. The sound of the creek carried faintly through the open door — steady, persistent, alive.

For the first time, Elias didn't feel the need to narrate it. He didn't need to label what was beginning between them, or what was ending within himself. It was enough to stand there, coffee warm in his hands, the house breathing beside him, the world softening back to life.

Outside, a bird broke into song — tentative at first, then sure. Elias smiled. "Guess we're not the only ones starting over."

Jacob nodded. "Spring's generous that way."

By the time the snow began to melt, the mountain was already humming again.

Not loudly — not the way it sang in July when the trails filled with voices and sunburned laughter — but quietly, like an instrument being tuned. The creek behind the Inn woke first. Elias could hear it from the kitchen each morning, that quicksilver sound of ice surrendering to water. A slow undoing. A reminder that not all breaking is loss.

He moved through his routine the way the mountain moved through thaw — unhurried, attentive. Bedding turned down. Curtains drawn back. Fresh grounds tamped, perfectly even. The first espresso pull released its steady hiss, and the scent of roasted caramel filled the room. He poured the shot into the same demitasse as always, the one with the faint chip on the rim, and watched the crema rise like dawn.

Outside, the street was still lined with snowbanks, but the edges had begun to sink, revealing patches of wet earth. Frisco smelled different now — not like winter's clean cold, but like something green remembering itself.

He wiped the counter. The sunlight hit the marble in a way that made it glow like poured honey. The house was warm, but the warmth was honest. Earned.

When August appeared, he was already rolling up his sleeves. "You feel that?" he said. Elias smiled. "The mountain breathing again." "Mm," August said. "She's generous today."

By midmorning, the guests had begun to drift outside again — scarves undone, cheeks open to air. The porch railings dripped steadily, each drop a note in the song of return. The Traveler was there too, sitting on the step, sketching the outline of Mount Royal where it rose like a story too big to finish.

Elias brought out two cups of coffee and set one beside them. "For the artist," he said. They looked up, smiling. "For the caretaker, then. Balance."

He sat. For a while, they said nothing. The silence between them wasn't empty; it was a place to rest.

From somewhere across the street, a dog barked once — joyful, startled by its own echo. A delivery truck rumbled past, tires splashing meltwater. The air was filled with those small, ordinary sounds that only arrive when the world remembers it's alive.

"You ever notice," the Traveler said, sketching a line that curved like a current, "that this house changes color depending on how you feel?"

Elias glanced back at the Inn. The morning light made the cedar siding glow amber. "Maybe it just reflects whoever's paying attention," he said.

"Then you must make it look beautiful," they answered.

He didn't reply. He didn't need to.

At noon, he was polishing glasses in the dining room when he saw it — a small blue car easing into the front lot, sun glinting off the windshield. The driver's door opened.

He froze.

Alyssa stepped out, one hand shielding her eyes, her hair wind-tangled and bright against the melting snow. She wore a denim jacket and an expression that belonged more to memory than distance. For a moment, the world tilted. The house, the mountain, even the air seemed to wait.

She looked up and saw him through the window.

Her smile wasn't sudden — it was the slow, inevitable kind that happens when the world finally makes sense again.

He met her at the door before she had time to knock.

"Hey, stranger," she said.

"Hey, bossy," he replied, and before either of them could think about it, she was in his arms — quick, solid, real. Her hair smelled faintly of cedar and wind. He hadn't realized how much of himself had been waiting for this exact weight against his chest.

When they pulled apart, her eyes were shining. "You look like you belong here."

"I think I do," he said.

They sat in the kitchen, mugs in hand, sunlight spilling over the counter. August pretended to busy himself with the lemons, though his smile gave him away.

"So this is the famous Alyssa," he said. "And you must be the saint," she answered. "He writes about you like you built this place from prayer and caffeine."

August laughed. "Close enough."

They talked through the afternoon — the Inn, the letters, the storm. Alyssa listened more than she spoke, her gaze soft but alert, taking everything in.

When she finally stood, she said, "Show me everything. I want to see the rhythm."

Elias grinned. "You sound like him," August muttered, but he followed anyway.

They walked through the Inn together — the soft creak of the floors, the smell of cedar and espresso, the muffled laughter from upstairs. Alyssa touched everything like it was sacred — the bannister, the bookshelf, the warm glass of the windows catching mountain light.

When they reached the lobby, she paused by the desk. "This is where you stand every morning?"

He nodded.

"It feels like a heartbeat," she said.

"That's because it is," he answered.

She smiled. "I see it now."

That evening, they stood on the porch watching the last of the snowmelt glisten down Galena. The town was alive again — children on bikes weaving between puddles, the sound of laughter spilling from the bakery, a busker strumming slow chords outside the café.

Alyssa leaned against the railing. "You've made something real here."

"We've both had to," he said.

She turned toward him. "Do you miss running?"

He thought about it. "Not the running itself. Just the feeling of moving toward something."

She nodded. "Then maybe this is it. Maybe you were never running away. You were just trying to arrive."

The sun dipped low, catching her hair in gold. Elias didn't answer. He didn't need to.

Later that night, the Inn was quiet again — a soft, golden quiet, alive with the hum of pipes and the scent of cinnamon cream from the kitchen. Alyssa was upstairs reading, August was in the library pretending to lose at chess, and Elias stood by the window in the dining room, looking out toward the dark ridge of the mountain.

The creek whispered below, alive and unbroken.

He touched the glass, the same way he always did.

"You're still here," he said to the reflection. It looked back and smiled. "I know," he whispered.

—~—

Meltwater

—~—

THE FIRST TRUE DAY OF SPRING ARRIVED WITHOUT CEREMONY. No trumpet of birds, no sudden blue sky. Just warmth, unexpected and shy, spilling through the cracks of the morning.

Elias woke to it the way you wake to music from another room — softly aware before fully conscious. The light was softer, rounder. When he swung his feet onto the floor, it wasn't cold anymore. It was forgiving.

Downstairs, the kitchen windows were fogged from the inside. The air smelled of orange peel, cinnamon, and wet earth — a recipe the house invented without asking. The steam on the glass blurred the outside world until it looked like a watercolor. Through it, the mountains had lost their edge, and the sky was the color of cream.

He moved through the Inn like someone turning the pages of a hymnbook. Slowly, reverently. Boots by the door. Two cups by the espresso machine. Alyssa's scarf still hanging from the hook, forgotten but deliberate.

On the counter sat a folded napkin — August's handwriting across it, uneven from haste:

Every thaw is a promise you've kept, whether you remember it or not.

He smiled when he read it. Not the outward kind of smile — the kind that lives just behind the ribs, small and steady.

From upstairs came a laugh — Alyssa's — chasing another voice down the hallway. Someone had opened a window. The sound of meltwater trickled down the gutter, soft and silver, the first true music of the season.

Elias leaned against the counter, listening.

There was no rush. No beginning or end. Just this — the sound of things learning to flow again.

He took his coffee to the window and stood there a long time, watching the light move over the snow, melting it one slow drop at a time. The world was remaking itself without asking his permission.

And for once, he didn't feel the need to interfere.

The Weekend Thaw

B Y MIDMORNING, THE SUN HAD CLIMBED HIGH ENOUGH TO MAKE THE snowmelt glitter like broken glass. Water rushed down the gutter beside the Inn, singing its way toward the lake. Elias propped open the front doors to let the air move freely through the lobby. It carried scents that had been missing for months — wet bark, metal, thawed pine, something wild and green just beneath the surface.

The house felt awake in every corner.

Lena moved through the kitchen with her sleeves rolled up, whistling over a bowl of dough. She'd switched from cinnamon rolls to lemon poppyseed scones, announcing that "winter's done with butter, now it wants brightness." The scent drifted through the hall, mingling with the faint sweetness of espresso and wax polish.

Alyssa appeared from the laundry room carrying a basket of folded linens. "The sunshine's making the rooms feel bigger," she said, balancing the basket against her hip. "I opened the windows in 205 — smells like wind again."

"Perfect," Elias said. "They'll love it."

"Who's checking in?"

"Couple from Santa Fe," Elias replied. "Anniversary trip."

"Another one?" she teased. "You're becoming the patron saint of second chances."

Elias smiled faintly. "Guess I'm qualified."

Outside, Marco was oiling the porch furniture, singing softly in Spanish, voice trailing up toward the rafters. The wooden chairs gleamed under his rag, sun warm on his neck. "Gonna be a good season," he called over his shoulder. "Feels different this year."

"It is different," Elias said, stepping out onto the porch. "The air's softer."

Marco laughed. "That's because you're finally breathing it."

Elias didn't argue.

The guests arrived just after noon — a flurry of motion and laughter, boots stomping the mud from the walkway. The couple from Santa Fe entered first, cheeks pink from the drive, arms wrapped around each other like they'd been waiting all winter to do so.

Behind them, a father and his teenage son checked in for a weekend of skiing; the boy's board clattered lightly against the counter as he leaned it down. There was also a woman traveling alone — writer's eyes, soft hands, the kind of quiet curiosity that made her seem at home the moment she crossed the threshold.

Elias welcomed each of them with the same gentle rhythm: a smile that reached his eyes, a tone that made every name sound like it had always belonged there.

By afternoon, the Inn had returned to life in full color. The common room was filled again — mugs clinking, soft conversation rising and fading. Sunlight fell across the chessboard near the window. The writer sat there, notebook open, hair falling across her cheek as she wrote. The father and son argued cheerfully about slopes and bindings. The couple from Santa Fe shared one chair between them, legs tangled.

Jacob came in from the porch, brushing sawdust from his hands. "Handrail's fixed," he said. "And the steps won't squeak anymore."

Elias looked up from behind the counter. "You trying to work your way into the payroll?"

Jacob grinned. "Depends on the benefits."

"Free coffee," Elias said.

"I was hoping for something more creative."

Elias didn't answer — just turned back to the espresso machine, hiding a smile that wouldn't leave his mouth.

Evening Settling

B Y SIX, THE LIGHT HAD TURNED GOLDEN AGAIN, THE MOUNTAINS rimmed in rose and blue. The sound of the creek deepened — fuller now with snowmelt, a living heartbeat under the porch. The guests gathered near the fire as the first chill returned to the air.

Alyssa had found the Inn's old string lights in storage and draped them along the mantel. Their glow reflected off the glasses on the bar, scattering tiny halos across the walls. The record player hummed to life — LANY's "Thru These Tears" — its melancholy softened by warmth.

Elias moved through the room like someone tuning an instrument. He refilled cups, adjusted the fire, collected empty plates. Every motion was small, deliberate, grounding. The kind of quiet work that made the night feel held.

Jacob leaned against the doorway, watching. "You ever stop moving?"

Elias looked up. "Not when there's life happening around me."

Jacob stepped closer. "Maybe life's trying to meet you halfway."

Something about the way he said it — easy, but earnest — landed like a hand against Elias's chest. He looked away, pretending to study the embers.

"Maybe," he said.

Later, when the guests had gone up to their rooms and the house had dimmed to its quiet hum, Elias lingered in the kitchen. The scent of baked citrus still clung to the air. He poured the last of the coffee into a small mug and stepped out back.

The night was clear — stars sharp as frost, the sound of dripping water steady from the eaves. The snow was retreating inch by inch, revealing the dark soil beneath. He crouched, pressed a hand to the cold ground, and felt the faint pulse of thaw — slow, steady, forgiving.

Behind him, the back door creaked. Jacob stepped out, holding two cups.

"Thought you'd be here," he said.

"I always am," Elias replied.

They sat on the porch steps, the wood still cold beneath them. The silence between them wasn't emptiness anymore; it was shared breath.

"Do you miss it?" Jacob asked finally. "The city, the noise, that old rush of being everywhere at once?"

Elias shook his head slowly. "No. I think I just used to confuse movement with meaning."

"And now?"

He looked at the mountains — their shadows long and sure in the moonlight. "Now I think meaning's what stays when the motion stops."

Jacob nodded. "You sound like someone I'd follow."

Elias smiled, eyes soft. "You already did."

The creek murmured on. The Inn glowed faintly behind them — warm, alive, listening.

Inside, Lena had left a note on the counter in looping cursive: "Tomorrow, blueberry pancakes. Don't argue."

Elias folded the paper into his pocket, looked up at the stars, and let the night breathe through him — deep, rhythmic, forgiving.

The thaw was happening everywhere now — in the hills, the walls, his chest.

He didn't need to name it. He just needed to keep showing up for it.

He left before the light decided what color it wanted to be. The street lay cool and empty, the mountain a darker shape against a sky still inventing itself. Elias jogged past the bakery —ovens already humming, sugar drifting through the air—past the shuttered gear shop and the lake path where the water kept its slow, mirrored beat.

His breath fell into rhythm: four counts in, four counts out, the soft thud of shoes syncing with the town's pulse. He didn't bring music. Summer had its own metronome— sprinklers ticking, a distant truck shifting down on the highway, the hush of pines in a wind too early to be named. He ran because motion turned worry into pattern, and pattern into prayer.

By the trailhead the path narrowed to packed dirt, cool beneath the aspens. The air smelled clean—wet stone, sap, something green and ancient. His body read the terrain before his mind did: knees warming, calves waking, lungs opening like windows. A bead of sweat traced his temple. He let it fall. Discomfort passed faster when you didn't resist it.

The mountain breathed differently than the Inn. The Inn inhaled and exhaled with people—steam, laughter, music. The mountain's breath was older, indifferent. Up here, no one asked if you were okay. It offered climb and descent, root and rock. Take or leave. Stay or go. Some mornings he needed something larger than kindness.

A jay flashed through the trees, blue as flame. Pebbles scattered underfoot. He counted steps—thirty up, fifteen even, thirty again—steadying thought into motion. Beneath the counting, a quiet vigilance: measure the drop-off, remember the slick clay curve after last night's rain, keep breath enough to turn back if needed. Attention, not fear.

A memory brushed him like a low branch—himself, smaller, running from sound that followed anyway. He smiled at the difference. He wasn't fleeing now; he was meeting.

Halfway up the second switchback a figure appeared ahead, tall, sure-paced—the kind of runner who didn't force the climb. Elias gained without trying. Faded cap, gray shirt, laugh rising through the trees.

"Didn't think you were a morning person," the man said as Elias drew even.

Elias knew the voice before the face. A flash of bar-light memory, a smile across a table he should have left earlier. Jacob.

"Didn't think you were still in town."

Jacob grinned. "Got in last night. Work thing. Or that's what I told myself."

They ran side by side for a few strides, the trail lifting beneath them like breath held. Elias counted steps to keep from counting months. The forest opened to sky, then closed again. A raven crossed the clearing, black wing against pale morning.

"Place looks good," Jacob said. "The Inn. Saw the porch lights on. Felt... familiar."

"It should," Elias said. "Not much changes."

"Except you."

Elias let the next incline answer. Heat bloomed across his shoulders. The trail widened, revealing the lake below—glass, town glinting like coins, mountains layered in blue.

Jacob slowed, hands on hips, catching breath. "You always stopped here," he said. "Pretending it was for the view."

"It was for the view," Elias said.

Jacob's laugh softened. "And for learning how to be still."

Elias watched sunlight choose its color—gold, generous. He thought of morning coffee, the ledger's clean page, August's crooked handwriting. The restlessness still lived in him, smaller now, like a dog learning to lie down.

"Still learning," he said.

Jacob's glance held approval. "You look steadier."

"I am. Most days."

They started again, feet finding a shared tempo. Silence felt less like avoidance, more like respect. A stream stitched the path with silver; they crossed in two steps. Cold water through mesh shoes woke his arches—sensation reminding him he was here.

"You ever miss it?" Jacob asked. "Before the Inn?"

Elias thought of noise that never stopped, of nights that didn't close, of the first key August placed in his hand—the first time he believed the word home without arguing with it.

"I miss the versions of me I thought I had to be," he said. "Not the life that asked for them."

Jacob nodded, jaw set like he'd been carrying the same truth. "Yeah. Same."

At the ridge they stopped. The whole valley unfurled below —rooftops catching light, a road ribboning toward the lake, wind moving the water like breath over silk. Elias braced his palms to his thighs, breathing through the stitch that always came and always left if he welcomed it.

Jacob watched him, eyes steady. For a heartbeat the old gravity flickered. Elias let it pass. Attraction didn't need instruction.

Down the slope, a band of cloud drifted like an undecided thought. The air tasted faintly of iron and pine. Need simplified here: air, water, daylight enough to get back.

"Breakfast still the best show in town?" Jacob asked.

"Some mornings," Elias said. "Today will be good. The scones are right."

"Then I'll come by. Pay too much for coffee. Pretend I'll hike again."

"Deal."

They descended together, gravity doing the work. The town's sounds returned—doors, dishes, a laugh that could have been anyone's. Elias checked in with himself: legs steady, mind kind. He didn't keep score anymore, but he noticed when the sum felt honest.

At the bottom, the trail split. Jacob pointed toward the lake. "I'll circle the water."

Elias nodded toward the Inn. "I'll open the day."

They didn't shake hands. They didn't need to. Jacob tipped two fingers from his cap, a gesture that felt like both apology and permission.

"See you soon, Eli."

Elias watched him go until the trees folded him away. Then he turned toward the Inn, heart working in a way that felt useful. He moved at the speed the morning asked for. When he reached the corner where sunlight touched brick, he set his palm against the warmth and let it answer back.

The mountain had its breath. The house would have its own. And he—between them—was learning to keep both.

CHAPTER FIVE

THE RETURN

———

G

THE ESPRESSO MACHINE HISSED ALIVE, STEAM CURLING LIKE BREATH. Elias caught his reflection in the brass—hair damp from the run, collar open, pulse too quick—and steadied it before stepping into the dining room.

"Good morning," he said, low and easy. The room lifted in response. The Traveler looked up from the corner; a couple whispered over plates; an older woman buttered a scone as if it were prayer.

Jacob sat near the window, backlit, already belonging. Elias tried not to notice. Failed.

"Elias!"

August's voice carried from the kitchen, sleeves rolled, flour dusting his forearm. He was polishing the copper French press like a relic.

A man in hiking gear leaned over the counter. "Hey, is that the handyman? This place looks immaculate."

Elias blinked, then laughed. "That's August. He owns the place."

The hiker flushed. "Oh—sorry, I didn't mean—"

August waved it off. "Better handyman than businessman some days. Welcome to breakfast."

Laughter rippled, and the room exhaled. Across the tables, August's look said you handled that well.

He carried out a tray of egg scones, butter and vanilla trailing behind him like music. Elias moved through the room with practiced grace, but the air felt different—every pass by Jacob's table brushed memory and unfinished thought.

The Traveler set down their cup. "There's something about this place," they said. "It feels... intentional. Like it was designed to make you remember who you are."

"That's the idea," Elias said. "Everything here is by design. Even the stillness."

"Stillness," they repeated. "It suits you."

He turned back to his work, letting the noise cover the heartbeat. Taylor Swift's Cornelia Street floated from the radio—I hope I never lose you, hope it never ends... For a moment he couldn't tell if what he felt was longing or peace.

Outside, Jacob stirred sugar into his coffee, smiling at something unseen.

Some mornings, Elias thought, you don't choose who walks through the door—only how you greet them when they do.

And this morning, the house had chosen to open its heart.

—∽—

The Heartbeat After Breakfast

—∽—

B Y TEN-THIRTY, THE DINING ROOM HAD THINNED TO ECHOES—EMPTY plates, sunlight on crumbs, a final sigh from the coffee pot. Elias moved quietly through the aftermath—stacking, folding, wiping in slow, reverent circles. Joy left a mess too.

August entered with a tray and that unhurried gait that made people believe he owned time. "Good crowd," he said.

"Good scones," Elias replied.

"I heard the compliment about my handyman skills. Maybe I missed my calling."

"You could fix anything," Elias said.

"I could," August answered. "But not everything should be fixed."

The line landed heavier than intended. Elias looked up. "Did you mean me?"

"I meant all of us. This place. Sometimes we're not broken —we're just in repair. There's a difference."

Elias nodded, throat tight.

"When people see me wiping tables," August went on, "they think it's small work. But maybe that's what keeps me steady. The quiet work no one notices."

"That's the only kind that ever mattered to me."

Outside, the porch chimes sang once in the wind. The Traveler's napkin lay folded on their table, ink pressed into the fibers:

Stillness is a kind of courage.

Elias tucked it into his pocket.

"Jacob might come back later," he said.

August didn't look surprised. "And how does that sit with you?"

"Like something unfinished that doesn't need to be finished—just acknowledged."

"Good," August said. "You don't have to rewrite every old chapter. Sometimes turning the page is enough."

The house was still again, but not silent. The hum, the warmth, the breath in the walls—all of it pulsed with his own. The Inn didn't heal by accident. It healed because they did the small work together.

— ~ —

Evening Light

— ~ —

B Y FIVE, THE SUNLIGHT THICKENED INTO COPPER. IT BRUSHED THE walls like a farewell. Elias poured an americano, watching crema bloom gold before fading.

"Careful," he said to the woman in the pale green sweater as he set it down.

She smiled, the gold cross at her neck flashing against the light. Moments like that—the poetry of light finding something to love—stilled him.

Around the room, guests settled into rhythm: hikers comparing dust, friends arguing over board games, the Traveler writing in their corner. August moved easily among them, gravity disguised as calm.

Through the window Elias caught Jacob's reflection—outside, phone in hand, looking toward the mountain. Something inside him shifted—not longing, but recognition.

"Some people don't return to places," the Traveler said softly without looking up. "They return to versions of themselves they lost there."

Elias paused. "Is that what you're writing?"

"Something like that."

The espresso machine hissed again, steam blurring the view. Malibu Nights played low, more pulse than melody. Outside, Jacob turned toward the door. Inside, Elias brushed an invisible crumb from the counter.

Stillness wasn't absence. It was attention.

And for the first time all day, he wished the moment wouldn't move on.

Nightfall

By nine, the Inn was soft around the edges. Laughter faded up the stairs, doors closing like breaths. Elias dimmed the lamps one by one.

The fire had turned to embers, pulsing under ash. He stirred them just enough to keep the glow alive. The gramophone whispered I Don't Wanna Love You Anymore, the melody gentle, reminding, not hurting.

He sat near the window, moonlight pooling over the floor. The Traveler's notebook lay open on the couch. A line in dark ink:

Perhaps stillness is the bravest kind of motion.

He smiled. "I'll give you that one," he murmured.

CHAPTER SIX

THE WEEK AFTER THE THAW

———

G

CHAPTER SEVEN

THE LIGHT THAT WAITS

———

G

THE BELLS FROM MAIN STREET DRIFTED UP THROUGH THE STILL morning air, echoing against the mountains. Elias stood barefoot in the kitchen, the first pot of coffee gurgling to life behind him. The windows glowed with pale sunlight; frost still rimmed the edges, but you could feel warmth pressing through.

He liked Sundays because they carried no performance. Guests slept in; the house spoke in low tones — the sigh of pipes, the faint hum of heat, the creak of beams adjusting to temperature. It was a living thing, this quiet.

Lena entered, half-awake, her hair tied up with a pencil. "Couldn't sleep," she said. "Dreamed the scones burned."

"They didn't," Elias said, smiling. "But the oven's ready for them to live their best life."

She snorted, reaching for the flour. "You always talk like this before coffee?"

"Only when I mean it."

They moved in rhythm — the familiar choreography of mornings. She measured, he wiped the counter; she whisked, he ground beans. The music that played — soft LANY again, 'Thick and Thin' — was low enough that it felt like breathing.

By seven, the scent of butter and lemon filled the kitchen. The first guest wandered in — the writer from earlier in the week. "That smell should be illegal," she said, voice still wrapped in sleep.

"Tell that to the mountains," Elias replied, pouring her a cup. She took it like it was communion, smiled, and sat near the window, sunlight painting her notebook gold.

Outside, Jacob was carrying logs to the porch stack, his breath visible in the cold. The sleeves of his flannel were rolled to the elbows, and for a moment Elias thought — not for the first time — how good it was that someone like him looked like that in this light.

Alyssa joined him a few minutes later, yawning, mug in hand. "The snow's almost gone," she said.

"Almost," Elias answered, watching the glint of meltwater run along the curb. "Some things take their time."

She nudged his shoulder. "You talking about snow or you?"

He smiled. "Both."

— ~ —

The Guests Who Stayed

— ~ —

THE MORNING CAME GRAY, THE KIND THAT SMELLED LIKE RAIN BEFORE it arrived. Elias ran early — not far, just to the ridge and back. The ground was soft, the trail dotted with patches of lingering snow. When he returned, the clouds had lowered over the town like heavy thoughts.

Inside, the Inn was bright against the weather. Lena lit candles on the tables. Marco stacked fresh towels by the sauna. The couple from Santa Fe lingered in the lounge, unwilling to check out.

"Can't leave yet," the woman said. "We're waiting for the mountains to tell us goodbye."

Elias nodded. "They always whisper something if you're patient."

She touched his arm. "I think they already did."

When they finally left, the room felt larger for their absence. He cleaned their table slowly, noticing the faint ring of two coffee cups — side by side, perfectly aligned. He didn't wipe them away right away.

Jacob walked by with a toolbox. "You keep that look on your face, people will start thinking you're in love."

Elias glanced up. "People think a lot of things."

Jacob smirked. "Only the true ones stick."

The Ordinary Miracle

I T SNOWED OVERNIGHT — BARELY HALF AN INCH — AND MELTED BEFORE noon. The brief return of white made the Inn look newly painted. Elias watched it slide from the roof in sheets, each one breaking apart mid-air into glittering fragments.

He brewed a new blend — cinnamon and dark roast with a hint of cream — and decided to serve it as "House Revival." Guests smiled at the name; he liked that.

Alyssa organized the gift shop downstairs, humming a tune from their childhood — the one their mother used to play when cleaning. Hearing it again felt like an open door.

By afternoon, the sky cleared into impossible blue. The father and son from earlier returned from the slopes, faces flushed. The boy ran up to Elias, holding out his phone. "We saw a fox! Right by the lift!"

Elias smiled. "Lucky sighting."

"Maybe he lives up there," the boy said.

"Or maybe," Elias replied, "he just visits to remind us that wild things still do."

Jacob laughed from the counter. "That sounded like a proverb."

"It probably was," Elias said.

That evening, the house smelled of roasted apples and cedar. Lena's laughter rolled out from the kitchen like a song that made even the walls relax. The guests lingered longer after dinner, as if no one wanted to end the day. When the last cup was washed, Elias turned off the lights one by one, whispering goodnight to the house like he meant it.

The Letter

THE MAIL CAME LATE, WET FROM DRIZZLE. AMONG THE FLYERS AND invoices was an envelope written in looping script — Alyssa's handwriting, though she lived only twenty minutes away. Inside, a single sheet:

"You've built something sacred, El. Not perfect, not easy — but sacred. Don't ever mistake peace for boredom. Some of us are still learning how to find what you already have."

He read it twice, then tucked it into the Inn's ledger — a secret between them and the house.

That evening, a rainbow appeared over the ridge after a short burst of rain. Guests stepped outside, gasping softly, taking pictures. Elias didn't. He stood on the porch beside Jacob, hands in his pockets, watching the colors fade.

"Beautiful," Jacob said.

"Fleeting," Elias answered.

"Maybe that's what makes it beautiful."

He turned to look at him then, the light refracting faintly in Jacob's eyes. "Maybe," he said. "Or maybe it's that some things come back."

—~—

The Small Work

—~—

THE DAY BEGAN WITH REPAIRS. MARCO ON THE LADDER, LENA sanding a new counter finish, Alyssa sewing curtains in the lounge. The house sounded alive — hammer taps, low conversation, a radio somewhere playing Fleetwood Mac.

Elias polished the espresso machine until it shone. The smell of oil and coffee filled the air. The polished curve gave him back to himself, small and bent in the brass—eyes tired, but steady. Not the man who had arrived here two years ago, but not entirely someone else either. Just... integrated.

Jacob came in carrying a new doormat. It read: Welcome Home.

Elias raised a brow. "A bit on the nose."

Jacob shrugged. "I figured sometimes the obvious is what people need most."

When the guests came down for breakfast, the Inn looked newer, but not unrecognizable. Just refreshed — like spring had repainted it without erasing the lines.

That night, they hosted a spontaneous dinner — stew, bread, laughter spilling through the open doors. No one wanted to call it an event, but everyone stayed until long after dessert. The record spun 'I Don't Wanna Love You Anymore.' The song hurt a little, but in the best way.

The Return

MORNING BROKE BRIGHT AND RECKLESS. SNOWMELT RAN IN SILVER streams down the street. Birds had returned to the pine boughs, calling sharp and clear.

Elias laced his shoes. "Run?" Jacob asked from the doorway.

"Always."

They took the lake path together — breath for breath, step for step. The air smelled of sap and thawing earth. The mountains glowed pale pink with sunrise.

At the overlook, they stopped. The valley spread below, the Inn small but shining.

Jacob leaned on the railing. "You ever think about leaving again?"

Elias shook his head. "No. I think about staying better."

Jacob smiled. "You're getting good at it."

The wind shifted — soft, fragrant, full of promise. Below them, the Inn caught the light, windows flashing gold.

For the first time in years, Elias didn't feel like he was looking at a story he'd left behind.

He felt like he was standing in the middle of one that was still being written.

The Gathering

T HE DAY ROSE EASY AND BLUE, THE KIND OF MORNING THAT CARRIED warmth even before the sun cleared the ridge. The Inn felt different — expectant, like it knew something was about to happen.

Elias moved through the halls quietly, checking the lights, the tables, the way the air smelled. Lemon and cedar. Fresh sheets. Piano dusted. Every detail a kind of prayer. By midmorning, the first of the spring light had filled the lobby — slanted gold catching on the brass rails and glass frames.

"Tonight's the night," Alyssa said from the staircase, holding a bundle of café lights. "If this goes well, you'll have to start charging tickets."

Elias laughed softly. "We don't charge for magic."

"Then you'd better hope it shows up anyway," she said, grinning as she disappeared up the stairs.

He turned toward the window. Outside, the street shimmered with the last of the meltwater, reflecting the sky like liquid glass. The mountain beyond looked almost tender — green reemerging, snow retreating in thin veins.

He whispered under his breath, "Here we are."

By afternoon, the preparations had turned the Inn into something halfway between a home and a sanctuary. Lena baked tray after tray of lemon shortbread and honey bread, their scent spilling through the rooms. Marco brought up wine glasses — not for wine, but for the sparkling cider Elias had picked out instead. He'd learned long ago that celebration didn't need a drink to be felt.

On the side table sat the new menu cards: cream stock, simple serif, embossed title. "Still, by Design — An Evening of

Small Rituals." Below it, in smaller print: To pay attention is our endless and proper work.

August would have been proud, he thought — proud and teasing. Finally learned to make beauty useful, huh, Eli?

Outside, Jacob was stringing café lights along the porch beams. His flannel sleeves were rolled, sawdust catching in the fading sunlight. From the open door, Elias watched him work — sure-footed, patient. Every so often, Jacob would step back, squint, then nod as if confirming some unspoken alignment.

"You're in my way," Jacob said, without looking.

"I'm admiring your craftsmanship," Elias answered.

"That's what people say when they don't want to admit they're staring."

Elias smirked, stepping aside. "Then I'm both."

Jacob laughed. "You sound like a writer."

"I've been living near one," Elias said, glancing toward the Traveler through the window — seated in the corner, notebook open, sunlight tracing the side of their face.

"Guess it's contagious," Jacob murmured.

As dusk settled, the lights flickered on one by one — warm, honeyed, like constellations arranged by hand. The first guests gathered in the lounge, wrapped in sweaters, cheeks pink from the evening air. The fireplace crackled, and from the corner record player, Ruel's "Suburbia" began to hum through the room.

The chords were clean, nostalgic, a little tender. The sound wrapped around them all like familiarity does — quietly, without announcement. The lyrics floated out softly: "These suburban streets keep me thinking of you..."

Elias adjusted the wick of a candle, feeling the room breathe with him.

He didn't stand at the center. He didn't need to. He was part of the rhythm — the slow inhale and exhale of a space finally at peace with itself.

Lena poured cider into glasses, passing them around with her usual command that nobody sit too still for too long. Alyssa arranged the dessert trays with reverence, dusting powdered sugar like snow. Marco adjusted the lights one last time before leaning against the counter, satisfied.

The Traveler was the first to speak, their voice even and low. "I wrote something this morning," they said. "I don't know if it's finished, but maybe it's enough."

Elias nodded. "Then it's ready."

They stood by the fire, notebook trembling slightly in their hands.

"I used to think stillness was what happened when nothing did. But now I see it's what happens when everything belongs. The sound of a cup being set down, the sigh of the floorboards, the breath you didn't know you were holding — all of it part of the same design."

The silence afterward was a living thing — full, tender, luminous. Then a soft wave of applause, quiet laughter, a few tears.

Jacob caught Elias's eye across the room. "She read your soul," he mouthed.

Elias only smiled. "She read the house."

Later, when the crowd thinned and the record shifted to "You Against Yourself," the tone deepened — intimate, introspective. Ruel's voice threaded through the air like memory. The sound of glasses clinking, of laughter blending with soft melody — it all felt like a home that had finally exhaled.

Elias stepped out onto the porch to catch his breath. The air was cool, the stars clean and countless. He could hear the creek running, the trees shaking off their frost. Jacob joined him, hands in his pockets.

"Looks like you did it," Jacob said.

"It wasn't me," Elias said, eyes on the lights reflecting off the window. "It was us. The house. The people. The small things that kept showing up."

Jacob studied him for a moment, the way people do when they're about to say something that matters. Then quietly, "I think you've stopped running."

Elias looked down at his hands — steady, warm, no tremor. "I think I finally found somewhere worth staying."

Jacob smiled. "You make it sound easy."

"It's not. But it's simple."

The record faded. The guests said goodnight, leaving behind the traces of their laughter, their warmth, their human proof.

Elias lingered by the fireplace, candlelight flickering across his face. He thought of August's old note — Beauty's in the doing. He thought of his sister's words — Some of us are still learning how to find what you already have. And he thought of every morning, every ritual, every act of care that had built this night brick by brick, cup by cup, breath by breath.

He closed his eyes and listened. The Inn hummed its steady tune — pipes, floorboards, wind, light — all tuned perfectly to the key of being alive.

Outside, the stars shimmered like windows into other lives, and Ruel's voice floated one last time through the open door:

"Maybe I don't need saving this time..."

Elias whispered, "Neither do I."

The house, in its gentle wisdom, seemed to agree. And just like that — with music and warmth still clinging to the walls — the week folded into itself, perfectly, by design.

---~---

The Morning Return

---~---

T HE AIR IN FRISCO WAS CRISP ENOUGH TO TASTE — PINE AND RIVER mist, that alpine tang that felt like truth. The streetlights were still on, their glow faint against the widening blue. Elias jogged the edge of Main Street, his breath puffing clouds into the morning.

It had become his ritual again — movement before noise. The body in rhythm before the day could ask for anything. He didn't time himself anymore; he didn't need to. The goal wasn't distance. It was return.

He slowed near the creek, watching the water move with purpose. Its sound — soft, relentless — mirrored his heartbeat.

There was peace here, but not the quiet kind. It was earned peace. The kind that hums under scars and fresh skin alike.

When he made it back to the Inn, Alyssa was sitting on the front steps, her hoodie pulled tight. She smiled when she saw him, a coffee mug balanced between her knees.

"You're glowing," she said.

"Endorphins," he teased.

"Or you finally slept."

"Maybe both."

He sat beside her, their shoulders brushing. The town below was just beginning to wake — delivery trucks, birdsong, the faint smell of bread from the bakery. The Inn stood still and steady behind them, its windows reflecting the first sunlight spilling down from Mount Royal.

"Do you ever think," she said softly, "that maybe you were always meant to come back here?"

Elias looked down at his hands — calloused, steady, alive. "Every day."

They didn't speak for a while. The sound of water, the hiss of coffee, the breath between them — all of it part of the same rhythm.

When the church bells rang eight, he felt something loosen in him. Not an answer — just release.

He smiled to himself. Progress, not perfection.

He stood, stretching. "Come on," he said. "Let's wake the house."

The House Wakes

By the time the sun found its place above Mount Royal, the Inn was humming again — not loud, not rushed, but alive.

Steam rose in thin curls from the kitchen, wrapping the smell of Guatemalan dark roast around every beam and banister. Elias moved through the space like someone who had learned to listen first. He didn't direct the morning; he tuned it. A nod here, a smile there — enough to keep everyone steady without ever breaking the spell.

Zach was already at the griddle, humming an off-key version of Here Comes the Sun. Alyssa darted in behind him, setting out the trays of scones and marmalade. The kitchen was a choreography of small noises — butter knives, porcelain, the clatter of a pan landing just right.

"Morning, maestro," Alyssa said, teasing.

Elias grinned. "You mean conductor."

"Same thing. One uses music, the other uses caffeine."

He laughed softly, the kind that lingered. "I'll take that."

Outside, the front porch glistened from last night's rain. He pushed open the door to check the tables — each one set with fresh blooms Alyssa had gathered from the side garden before dawn. The air was cool, spiced with pine and cinnamon, and when the wind passed through, it carried the faint sound of the town — a shopkeeper unlocking a door, a cyclist gliding by on wet pavement.

Elias watched it all and thought how strange it was — the way routine could feel holy when done with care.

The Guests

B Y NINE, THE DINING ROOM HAD TURNED GOLDEN. A YOUNG COUPLE sat near the window, their hands brushing occasionally between sips of coffee. A woman in a red scarf read a worn paperback of The Alchemist, stopping now and then to underline something. And in the far corner, an older man was sketching the mountain — his lines steady, his expression calm.

Elias moved among them quietly, refilling cups, straightening napkins, offering warmth in the smallest ways.

"Everything all right this morning?" he asked the man with the sketchbook.

The man looked up, eyes bright behind his glasses. "More than all right," he said. "Your place makes me remember the world is kind."

Elias blinked, caught off guard by the simplicity of it. "That's the idea," he said softly.

Across the room, Alyssa whispered something that made the couple laugh. The sound rose and stayed, threading itself into the air. Elias turned, watching her work the room with that easy grace — the kind that made people feel both at home and seen.

He thought how proud he was of her — not in the way of ownership, but of recognition. She had learned the rhythm too. She had learned the listening.

The Midday Quiet

AFTER BREAKFAST, THE INN SOFTENED AGAIN. GUESTS DRIFTED OUT toward the lake trail, their laughter fading down the hill. The sound of dishes being washed echoed faintly through the kitchen — water, porcelain, the occasional clink of silver.

Elias stayed behind at the counter, wiping it down with slow, circular motions. He loved this hour. The lull after motion. The residue of joy.

He made himself another coffee — cream and cinnamon, stirred until the colors swirled like marble. The first sip was grounding, and he closed his eyes just long enough to hear the rain gutters ticking as they dried in the sun.

He sat in the window seat that overlooked the garden. Birds dipped between the lilacs. The sky had that clean, late-morning blue that always made him think of forgiveness.

Jacob Returns

HE DIDN'T HEAR THE DOOR OPEN. HE JUST FELT THE AIR CHANGE — a draft that carried something familiar. When he looked up, Jacob was there again, standing half in shadow. His shirt was damp from the walk; his hair pushed back; his eyes, unreadable.

"You weren't going to tell me the cinnamon was your secret," Jacob said, leaning on the counter.

Elias smiled without standing. "You didn't ask."

"I shouldn't have to. I thought we shared everything now."

Elias raised a brow. "We?"

Jacob grinned, slow and easy. "Don't get nervous. I meant this place. You. Me. The silence between us. It's starting to feel like part of the landscape."

Elias tilted his head, pretending to study him. "You're not supposed to get poetic before noon."

Jacob shrugged. "Blame the altitude."

They laughed, and for a brief second, it was simple — two people suspended in a space that didn't demand anything more.

Elias poured another coffee, added cream and a pinch of cinnamon, and slid it across the counter. "For your altitude."

Jacob accepted it, their fingers brushing. "Careful," he said. "You'll make me stay longer than I planned."

"That's the idea."

G

CHAPTER EIGHT

THE AFTERNOON PULSE

———

G

B Y TWO, SUNLIGHT DRIPPED THROUGH THE SKYLIGHT, SPILLING GOLD across the lobby. Alyssa was cleaning the banister, humming Ruel's Growing Up Is___, her voice gentle, nearly a whisper.

Elias was back in the spa area, checking on linens, straightening towels, feeling the soft ache in his shoulders that only came from purpose.

Through the thin walls, he could hear the faint hum of the massage room, a guest laughing quietly with the therapist. Life moving on, gently, fully, without noise.

He found himself thinking about his morning run — the cool air, the mist on the lake, the way the mountain reflected on the still water. It had felt like running inside a mirror. He wondered if healing looked like that: progress disguised as reflection.

—∼—

Evening, Again

—∼—

B Y DUSK, THE INN GLOWED. CANDLES FLICKERED ALONG THE hallway; the scent of dinner drifted through — thyme, garlic, lemon. The guests gathered in small clusters, voices low, laughter soft.

Elias stood behind the counter polishing the wine glasses — not because anyone would use them tonight, but because the act itself was calming. The reflection of the flames in the glass made him think of movement within stillness — the quiet fire he'd learned to live beside.

Jacob appeared again near the doorway, his jacket slung over one shoulder. "Need a hand?" he asked.

Elias shook his head. "I'm good."

Jacob leaned on the frame. "You always say that."

"Because it's true."

"Or because it's safe."

Elias looked up, meeting his gaze. The air thickened, the kind of quiet that asks for honesty.

"Maybe both," Elias said finally.

Jacob nodded, stepping closer. "You don't have to be safe all the time."

"I know," Elias said. "But I've worked hard for this peace. I don't want to trade it for chaos."

"Who said it had to be chaos?" Jacob's voice was softer now. "What if it's just... living again?"

Elias didn't answer. He just looked at the light catching on Jacob's face — the warmth of it, the recognition. The music from the speaker changed — LANY this time, "Thick and Thin" spilling slow through the air.

Jacob smiled faintly. "You and your playlists."

"They're maps," Elias said. "Of where I've been."

"And where you're going?"

Elias looked around the room, at the guests, the glow, the heartbeat of the Inn itself. "Maybe," he said. "If I'm lucky."

— ~ —

The Night Breathes

— ~ —

AFTER EVERYONE HAD GONE TO BED, ELIAS WALKED THROUGH THE empty dining room. The moon hung low above the mountain, spilling silver across the tables.

He ran his hand over the wood grain of the counter — smooth, warm from the day. The coffee machine clicked softly as it cooled. The whole house seemed to exhale.

He stood by the window, watching the reflection of the porch lights shimmer against the glass. His own image was faint there — a man shaped by silence, stillness, and the smallest, fiercest kind of hope.

He whispered the words he'd written on his first day back: Stillness is a kind of courage.

And somewhere outside, a train's distant horn answered — long, low, and steady, like agreement.

— ∾ —

What the Walls Remember

— ∾ —

T HE INN SEEMED TALLER AFTER RAIN, AS IF THE TIMBERS HAD DRUNK
enough to stand a little straighter. Elias moved through
the dim with a damp towel over his shoulder, touching the
places only he and the house knew: the second baluster that
wobbled if you leaned, the window latch that liked a leftward
nudge, the piano lid that closed if you breathed too hard.

From the kitchen came the steady whisper of milk
steaming. He didn't need to look to know Alyssa was at the
machine—her angles were different from his, more playful, like
she was drawing hearts into the crema even when no one
asked. Cinnamon sat in a small brass dish beside the grinder, a
warm, friendly note that made strangers think they'd been
here before.

"Try this," Alyssa said, sliding a mug into his hand. "Less
sugar. More light."

He tasted. The balance was perfect—cream rounded the
coffee without smothering it; the cinnamon stayed polite.
"You're getting dangerous," he said.

She bumped his shoulder. "You taught me to listen. I'm just
listening to sugar."

A laugh drifted from the foyer—Avery and Kit, the road-
tripping twins, arguing about whether the lake smelled like
coins or cold bread. In the reading room, a woman traced
underlines in a paperback and then underlined her underlines,
as if certainty needed reinforcement. Someone upstairs sang
one confident line of a song and then went quiet,
embarrassed by their own happiness.

Elias stood in the doorway and watched it all. The Inn
wasn't busy-busy; it was held. The air had that good weight a

room gets when every person inside is exactly the size of themselves.

The bell chimed with a breeze, and Jacob leaned in, hair pushed damp against his cap, hoodie unzipped like he'd peeled off a longer day. The old familiar spark rose and scared nobody this time.

"You ever notice," Jacob said, closing the door behind him, "that this place always smells like the first morning of someone's life?"

Elias wiped a ring of condensation from a table. "I always hoped it would."

"Then it does."

They didn't meet in the middle of the room; they met at the edge—Jacob's shoulder to the wall, Elias's hip to the counter, a line of sight with enough room for breath. Alyssa glanced up, saw the weather between them, and set three more mugs to warm because hope likes preparation.

"You hungry?" Elias asked.

"Only for something I can stay to finish."

Elias pretended not to hear the double meaning. "There's orange-cardamom bread. We're testing it for the holiday book."

"Bring me the chapter," Jacob said.

They ate in Plato's Corner—two slices, three napkins, one knife that squeaked against the plate and made them wince in the same instant. Ruel's "Suburbs" visited from the stereo, soft as fog. The fire in the hearth took its time deciding whether to catch. Alyssa moved through with a tray, a comet of efficiency and bracelets.

Jacob set the last crumb like a period on his plate. "Do you still run before sunrise?"

"When I need to remember I have a body."

"And when you don't?"

"I run anyway. It's easier to hear the mountain's yes if I'm already moving."

Jacob smiled in that quiet, proud way he had when he wanted to reach and also wanted to respect the space. "Come tomorrow," he said. "I'll keep pace."

"You never keep pace," Elias said. "You escalate."

"I adapt."

A young girl—Alyssa's age ten years ago—stood at the threshold with a pen clutched like a wand. Her name tag said Maya; her freckles said August. "Excuse me," she asked the room, brave and trembling, "do you have... um... postcards?"

Elias pointed to the oak desk. "Bottom drawer. The ones with the mountain are free. The ones with the Inn cost one story."

Her face lit up. "I have so many."

"Start with your favorite," Alyssa said, appearing at her side like an older sister who'd been conjured instead of raised.

Maya began to talk—about a fox she'd seen by the bike path, about how the steam from hot cocoa made tiny ghosts that ran away if you tried to name them. The grown-ups listened like it was their job. When she finished, Alyssa placed two postcards in her hand. "That's a two-story night."

Maya skipped away, dragging a parent-shaped shadow behind her.

Jacob watched, head tilted. "You ever going to tell me how you built this—this church of ordinary?"

"Brick by cup," Elias said. "And by mistake. And by getting up tomorrow."

"Then I'll get up with you."

The fire finally chose flame. It found the dry part of the wood and drew itself taller, resolving into a steady ribbon. Heat nudged the room wide. Elias felt that familiar ache—the good kind, the one that arrived when stillness tugged at the same place longing used to live.

He stood. "Walk with me. I need to check the porch light."

They stepped into the night. The boards were cool. The street smelled like rain rinsed with stars. Somewhere, a dishwasher in another life clattered into silence. Jacob took the far rail, not the near one. Elias appreciated him for that— the kindness of not encroaching and not retreating.

"Do you miss the noise?" Jacob asked again, not quite the same way as before.

"I miss the part of me that thought noise meant aliveness." He tightened a bulb; the warm pool widened on the wood. "But the quiet here isn't empty. It's listening."

"Listening to what?"

"Whatever you'll say if I don't hurry you."

Jacob did not hurry. The pause had texture, a soft ribbing like knit wool. "I want to stay longer than I told myself I would," he said at last. "Every time."

Elias breathed out through his nose, a smile he'd learned to deliver to the dark. "Then stay. The room is already made. You can pay with a story."

Jacob turned a fraction, enough to show the thought hit clean. "What if it's a hard one?"

"Then we make tea."

"And if it's a good one?"

"We make the same tea and sit closer."

They didn't sit. Not yet. He felt the porch decide to keep the night exactly as it was, unruined by outcome. Somewhere inside, Alyssa laughed—a bright, startled sound that pushed back the edges of their separate histories.

"Tomorrow at six?" Jacob said.

"Five-fifty-eight," Elias replied, because leaning into joy deserved precision.

They went back inside, and the house rearranged itself around their return.

Anatomy of Care

S TEAM CLOUDED THE KITCHEN WINDOW UNTIL THE MOUNTAIN blurred like a watercolor that had been rained on and forgiven. Elias lined mugs in twos even when single orders came in; the symmetry calmed him. He wiped the steel wand, purged the hiss, tapped the portafilter with the same three-count he'd taught himself when he needed a beat that wouldn't argue: one, two, steady.

A guest with travel-tired eyes asked, "How do you make the foam do that swirl?"

"Whisper to it," he said.

"Does it whisper back?"

"If you're patient."

In the lobby, a stack of board games became a small civilization. An older couple negotiated a truce over Scrabble by inventing a rule where any mountain counts as a proper noun. Maya walked past with her postcards held like tarot and informed them gently that summit is common, but Quandary scores more.

Alyssa put out a plate of citrus slices beside the water carafe. "Hydration by seduction," she declared.

"Trademark it," Elias said.

She lowered her voice. "You're different," she said. "This month. Not performing the calm. Owning it."

He thought of the long bike rides that had reset his lungs, the appointment where the nurse had said, Let us carry part of the weight for a while, the afternoon Alyssa had shoved a journal into his hands and said, Write the truth before it chases you through the day. He thought of the mountain's yes.

"I think I found the pace that lets me hear myself," he said. "Every day I keep it is a win."

Alyssa's grin flickered, soft and proud. "Progress, not perfection."

He touched his watch, a private amen.

The Lift in the Room

LATE LIGHT FOUND THE HONEY IN THE FLOORBOARDS. LANY FLOATED in from the speaker—soft, not sad, the kind of melancholy that invites company. Elias polished champagne flutes for the couple in Room 205, who'd shyly whispered anniversary like a password. The ritual mattered even if he'd pour sparkling cider instead—his recovery was a boundary, not a wall. He tied a ribbon around the tray, slid a handwritten note beneath it: Beauty is in the doing. May it keep doing you good.

He carried the tray upstairs. From 205 came a whisper, a gasp, the unmistakable sound of two people seeing each other with new eyes even after years. He set the gift outside and didn't knock. Some moments deserved to be found rather than delivered.

On his way down, he passed the landing window and paused. The lake threw back the color of the sky like a promise. He let himself want the simple things out loud: a run that felt like prayer; a night without interruption; Jacob's shoulder near enough to lean and not have to; Alyssa's laughter protecting the fragile parts of the world.

When he reached the lobby, Jacob was there with a basket of lemons and a look that asked, Can I belong here without breaking anything?

"You already do," Elias said, out loud before the fear could edit him.

Jacob set the basket on the counter and made it a shrug. "Then I'll earn it."

"You don't have to."

"I want to."

"Then stay for dish duty."

Jacob saluted with a towel. "Finally, a promotion I understand."

They worked in the narrowed quiet—August blue deepening outside, the house choosing its softer voice. The clink of plates became percussion; the sweep of towel, a brushed snare; water, a low synth under everything. Alyssa conducted with a stack of clean napkins and an unshakable tempo.

"Tell me a hard story," Elias said softly, not looking up.

Jacob rinsed, considered. "I kept moving because I thought distance meant safety. Turns out I was just teaching myself how to be gone."

Elias set a glass to dry. "And now?"

"I'm practicing arrival."

"Me too," Elias said, and the quiet after held.

They finished the stack. Alyssa flicked the lights to evening and pressed play on a record that began with a single piano note—a lean, amber thing that felt like cinnamon when it lands on milk. People drifted in for decaf and herbal tea. No one asked for anything the house couldn't give.

Elias wrote salon, Thursday in the ledger's margin and added small rituals welcomed. He looked up to find Jacob reading over his shoulder, smiling.

"So it's official?" Jacob asked.

"It's already happening," Elias said. "We're just naming it."

Jacob's knuckles brushed the paper, an accidental vow. "I'll read."

"Then I'll pour."

From upstairs, door 205 opened. Two voices laughed softly, the buoyant, after-gravity kind. Elias felt something in the room lift with them, as if love were a window you could crack for more air.

He breathed it in and believed, for a clean, shimmered second, that the life he had built was not a detour but the road itself.

The mountain was still wearing its first light when Elias stepped out, shoes crunching the frost-soft gravel. Breath misted, hanging like pale ribbon in the air. The town below was quiet except for the hum of someone's radio and the rhythm of a broom against concrete. The world hadn't quite decided to be loud yet, and he loved that.

Inside, the Inn held the kind of warmth that doesn't come from temperature alone. Someone—Alyssa, he guessed—had already lit the fire in the lounge. The smell of cedar and espresso mingled in a way that made the place feel newly built, even though it had stood here for generations.

He ran a cloth over the counter, not because it needed it, but because the motion settled his mind. Behind him, the kettle whistled. He poured hot water over the grounds, the scent rising like memory: cinnamon, caramel, earth. The sound of dripping filled the silence like punctuation.

Alyssa appeared barefoot, hair still wet from a quick shower. "You ever sleep?"

"I nap in sections," Elias said.

She grinned. "You should patent that."

He handed her a mug. "Here. The first pour always tastes better if you don't ask why."

They stood for a moment, side by side, sipping coffee, watching the light crawl through the windowpanes. She leaned her head against his shoulder the way younger sisters do when they think you won't notice.

He did. He just didn't move.

The front door opened and Jacob came in, wrapped in a navy hoodie, cheeks flushed from the cold. "You two look like an ad for calm," he said.

"Fake it till we make it," Alyssa replied.

Jacob laughed, and it was such an easy sound that even the fire seemed to lean closer. He set a small paper bag on the counter. "I brought muffins. Don't ask from where. You'll judge me."

Elias raised an eyebrow. "Gas station again?"

"Local artisan," Jacob insisted. "Artisan of convenience."

They ate in that companionable quiet that only early mornings allow. Jacob's leg brushed Elias's under the counter —by accident, maybe, but it stayed there for half a breath too long.

"Sunrise run today?" Jacob asked.

"Later," Elias said. "I've got a guest checkout and a new batch of roast to test."

Jacob leaned closer. "You always have a reason not to."

Elias smiled faintly. "And you always have a reason to."

"Balance," Jacob said.

"Annoyance," Alyssa muttered into her coffee. They both ignored her.

The doorbell rang—a family arriving early. Elias slipped back into motion, soft but sure, his hands finding purpose before his thoughts could. Alyssa followed, and the day began in full: the shuffle of boots, the low chatter of introductions, the clink of keys on the marble desk.

By noon, the Inn was alive again. The sound of suitcases bumping up stairs, water running through pipes, someone practicing a guitar in the far lounge. Sunlight poured through the stained glass, painting the lobby in muted amber and blue.

Jacob found him again around two, out on the porch mending a planter box. "You always fix things that don't need fixing," he said.

Elias didn't look up. "They all need something eventually."

Jacob crouched beside him. "Maybe that's true for people too."

Elias smiled without answering. The mountain wind swept through, cool and clean. He could smell snow higher up the ridge even though spring was trying hard to stay.

They worked like that for a while—no plan, just proximity. Jacob brushed sawdust off Elias's sleeve once, and his hand lingered in that small, suspended space between apology and intention.

Later, when the sun slipped behind the slope and the porch lights blinked on, the guests began to gather in Plato's Corner again. Alyssa played soft Ruel tracks, the kind that made people talk quieter. The room felt like it was holding its own breath.

Elias poured coffee, set down plates, laughed at things he barely heard. Across the room, Jacob caught his eye and lifted his mug slightly, a wordless toast.

The moment wasn't loud. It didn't need to be. It was enough that Elias felt it—the small, exact click of something aligning.

Outside, snow began to fall again, soft as breath, erasing every footprint from the morning.

Snow came early that year. Not the kind that shouted its arrival, but a soft, confident fall that blanketed the streetlights in calm. By morning, the Inn looked like a confection itself—frosted edges, powdered roofs, chimney smoke curling like icing.

Elias stood at the window, mug in hand, watching flakes cling to the railing. Behind him, the kitchen was already alive with motion: Alyssa in her red apron, stirring a bowl big enough to be a small planet. The air smelled of molasses and citrus zest.

"Gingerbread Week," she declared, voice half-buried under the hum of the mixer. "Our Mount Royal Olympics."

He smiled, setting his mug down beside the recipe binder— old pages flecked with sugar, corners stiff from years of use. The Frisco Inn on Galena Presents: The World-Renowned Gingerbread Invitational. The title still made him laugh. They'd invented it once as a joke, and now families booked entire Decembers around it.

You were in the boutique next door, stringing garlands in the window display—evergreen, gold ribbon, and hand-stitched felt ornaments that smelled faintly of cedar. The little bell above the door jingled every few minutes as guests wandered in, leaving trails of snow that melted into tiny, perfect stars on the floor.

Jacob arrived midmorning, dusted in white like he'd walked straight out of a snow globe. "I come bearing gifts," he said, lifting a box. Inside: ginger, cinnamon, cardamom, and three kinds of molasses.

"You're early," Elias said.

"I'm late from last year," Jacob replied, shaking snow from his hair. "Besides, it's tradition."

Alyssa handed him a whisk. "Then get to work, tradition."

By noon, the kitchen had become a warm kind of chaos—bowls stacked, timers beeping, the radio alternating between Ruel's "Distance" and old jazz standards. Guests drifted in and out, drawn by the scent. Someone from Room 4 was sculpting a cathedral out of dough. The couple from Denver was attempting a ski chalet complete with pretzel-rod lift towers.

"Judging's at seven on Friday," Alyssa announced to the room, as though she were addressing a royal court. "Points for creativity, structural integrity, and festive spirit. Extra credit for stories attached to your house."

Elias nodded toward her clipboard. "You've been practicing your tone again."

"I like authority," she said. "It makes people brave."

He looked around at the floured faces, the laughter, the faint music. Brave, he thought, is exactly what this is. People building fragile things that might collapse—but doing it anyway, together.

Jacob leaned close enough for his breath to warm the back of Elias's neck. "You realize this is the only place in the world where adults argue about gumdrop placement like it's theology."

"That's why it works," Elias said.

Outside, snow continued in slow confession. Inside, time folded. Every sound—the clink of spoons, the hum of ovens, the faint echo of you laughing from the boutique—wove into something whole.

Evening settled without announcement. Alyssa lit the window candles one by one, each a small promise. The inn's sign gleamed against the falling dark: Still, by Design.

Elias stepped outside to hang a final wreath. The air tasted like pine and sugar. Across the street, the lake's edge glimmered beneath a thin layer of frost. Jacob joined him, hands shoved deep in his coat pockets.

"Do you ever stop and think how lucky this is?" Jacob asked quietly.

Elias tilted his head. "Luck feels too easy. I'd call it grace earned the hard way."

Jacob smiled, snow gathering in his eyelashes. "Then here's to earning it again tomorrow."

Inside, laughter broke out—the sound of a roof collapsing in the great gingerbread war of Room 7. Alyssa's voice carried: "Ten points for effort!"

Elias laughed, and Jacob's joined his, their breath meeting in the cold.

The Inn glowed behind them like memory made visible. And for the first time in years, Elias didn't feel like he was tending something fragile. He felt like he was part of something strong enough to hold him, too.

By dusk, the Inn shimmered like something remembered from a dream. Snow kept falling in slow, deliberate spirals, the kind that hushes the whole world. Through the wide front windows, the glow of the fire turned the snow outside amber, as if the warmth were leaking into the night.

Inside, it was all soft sound and laughter. Every lamp was dimmed to that perfect golden tone — the kind that turns conversation into music. Wreaths framed the windows, pine-scented and threaded with tiny white lights. Candles flickered along the tables, their reflections trembling in the glassware like little stars.

The dining room had been transformed into a wonderland of sugar and story. The gingerbread houses stood like a village reborn — crooked roofs, sugared trees, chocolate chimneys exhaling faint wisps of steam. Each one carried fingerprints and intention, joy baked right into its walls. The centerpiece was unmistakable: a perfect miniature of the Inn itself, its red door glowing, its windows framed in icing.

Elias stood near the hearth, coat dusted with flour and snow, tie askew, smile unguarded. He looked out over the room — guests, locals, travelers who'd stumbled in by luck — and thought that maybe this was what belonging actually looked like.

Alyssa took the floor with her clipboard. "Alright, everyone! The results are in!"

The crowd hushed, warm and bright and expectant.

Jacob leaned against the bar, arms folded, eyes locked on Elias with a look that said he'd already won something.

Alyssa cleared her throat with exaggerated ceremony. "Third place goes to Room 4, for their audacious but slightly leaning Alpine chapel!" Applause and laughter. "Second place—

Room 7, for demonstrating the importance of architectural humility after gravity's intervention."

She paused for effect, grin wide. "And first place... to our youngest entrant, Miss Lila from Room 2, for her 'Frisco at Christmas'—featuring actual light-up windows and more heart than any blueprint could hold!"

The little girl gasped, cheeks red as cranberries. The crowd erupted. Someone lifted her onto a chair. The lights blinked as if joining the celebration.

Elias caught her eye, hand over his heart. "You built the feeling of this place," he said softly, and she smiled, shy but proud.

As the applause softened, the fire popped once, loud and bright, and Alyssa raised a mug. "To the Inn!"

Everyone echoed her: "To the Inn!"

Elias turned slightly, catching Jacob watching him again — that quiet, steady look, no longer heavy with what-ifs but light with recognition. Jacob crossed the room slowly, stopping just close enough for Elias to feel his presence more than his touch.

"See?" Jacob murmured. "You built this too."

Elias looked around: Alyssa laughing with guests, the scent of cinnamon and citrus, the glow of snowlight on wood beams, the gentle hum of LANY's 'Thru These Tears' playing low from the stereo. Everything was alive, threaded with warmth.

"Not alone," he said.

Jacob nodded. "That's the best part."

Outside, the snow thickened, but no one noticed. The Inn was its own weather system now — glowing, pulsing, safe. Someone started a slow carol on the piano; a few guests joined, voices low and unpolished but sincere.

Alyssa dimmed the last light above the hearth. "Perfect," she whispered, stepping back to admire the glow.

Elias felt it then — the pulse of the Inn itself, deep and rhythmic, like a heart content to keep time. The walls breathed warmth. The floor remembered footsteps. The fire hummed approval.

Jacob reached out, barely touching Elias's sleeve. "Still," he said quietly.

Elias smiled, the kind that belongs to people who finally stopped running. "By design."

The snow fell harder, soft as grace, wrapping the Inn in silence. Inside, the warmth didn't waver. It only deepened.

Light in the Quiet

S NOW STILL COVERED FRISCO LIKE A HELD BREATH. THE STORM HAD passed overnight, leaving the world sculpted in silence. The Inn rose from it like a memory reborn — eaves hung with icicles catching the first threads of gold light, smoke curling soft from the chimney.

Inside, the warmth lingered. The fire had burned down to its patient embers. The dining room was a soft ruin of celebration — plates stacked, crumbs of gingerbread dusting the tables, ribbons left half-curled. The air smelled faintly of sugar and pine and something human — laughter that hadn't quite left.

Elias moved through it slowly, sweeping, collecting, tending. He didn't rush. Every sound — the whisper of the broom, the distant creak of the floorboards — felt like a language he'd finally learned to understand.

In the kitchen, Alyssa was already humming to herself, hair tied up messily, a mug of coffee balanced dangerously on the counter. "Morning," she said, her voice still sleep-rough.

"Morning," Elias replied, his tone carrying that soft awe that only followed nights that meant something. "How'd you sleep?"

"Like someone who doesn't have to run tomorrow," she said, smiling. "You?"

"I didn't dream," he said. "And that feels like enough."

Outside, the light shifted — a pale shimmer climbing over Mount Royal, brushing the windows with warmth. Elias stepped closer to the glass. Down below, the snow along Galena glittered like someone had spilled stars on the street.

Then he saw him.

Jacob was outside, bundled against the cold, sweeping the front steps clear. He worked slowly, rhythmically, every exhale a visible cloud. When he looked up and caught Elias's gaze through the window, he didn't wave — he just smiled. The kind that said good morning without needing words.

Elias's chest tightened in that new, steady way. He grabbed a second mug from the rack and poured coffee into both — rich, dark, the house roast he'd blended himself. He hesitated for a moment, then added a dash of cinnamon and cream, stirring until the color turned the shade of late morning.

He stepped outside, the door creaking softly behind him. The air bit cold, but clean — the kind of cold that woke you into gratitude.

Jacob straightened, leaning on the shovel. "You didn't have to."

"I wanted to," Elias said, handing him the cup. "House blend. Strong enough to bring the dead back."

Jacob laughed, took a sip, and winced. "Or kill the living."

"That's how you know it's working."

They stood there in companionable silence, watching the town stir awake — a dog trotting through fresh snow, a delivery truck rumbling in the distance, a child in a red coat dragging a sled toward the slope behind the library.

"This place," Jacob said softly, looking at the Inn. "It's like it keeps its promises."

Elias nodded. "Only the ones you make to yourself inside it."

Jacob tilted his head, studying him. "You ever think about what's next?"

Elias smiled, that quiet, knowing smile. "No. I think about now."

The light caught his face — softening the lines around his eyes, turning the steam from their mugs into halos. Somewhere behind them, Alyssa's laughter floated through the door as she called out to a guest. The scent of scones drifted on the air again — cinnamon and butter and warmth.

Elias turned to look back at the Inn — its red door glowing against the snow, its windows alive with firelight, the wreath above the entry twinkling in the morning sun. It was perfect in its imperfection. Still, by design.

And for the first time in a long time, he didn't feel like he was watching a life unfold. He felt like he was inside it.

The wind shifted, carrying a bell tone from somewhere down the street — the sound that marked the first chairlift opening on the mountain, the first spark of another day beginning.

Elias took one last sip of coffee, let the warmth linger, then glanced toward Jacob. "Come on," he said, nodding toward the path. "Let's take a walk before the guests wake up. The world's still new."

Jacob grinned. "Lead the way, caretaker."

Elias laughed softly. "Not caretaker. Just someone learning to stay."

And together they walked out into the fresh snow, their footprints side by side — vanishing behind them almost as soon as they were made.

Above them, the mountain breathed. Behind them, the Inn glowed. And in the hush of that bright morning, everything felt possible again.

The Sound of Water Returning

B Y March, the snow had begun to retreat — slowly, stubbornly, like a guest who didn't want to check out. The roofs wept at noon, the gutters trickled, and the creek behind the Inn loosened its frozen throat. It began quietly, with a single thread of water running under the ice, then another, then a chorus — a thousand rivulets whispering: we're back.

Elias heard it first before he saw it. That thin, rhythmic music of thawing ice carried through the floorboards, blending with the hush of the espresso machine. It was the mountain's pulse returning — the signal that the season had turned, even if the snowdrifts refused to admit it yet.

He'd cracked open the kitchen window earlier that morning, just an inch, to let in the air. It came cold and clean and full of scent — pine sap, damp earth, the faint sweetness of decay that promised growth. The light was different now too: warmer, more forgiving, the kind that slipped around edges instead of cutting through them.

He moved through the morning the way he always did — with ritual, but not routine. Wiping the marble counters. Folding the dish towels into perfect thirds. Turning the cups so their handles faced east. He didn't do it for guests. He did it for rhythm, for sanity. For the quiet promise that some things could be tended into peace.

Behind him, the radio played softly — Ruel's "Suburbia" drifting in and out through static. He hummed along, not quite on key, and smiled when the chorus hit that line about "missing the small things."

The coffee brewed dark and strong. He poured it into two cups — one for himself, one for Jacob, though Jacob was still asleep upstairs. He'd been helping Alyssa move boxes late into the night: new stock for the boutique, jars of local honey, lavender candles, tiny soaps shaped like alpine flowers. Their laughter had carried through the vents. It had been a long time since laughter felt like part of the walls again.

Elias set Jacob's cup by the stairs, a quiet offering.

By midmorning, the light had turned molten. He moved upstairs to strip the beds, humming under his breath. Room 3 faced Mount Royal, and the view from its window always reminded him why he stayed. The snowline had already crept higher up the ridge. You could see streaks of wet stone now, veins of earth showing through.

He paused, one hand resting on the window frame, eyes half-closed. The reflection looking back at him had changed since the year before. Softer in some ways, sharper in others. His hair had grown longer — a wave that caught the light like it had something to say. His face was leaner, more lived-in, but the eyes — those same storm-colored eyes — held something steadier now.

He opened the window wider, breathing in the melt. Somewhere down in town, a dog barked, a snow shovel clanged, and a car door slammed twice before the engine caught. Frisco was waking up from its long, beautiful sleep.

"Elias?"

Alyssa's voice carried up from the lobby, bright and insistent.

"Yeah?" he called, folding the sheet into a crisp square.

"Can you come down for a sec? I think we have a situation with the new display."

He grinned to himself. "Of course we do."

When he reached the bottom of the stairs, he found her kneeling in front of the front desk, surrounded by a battlefield of gift items — half-unpacked boxes, tissue paper, twine, tags. A hand-lettered sign read Spring Boutique Collection, though the "B" was already smudged.

"It collapsed," she said solemnly, gesturing to a pile of honey jars. "Gravity's rude."

Elias crouched beside her, suppressing a laugh. "Maybe it's an aesthetic choice?"

"Minimalist chaos?"

"Rustic entropy."

They looked at each other and broke into laughter.

Nora, the new college intern, appeared behind them carrying a stack of folded linens. "I think we can fix it," she said earnestly. "We just need balance. You know — heavy things on the bottom, lighter things on top."

Alyssa winked. "See? Wisdom of youth."

"Or common sense," Elias added.

They rearranged the table together. When it was finally upright again — the candles gleaming, the soaps in neat rows, the jars of honey glowing amber in the light — it felt like more than a display. It felt like a small declaration: spring is coming. we are still here.

The front door opened then, letting in a breath of mountain air. Jacob stepped inside, hair wind-tossed, cheeks pink from the cold, his flannel half-buttoned. He carried a crate of paintbrushes in one hand and a bouquet of tulips in the other.

"Don't ask," he said, setting them on the counter. "The flower shop lady insisted. Said the lobby looked like it needed a pulse."

Elias tilted his head. "She's not wrong."

Alyssa clasped her hands. "Finally! Color!"

Jacob's gaze found Elias's — a brief, quiet connection in the middle of the bustle. It wasn't heavy like before, but easy. Like they'd stopped needing to solve the past and just started living in it.

He gestured toward the window. "The creek's moving again. Want to take a walk after lunch?"

Elias nodded. "Yeah. Let's see what's left of winter."

That afternoon, the Inn filled with motion again. The sound of footsteps, the clatter of cups, the small talk of guests returning after months away. A couple from Denver checked in for their anniversary — the same couple who'd built the leaning gingerbread chapel in December. A writer from Santa Fe arrived with a vintage typewriter and a promise to "finally finish something here."

Everywhere Elias went, there was a trace of thaw. Condensation on the windows. The smell of polish. The glint of sunlight off brass.

And everywhere he went, he felt the same thing: That gentle, grounding sense that life was beginning again — not loudly, but truthfully.

When dusk came, he stood on the porch with Jacob, watching the last of the snowmelt drip from the eaves. The tulips Alyssa had placed in the window behind them caught the fading light, their petals glowing like tiny lanterns.

Jacob handed him a mug of coffee — their second of the day, both still warm.

Elias took it, smiled. "You know what I love about this place?"

Jacob leaned against the railing. "What's that?"

"It remembers."

Jacob nodded slowly. "Maybe that's why people come back."

The creek below kept singing, louder now, water rushing over stone. The wind carried the scent of thawed pine and promise.

And in that quiet, Elias realized something: Every season asked the same question — not will you change? but will you stay long enough to notice that you already have?

He closed his eyes and let the sound of the water answer.

THE MARKET PREPARATIONS

———

G

B Y THE FOLLOWING WEEK, THE INN HAD FOUND ITS NEW TEMPO —
lively, a little messy, humming with energy like an
orchestra tuning before the first note.

Alyssa had strung paper lanterns across the library's
windows, Nora had filled mason jars with fresh tulips, and the
faint smell of lemon polish lingered in every corner. From the
kitchen came the constant rhythm of something being
prepared: the clatter of trays, the hiss of steam, the soft
scrape of a wooden spoon against a metal bowl.

Outside, vendors were already claiming spots along the
walk. The air was crisp, edged with sunlight, and the sound of
hammering mingled with birdsong. Frisco's annual Spring
Artisan Market wasn't just a local event anymore; it had
become something people planned their trips around — a
weekend where art and memory blurred, and everything
smelled like lavender and dough.

Elias had been up since five, moving between the kitchen
and the front desk with that practiced, meditative grace of
someone trying not to think too much.

He liked motion. It kept the mind from asking questions it
wasn't ready to answer.

Jacob had left early that morning to "run an errand,"
though he hadn't said what. That wasn't unusual — Jacob was
a man of half-answers and long pauses — but something in his
tone had been different. Quiet, careful.

Now, as Elias wiped down the counter for the fifth time,
the unease he'd been trying to ignore began to settle in.

Alyssa appeared beside him, brushing crumbs from her
apron. "You've been cleaning that spot for twenty minutes,"

she said gently.

He forced a small smile. "Therapy."

"Maybe the kind that needs a co-pay."

He laughed, but the sound was thin.

"You okay?" she asked, leaning her hip against the counter. "You've been... somewhere else."

"I'm fine."

She raised an eyebrow. "You're lying."

"I'm—"

The front door opened then, and the conversation fell away.

Jacob stepped in, the mountain light catching in his hair, the doorbell chiming its delicate note. He wasn't smiling. His expression was composed, but not calm — like someone who'd been rehearsing a truth on the drive back.

He held a paper bag in one hand and something folded — a letter maybe — in the other.

"Hey," Elias said, trying for casual.

"Hey," Jacob echoed. "Got the supplies. And, uh... something else."

Alyssa looked between them, sensing the shift. "I'm gonna... check on Nora." She disappeared toward the kitchen without waiting for an answer.

Jacob set the bag down, then the paper. His fingers lingered on it for a second before he let go. "This came this morning. My brother sent it up from Denver."

Elias's stomach tightened. He reached for the letter but didn't unfold it.

Jacob exhaled. "It's from the design firm. They offered me a permanent position. Out east."

Silence. Not sharp — just heavy.

Elias glanced at the paper. Out east. That could mean a dozen things, but all of them far.

"You said you were done with the city," Elias said quietly.

"I thought I was." Jacob's voice was steady, but his hands weren't. "It's... good work, El. Real work. Building again. Creating."

"You're building here," Elias said before he could stop himself.

Jacob's eyes softened, almost with regret. "This is your building. I just help it stand a little taller."

Elias swallowed, the air suddenly too thin. "When do they need an answer?"

"Soon."

The word hung there, cruel in its simplicity.

Outside, a hammer struck wood — loud, decisive. Someone laughed down the street, a vendor calling for help lifting a canopy. The normalcy of it all made the moment stranger.

Elias looked down at the counter. A thin ring of moisture from Jacob's cup shimmered faintly in the sunlight, fading at the edges. He wiped it away without meaning to.

Jacob watched him, eyes full of something between apology and ache. "Say something."

Elias shook his head. "I don't know what to say that doesn't sound selfish."

"Try me."

He looked up then, meeting Jacob's gaze. "Stay."

It wasn't loud. It wasn't desperate. It was just real.

Jacob's face softened, then closed again like a curtain drawn too fast. "I want to. God, you have no idea how much I want to. But I've spent years running from things that ask me to stay still. Maybe I need to see what it's like to build something that doesn't depend on a season."

Elias wanted to say that this — this Inn, this fragile, luminous thing they'd built together — wasn't seasonal. That it was more permanent than any office or project or skyline. But he couldn't. Because deep down, he knew the truth: the world outside didn't stop for stillness.

Instead, he nodded. "You should do what's right for you."

Jacob blinked, as if he hadn't expected permission.

Elias smiled — small, tired, but kind. "Just don't forget to come home."

The chime above the door rang again as a guest entered, breaking the spell. Jacob stepped back, pocketed the letter, and said quietly, "We'll talk tonight."

Elias nodded again, though his throat felt thick. "Yeah. Tonight."

When the door closed behind Jacob, the air seemed to change temperature. The chimes kept ringing faintly, long after he'd gone.

Alyssa reappeared, reading his face before he spoke.

"What happened?"

He exhaled. "Nothing yet."

She set a hand on his shoulder. "Then maybe that's something."

Outside, the mountain wind carried the scent of spring — sharp, green, alive. The market stalls shimmered with color, vendors laughing as they strung up hand-painted signs. Inside, Elias poured another cup of coffee, though he knew he wouldn't drink it.

The house felt the shift too — the kind of quiet that comes not from loss, but from waiting.

— ~ —

The First Night of the Market

— ~ —

B Y SUNSET, FRISCO HAD TRANSFORMED. THE WHOLE TOWN GLOWED with color and sound — booths spilling out along Main Street, the smell of caramel and citrus threading through the cold. Paper lanterns swung gently overhead, their light reflecting off puddles left by the day's thaw. The Inn stood at the center of it all — not just a building, but the heartbeat of the evening.

From the porch, Elias could see everything. Alyssa had arranged a table of steaming cider and handmade truffles; Nora was tying green ribbons around napkin rolls with the focus of a surgeon. Even the local musicians — a trio with mismatched sweaters and perfect harmonies — had gathered by the fire pit, tuning their guitars as the first stars began to appear.

Inside, the warmth of the Inn pulsed outward — laughter spilling through the open doors, music threading softly beneath conversation. The boutique sparkled with new life: soft scarves, mountain-scented soaps, and that faint smell of cinnamon blended with cream that always seemed to linger when the fire was strong.

And yet, for all of it — the glow, the joy, the living pulse of spring — Elias felt slightly apart. Not lonely. Just... tender.

He moved through the crowd with practiced grace, nodding to vendors, helping a guest find their table, adjusting a lantern whose flame burned too low. His body did what it always did, but his mind was elsewhere — back at the counter that morning, at the sound of Jacob's voice saying out east.

He found himself by the window near the espresso bar, where he could see the reflection of the street's golden light

spilling over the snowmelt. Someone had left a mug half-full —
the foam now collapsed, heart-shaped residue clinging to the
porcelain. He wiped it away gently, the motion automatic.

"Still running a one-man show?"

Jacob's voice came from behind him — quieter, more
cautious than usual.

Elias didn't turn immediately. "Someone's got to keep the
wheels from falling off."

Jacob stepped beside him, holding a mug of cider. He
looked around the room — the guests, the laughter, Alyssa
trying to teach a group of kids how to make beeswax candles.
"You've built something, El. You know that, right?"

Elias smiled faintly. "We built it."

Jacob nodded, eyes tracing the flicker of candlelight across
the glass. "Yeah. We did."

For a moment, they stood there in silence, the kind of quiet
that feels louder than any sound. The music outside swelled
— something gentle and familiar, a local band's rendition of
Ruel's "Painkiller." The melody drifted through the open door,
soft and aching.

Elias looked over at him finally. "You're leaving."

Jacob didn't answer right away. He took a sip instead, eyes
down. "I haven't said yes yet."

"You will."

"Maybe."

Elias wanted to be angry — wanted to say how can you
build a life here and just walk away from it? — but he couldn't.
Because he understood. He'd spent so much of his own life

running toward places that promised purpose. Maybe this was Jacob's turn.

Jacob glanced around the room again. "You ever feel like this house is too alive? Like it's keeping track of us?"

Elias smiled softly. "Always."

They stood there, both watching as Nora carried a tray of cookies too large for her to manage. Alyssa caught it mid-wobble, the crowd applauding. Someone started clapping along to the music, and suddenly the entire room joined in — laughter rippling like light through the air.

Elias felt something shift in him then. Not peace exactly, but something close. A loosening. He looked at Jacob — at the tired kindness in his eyes, the way his hand tapped unconsciously to the beat — and thought, maybe it doesn't have to be forever to be real.

Jacob's gaze flicked up, catching his. "Dance with me."

Elias blinked. "What?"

Jacob set his mug down. "Come on. You never do. Always watching, never joining."

"I can't dance."

"You don't have to. Just move."

Before Elias could protest, Jacob took his hand — just long enough to pull him toward the open space by the fire. People shifted, laughing, making room. The song changed, slower now, softer. The air between them was thick with woodsmoke and memory.

They didn't really dance. They just stood close, moving slightly to the rhythm, breathing in the same beat. The world blurred: candlelight, laughter, music, everything.

Jacob leaned in just enough to say, "If I go, it's not away from you. You know that, right?"

Elias's throat tightened. "Then what is it?"

Jacob smiled sadly. "A way through."

The words lingered between them, fragile and bright.

When the song ended, Jacob stepped back, eyes unreadable. "Save me a coffee for the morning?"

Elias nodded. "Always."

Jacob smiled, then turned toward the door, disappearing into the cool night air, his silhouette swallowed by the lantern glow.

Elias stood there for a long moment, watching until he couldn't see him anymore. Then he exhaled, turned toward the fire, and felt the Inn breathe with him — a sigh of warmth, of life continuing.

Alyssa appeared beside him, wiping her hands on her apron. "You okay?"

He smiled faintly. "I think so."

"You'll be more than okay," she said softly. "You always are."

Outside, the night deepened. Snowmelt dripped from the eaves like ticking clocks, each drop marking time — patient, relentless, and kind.

G

CHAPTER TEN
MORNING AFTER

G

T HE INN WAS QUIET AGAIN. THE KIND OF QUIET THAT COMES NOT from stillness, but from something just finished — like applause fading after the last song. The lanterns were still lit in the lobby, their light pale against the blue-gray dawn. A few napkins lay crumpled on the counter, and the faint smell of cinnamon and cream still lingered in the air.

Elias moved through the space barefoot, his steps soft on the old wood. He'd fallen asleep late, or maybe early, he wasn't sure. His dreams had been full of fragments — a song half-heard, a voice calling his name, Jacob's hands steady on his shoulders, then gone.

He didn't turn on the lights. He liked the room this way — washed in the early light that made every imperfection tender instead of tired. On the counter sat last night's coffee pot, cold but fragrant. He poured a little anyway, took a sip, winced, and smiled.

Routine. Always routine. It didn't matter if the world shifted or if his heart did — the coffee still needed brewing, the tables still needed setting, the Inn still needed him to move through it like breath.

He began quietly: straightening chairs, wiping the marble, aligning menus. Little rituals of control that kept the noise in his head from getting too loud.

The mountain air coming through the window carried that same early spring scent — pine, snowmelt, and faintly, the smoke from a chimney somewhere down the street. He pressed his palm against the cool glass. Outside, the world looked washed clean — roofs dripping, birds tentative, the creek a little louder than yesterday.

For a while, he just stood there. Letting the light reach him.

Then he heard the creak of the floorboards. Alyssa's voice, still half-asleep, floated from the stairs. "You're up already?"

He smiled without turning. "You say that like it's new."

"I say that like you might actually sleep one day." She appeared beside him, a blanket draped around her shoulders. Her hair was wild, her expression soft. "You okay?"

He nodded. "Yeah. Just... processing."

"About Jacob?"

"About everything."

She was quiet for a moment, then said gently, "He cares about you, you know."

"I know," Elias said. "That's what makes it hard."

Alyssa rested her head on his shoulder, her voice low. "Sometimes love doesn't ask us to stay. It asks us to bless someone's leaving."

He didn't answer. The words settled in the air like dust, light but impossible to ignore.

Behind them, the espresso machine hissed to life, as if remembering its duty. Elias turned, wiped his hands on a towel, and smiled faintly. "Guess that's my cue."

"Guess so," she said. "I'll get the pastries ready."

As the first guests began to stir upstairs, the Inn came alive again — softly, gently, like a body stretching after a long sleep. The sound of running water, footsteps, laughter through walls. Life returning, even as something inside him still stood at a crossroads.

He moved behind the counter, grinding the beans. The sound filled the air, steady and grounding. The smell followed

— dark, bitter, familiar. He measured the cream carefully, watching the swirl of white into brown, and thought of the note Jacob had left by the register:

Be gentle with the day. It's new too.

Elias smiled, tucked the note into his pocket, and whispered to the empty room, "I'll try."

Evening

B Y DUSK, THE INN HAD TRANSFORMED. THE LIGHT THAT HAD POURED through the lobby windows all afternoon now lay in soft puddles along the walls, its last traces turning everything honey-gold before retreating entirely. In its place, candles flickered on tables and sconces, their glow breathing warmth into every corner.

The dining room buzzed — softly, intimately — with the kind of noise that made a place feel lived in. The clink of silverware, a burst of laughter, a chair scraping against the wood floor. A violin played somewhere in the background, its melody slow and unhurried, as though time had finally given permission to rest.

Elias moved through it all with the grace of someone both part of and apart from the moment. His apron was folded neatly at his waist, sleeves rolled up, a faint dusting of flour still on his forearms. He carried a tray of wine glasses, weaving between tables with an ease born not of repetition, but devotion.

"More Merlot?" he asked softly to a table of older guests, their cheeks pink from both laughter and altitude.

"Please," one of them said. "You're spoiling us, Elias."

He smiled. "That's the point."

When he turned toward the fireplace, he paused — Jacob was there, speaking with Alyssa and a couple from Denver who'd come up for the weekend. The light from the flames painted him in soft orange and gold, his smile unguarded, his hand resting lightly on the back of a chair. He looked at home here — or perhaps Elias's idea of home had begun to take his shape.

Their eyes met across the room, and for a moment, the noise fell away. It was that kind of silence that existed only between two people who'd already said too much and not enough.

Jacob's look was small but certain — a quiet acknowledgment. Elias felt his chest tighten, then ease. He exhaled, steady, and turned back to his tray.

Alyssa joined him near the counter, carrying a bowl of sugared almonds. "It's beautiful tonight," she said, setting them out near the hearth.

"It is," Elias said. "Feels like the Inn itself is exhaling."

She nodded. "You've built something special here."

"We've built it," he corrected.

She smiled, nudging him. "You always say that. Maybe start believing it."

A burst of laughter rose from the far corner where a young couple clinked their glasses together, whispering something only they could hear. The violinist shifted into something slower, sweeter. The melody curled through the room like smoke, warm and familiar.

Elias poured another round of coffee for a guest and felt the rhythm of the night carry him — the cadence of motion, the small kindnesses that kept the world turning.

Jacob approached the counter quietly, two empty wine glasses in hand. "Refills?"

"Always," Elias said, filling them carefully.

Jacob leaned on the counter, close enough that Elias could smell cedar and soap. "You know," Jacob said, "if you ever decide to stop running the place, you'd make a damn good magician."

Elias laughed softly. "Why's that?"

"Because somehow, every time I walk in here, everything feels lighter."

Elias didn't respond right away. He capped the wine bottle, set it down, and met Jacob's eyes. "Maybe it's not magic. Maybe it's just care."

"Maybe," Jacob said. "But you're the only one who makes it feel like that matters."

The fire popped. Someone in the corner toasted "to small miracles," and a few voices echoed it with cheerful sincerity. The violin swelled gently.

Jacob took one of the glasses, but instead of walking away, lingered. "You ever think about it?" he asked quietly.

"About what?"

"About staying."

Elias looked past him, toward the guests, the glowing hearth, the windowpanes glistening with condensation. The world outside was dark now, but inside — this little world he'd built — there was light enough for everyone.

"I do," he said finally. "Every day."

Jacob nodded. "Good."

They didn't say more. They didn't need to. The silence that followed was soft, forgiving — the kind that allowed room for everything left unspoken.

As the night deepened, the laughter softened, and the Inn's rhythm slowed to a heartbeat's pace. Elias stood by the window again, watching the reflection of candlelight shimmer against the glass. For a moment, he saw not his own reflection, but the shape of something larger — belonging, perhaps.

He took a slow breath, the air thick with warmth and cinnamon and the faintest trace of lavender. Somewhere behind him, Jacob's voice mixed with Alyssa's laughter. And for once, Elias didn't analyze the feeling.

He just let himself exist in it — fully, gently, completely.

— ~ —

Morning After

— ~ —

THE MORNING CAME SLOW. THE KIND OF SLOW THAT FEELS EARNED — like the world had taken a deep breath and decided to hold it just a little longer.

Elias woke before the alarm. The quiet felt clean. The light through the window was pale gold, threading its way across the quilt like the promise of a softer day. For a moment, he stayed still, listening — the pipes ticking gently, the hush of wind around the shutters, the low hum of the Inn waking in its own time.

The scent of roasted coffee reached him first, then the faintest trace of sugar and spice — ginger, nutmeg, cinnamon. They'd stopped baking those for the Gingerbread Competition months ago, but somehow, the scent never really left the walls. He liked that about this place. It remembered joy in layers.

He sat up, rubbed his eyes, and caught his reflection in the old mirror — sleep-tousled hair, tired eyes that didn't look as tired as they once did, the shadow of something lighter around his mouth. He wasn't sure if it was happiness or just the peace that came from living honestly. Maybe both.

He dressed quietly, pulling on a soft henley and jeans worn thin at the knees, and stepped into the hallway. The air was cooler there, alive with the smell of polish and mountain air. On the wall near the landing hung a framed photo — the Gingerbread Competition winners. Alyssa had insisted they hang it. A miniature of the Inn itself — crafted in sugar and light — every balcony, every window, every carved piece of trim replicated perfectly, down to the flickering candy-lamp in the front entry. It had taken a team of three guests, a retired architect, and two toddlers to pull it off, but it was still standing on the shelf in the lounge, its sugared roof glinting whenever the sun passed over.

Elias smiled at the sight of it, that perfect echo of December joy surviving through spring.

Downstairs, the faint hum of Mama's Boy drifted through the rooms, the speakers crackling slightly with age. The track was "Heart Won't Let Me," soft and slow, like memory itself had pressed play. He followed it.

The kitchen was already warm — the espresso machine sighing with steam, the scent of butter and flour blooming from the oven. Alyssa was there, hair in a loose braid, apron already dusted white, humming along with the song.

"Morning," she said without turning.

"Morning," Elias replied. "You're early."

"Old habits."

He smiled at that, heading for the grinder. The beans whispered against the steel, a small rhythm he knew by heart.

"I found another ribbon from the competition," Alyssa said, nodding toward the counter. "It was stuck in one of the pastry boxes. Red with little sugar crystals still on it."

Elias glanced at it — the ribbon curled on the counter, faded but still lovely. "You think it's trying to tell us something?"

"That we're supposed to do it again next year?"

He chuckled softly. "Maybe."

The espresso machine hissed to life — the sound as steady as breathing. He poured the shot, the crema forming smooth and golden, then poured a second without thinking. His old ritual. Two cups. One for the moment. One for whoever might walk in.

Right on cue, the door creaked open — the sound of morning slipping in. Jacob stood there, cheeks flushed from the cold, eyes bright but weary. He hesitated in the doorway like someone testing the temperature of a familiar room.

"Couldn't sleep?" Elias asked.

Jacob shook his head, smiling faintly. "The mountain looked too good to ignore."

Elias poured a cup and slid it toward him. "You always did chase the first light."

Jacob accepted the mug, their fingers brushing briefly — enough to notice, not enough to linger. "I missed this," he said. "The sound. The smell. You."

Elias looked up, surprised by the ease of the confession, then softened. "Then don't miss it. Stay long enough to remember it properly."

Jacob smiled, but there was a shadow behind it — something he wasn't saying yet.

Alyssa, catching the undercurrent, excused herself with a knowing glance. "I'll check the oven."

The silence that followed wasn't empty. It was filled with everything neither of them had found the words for last time.

Outside, the mountain was shedding the last of its snow, trickles of meltwater threading through the rocks. The sun was climbing higher, scattering gold across the rooftops of Frisco.

Jacob took a slow sip of coffee, then said, almost carefully, "You ever feel like the things that saved you aren't meant to last forever?"

Elias thought of the Inn, of its breath and bones, of how it had saved him by teaching him to stay still. "Maybe they don't have to last," he said quietly. "Maybe they just have to change with us."

Jacob nodded, staring into his cup. "Maybe."

The stereo clicked softly, looping back to track one. "One thing about me is I'm the same me..." The line fell perfectly between them — a quiet truth neither had to name.

Elias turned toward the window, watching the light settle over the porch, over the photo of the Gingerbread Inn on the wall, over the steam rising from the cups. Everything shimmered just a little — familiar but newly alive.

He took a slow breath, felt the warmth fill him, and smiled.

The house was awake again. And so, it seemed, was he.

The Thing He Brought Back

A FTERNOON THINNED INTO THAT SOFT GOLD THAT MAKES THE INN look older in a good way—like it remembers more than it tells. Mama's Boy spun low from the shelf speaker—"Good Guys," then "If This Is the Last Time," both songs moving through the rooms like warm air.

Elias was labeling jars at the boutique counter—lavender soak, bergamot hand balm, cedar-honey polish—his handwriting small and certain. Cinnamon and cream threaded the air from the kitchen; Alyssa had a tray of chai scones cooling by the window. Outside, meltwater stitched a bright seam along the curb; the creek was louder than yesterday.

The bell over the door chimed. Jacob stepped in.

He looked like weather—hair wind-ruffled, cheeks pink, a brightness in his eyes that wasn't quite joy and wasn't quite fear. He held a rolled tube in one hand and a manila envelope in the other.

"Hey," Elias said, without looking up just yet. If he didn't meet the news right away, maybe it would soften on the approach. "You beat the 4 p.m. lull."

Jacob smiled. "Didn't want to miss your penmanship." He nodded at the neat row of labels. "Do they teach that here or is it genetic?"

"Trade secret." Elias set the pen down, finally taking him in —coat unzipped, breath just a little too quick. "You okay?"

"I brought something." Jacob unrolled the tube and slid out a glossy sheet: a weathered lighthouse, white against slate-blue ocean, a ring of wind-bent grass around it. Below the photo, a logo and a line of text: Atlantic Heritage Trust: Spring Coastal Restoration Residency.

"Rhode Island," Jacob said softly. "Three months. They pick a small team every spring—architects, designers, carpenters. You live on site. Restore the original interior, study the light patterns, rebuild the keeper's desk from the old plans. It's... stupidly romantic."

Elias let a breath out he didn't know he'd been holding. Not forever. Not a lifetime. But far. And soon.

"When?" he asked.

"Six weeks." Jacob laid the envelope beside the photo. "They want an answer by Friday."

Ruel's "Hard Sometimes" drifted in from the lobby—soft percussion, the kind of rhythm that keeps your hands moving when your mind wants to freeze. Elias touched the edge of the photo. The paper was cool under his fingertips.

"It's beautiful," he said, and meant it. "You'd be good at this."

Jacob's laugh was brief. "That's the problem. I think I would be."

Silence settled—gentle, not punitive. Alyssa's tray clicked in the kitchen. Somewhere upstairs, a door closed and a guest laughed once, a clean, surprised sound. The house breathed around them, the same way it always had.

Elias spoke first. "I can do three months," he said, like he was testing the sentence for cracks. "I think I can."

Jacob's face softened. "I didn't tell you because I was trying to protect... whatever this is. But that felt like the old me—hiding the truth to keep a kind of peace that doesn't last."

Elias nodded. "We don't do that anymore."

"I don't want to leave like I'm running," Jacob said. "I want to go like I'm carrying something from here to there. And bringing it back."

Elias looked out the window at the thaw. A thread of water glittered along the porch stone, finding the lowest line and following it. "The Inn can stand a season without you," he said quietly. "I can too. I just don't want to pretend it won't hurt."

Jacob's eyes shone, not with tears but with that full, honest brightness that arrives when someone names the thing in the room. "I don't want to pretend either."

They stood there a beat longer—two men in a small boutique that smelled like cedar and lemon oil, holding a lighthouse between them.

Alyssa appeared in the doorway, took in the scene, and set the scones down like a peace offering. "I heard the words Rhode Island and lighthouse and decided carbs were necessary."

"Always," Elias said, voice steadying. He broke a scone, handed half to Jacob, kept half for himself. Cinnamon sugar dusted his thumb; he didn't wipe it away.

"So," Alyssa said, leaning on the frame with conspiratorial softness, "do we like this for him?"

Elias glanced at Jacob, then back at her. "We like this for him," he said, and felt the truth of it land in his chest like a stone that sinks and then somehow makes the water clearer.

Alyssa's grin curved, both proud and protective. "Then I'll start a list. Care packages. Postcards. A Very Official Inn Pen he's required to use in the field."

Jacob laughed. The sound loosened the room. "Please don't send glitter."

"No promises," she said, and disappeared again, humming.

Jacob rolled the photo back into its tube, then didn't put it away. "There's more," he said, lighter now that the door was open. "They do an open weekend halfway through—keepers used to host families. You could come. You and Ally. We could walk the breakwater at dusk. I could show you the desk I rebuilt."

Elias pictured it: the Atlantic wind, the keeper's stairs, Jacob's hands explaining the grain of the wood the way he sometimes explained his own heart—indirectly, tenderly. He felt something ache and widen at the same time.

"I'd like that," he said. "I want to see the you that shows up there."

"The same me," Jacob said, almost quoting the album on loop. "Just at a different edge."

They moved to the lobby together, letting the boutique's bells settle behind them. Guests filtered through with paper flowers from the market, the creek's voice threading under it all. Elias poured two americanos, adding the smallest curl of cream to each—his quiet signature this time of year. He set one in front of Jacob.

"No alcohol for me," he said, as he always did when the hour carried that old habit's shadow. "But we can still toast."

Jacob lifted the cup. "To lightkeepers," he said.

Elias lifted his. "To leaving like you plan to return."

Their cups touched with the softest click. Outside, the mountain shouldered a cloud and let it pass. The track changed—"I'm not afraid of forever, I'm afraid of right now"—and somehow the line didn't land like fear, but like permission.

They took their first sip together. The coffee was strong and honest; cinnamon rode the edge of the taste and then dissolved. Jacob set his cup down and, without ceremony, took Elias's free hand across the counter—palm to palm, not gripping, just present.

"I'm not choosing between a life here and a life there," he said. "I'm choosing a life that includes both. If you want it to."

The old Elias might have looked for a promise, a guarantee, a plan with bullet points and dates. The man standing in this spring light just felt his own breath match the Inn's and said, "Yes."

They stayed like that until a guest asked about dinner and Nora came skidding past with menus and Alyssa announced she had located a postcard set with lighthouses wearing scarves. The room warmed another degree. The creek outside went on singing.

Later, when the trays were cleared and Mama's Boy had looped for the third time, Elias found the lighthouse flyer pinned to the corkboard beside the photo of December's sugared Inn. Winter's sweetness. Spring's distance. Both kinds of light, side by side.

He pressed the tack in a little deeper and felt the house approve—one quiet creak in the floorboards, the softest yes in the walls.

Not an ending. A direction.

CHAPTER ELEVEN

THE EVENING AFTER

———

G

E VENING CAME LIKE FORGIVENESS—SLOW, AMBER, AND PATIENT.
The Inn glowed in its soft ritual of light. Candles along the dining tables burned low; the scent of rosemary and citrus hung in the air from dinner service. Somewhere, a guest laughed, the kind of laugh that made other people look up and smile without knowing why. The air outside was cold again, though the snow no longer stuck to the ground—just a scatter of ice on the porch that caught the lantern glow.

Elias stood behind the counter polishing the silver tongs from the charcuterie tray. The movement was quiet and methodical—his mind tracing the same small circles his cloth made. Music drifted from the corner speaker—LANY's "If This Is the Last Time" giving way to "Cowboy in LA." The kind of songs that sounded like memory humming itself back to life.

He watched the reflection of the fire in the window, how it flickered between his outline and the mountain behind him. He thought about what Jacob had said that afternoon—about lighthouses, about leaving, about coming back. He'd meant it kindly, Elias knew. He'd meant it as a promise. But still, it felt like a wind had come through the room and rearranged everything.

Alyssa was setting plates in the dishwasher, humming under her breath, pretending not to see him retreating inward. She had that sibling intuition—the kind that caught storms before they broke.

"Dinner went well," she said softly, breaking the silence. "Guests were raving about your soup again."

He smiled. "It's just lentils and thyme."

"It's not the soup, Eli. It's the way you make them feel like they belong."

He looked up at her, warmth flickering behind the tiredness. "You really think that's what they feel?"

"I know it is," she said simply. Then, with that same knowing tone she'd had since they were kids: "You still thinking about him?"

He didn't answer right away. The dishwasher clicked shut. Steam curled into the air like a slow exhale.

"He's going to Rhode Island," he said finally. "Three months."

She nodded. "That's not forever."

"No," he said. "But it's far enough to hear the echo."

She walked over, drying her hands on her apron. "You can't keep someone by standing still, you know."

"I'm not trying to keep him," Elias said, eyes on the flickering candlelight. "I just want to be part of what he comes back to."

Alyssa leaned against the counter, studying him the way only a sister could. "Then you already are."

Outside, the wind picked up—gentle but insistent—rattling the chimes on the porch. Elias looked toward the sound. Through the window, he could see the reflection of the firelight trembling against the snow-dusted glass. For a moment, he thought he saw Jacob's shape there—half memory, half imagination—standing with his hands in his pockets, smiling the way he did when something beautiful scared him.

He blinked, and the space was empty again. Only the mountain, the snow, and the faint glimmer of Frisco's lights below.

Alyssa touched his shoulder, grounding him. "Hey. Want help closing up?"

He shook his head gently. "Go rest. I'll finish here."

She smiled, kissed his cheek, and left him to his quiet.

The kitchen settled into its soft postscript hum—the slow tick of cooling metal, the low purr of the espresso machine, the heartbeat of the house. Elias filled a mug with steamed milk and honey, carried it to the library, and sank into the corner chair by the window.

The Inn at night was its own kind of alive. Shadows breathing. Floors sighing. Firelight painting gold onto the old oak table. He liked that the walls seemed to remember every voice they'd ever heard. Sometimes, when it was this quiet, he imagined the Inn whispering back.

"You're doing fine," it might say. "Even when you don't think you are."

He looked down at the mug in his hands, the milk's surface catching the flicker of light. Outside, the moon rested low on the mountain ridge—silver, steady, endless. It reminded him of the lighthouses Jacob had described. Stations of hope, watching for those who leave and those who return.

He smiled faintly, whispering to the quiet: "Then shine, wherever you are."

The floor creaked in response—soft, approving.

Elias leaned back, the warmth of the chair and the room settling around him. Somewhere upstairs, a guest turned in their sleep. Downstairs, the chimes rattled once and then stilled. The night folded itself close.

The house, as always, listened.

Chapter: The Morning After the Pause

The mountain air smelled cleaner after the rain. Not new, exactly—just freshly honest.

Elias stood on the back porch of the Inn, mug in hand, steam rising into the thin light. He hadn't slept much. His mind kept replaying the afternoon: Jacob's quiet voice, the rolled-up blueprint, that word—Rhode Island—spinning like a compass needle.

The sky was pale blue-gray, the kind that made the peaks look softer, almost forgiving. Below, the stream ran full again, loud with meltwater and restless energy. The rhythm of it matched his pulse.

He leaned against the rail, the wood still damp. Progress, not perfection, he thought—words he'd scribbled once in a notebook back when he still believed recovery was a straight line. He smiled faintly. Some lessons took years to circle back.

Alyssa appeared in the doorway, two croissants on a plate and her hair a mess of morning light. "You've been out here since dawn," she said.

"I know. It's nice when the day doesn't ask for anything yet."

She joined him, handed over a croissant. "You gonna tell me what's spinning in that head of yours?"

"Maybe later," he said, though she already knew.

They ate in companionable quiet. From the kitchen came the sound of Nora unpacking boxes for the boutique, humming to herself. Upstairs, pipes creaked; a guest turned on a shower. The Inn was waking up in its usual, beautiful way.

Alyssa brushed a crumb from her sleeve. "You know," she said softly, "sometimes people leave so they can bring something new back. Doesn't mean they're gone."

Elias nodded. "I know." He meant it. Mostly.

He spent the rest of the morning working on the new labels for their bath oils—cedar-sage, mountain honey, and bergamot cream. The repetition calmed him. The scent of bergamot filled the air, sharp and bright, like sunlight made tangible.

By midday, the guests were trickling through the lobby, checking out, leaving little notes in the ledger:

"Best sleep I've had in years." "Felt like coming home."

He lingered on that last one. Coming home. Maybe that was what he was still learning—how to stay home within himself, no matter who came or went.

After lunch, he walked into town to drop a letter at the post office. The wind lifted the collar of his jacket and brought with it the scent of rain-damp pine. He passed the café window where Jacob used to sit when he worked remotely—the same seat, the same chipped mug. It wasn't grief exactly; it was remembering. The good kind.

Inside, he ordered a black coffee and sat by the window. A group of hikers laughed at a corner table. A couple shared a slice of blueberry pie. Outside, the mountain loomed like a constant—unchanged, unmoved, but somehow always watching.

He opened his journal.

Wednesday, May 27th, 2025 I feel like it's been a small day with a lot packed into it. The kind that sneaks up on you. I'm learning that peace doesn't have to mean quiet. Sometimes it's just knowing you're still here.*

He paused, pen hovering, then added:

Jacob leaves in six weeks. I'm proud of him. I'm also afraid. But I think those can live together.

He closed the notebook and sat back. Through the glass, the light shifted—gold spilling across the street, glancing off the puddles until everything shimmered. He smiled, almost shyly, at the reflection looking back at him.

That night, after dinner and dishes and Alyssa's teasing about his "mildly tragic" playlist choices, Elias returned to his room. The fireplace hummed. The Inn's walls breathed the faint smell of cedar and candle wax.

He sat at his desk, the journal open again.

Friday, May 29th, 2025 What a good day it has been. I didn't go to the gym; I didn't rush. I let myself rest, and it felt... holy. Maybe that's what healing looks like now—less chasing, more staying.*

He capped the pen, closed the book, and leaned back. For once, there was no ache, no anxious undercurrent. Just the quiet fullness of being alive.

He whispered to the empty room, "Goodnight," and the Inn, in its old, knowing way, seemed to whisper back, Goodnight, Elias.

The Postcard Arrives

T HE MORNING BROKE SOFT AND GRAY, CLOUDS RESTING LOW AGAINST the ridge like unmade sheets. The smell of rain lingered, mingled with espresso and lemon oil from the freshly polished counter. Guests trickled down early—travelers heading to Denver, couples in matching fleece, one woman reading by the window with her tea untouched.

Elias moved through it all with a steady rhythm, polite smiles, warm tone, practiced ease. It was his armor—the routine that made everything seem right, even when the inside of him still felt quietly rearranged.

He was refilling the pastry case when Alyssa called from the front door.

"Hey, mail came early!"

She tossed a small bundle of envelopes onto the counter. Bills. A local flyer for the farmer's market. And then— something smaller. A postcard.

The edges were worn, the corners smudged from travel. On the front: a photograph of a lighthouse standing alone on a rocky shore, its lantern lit against the fading light. Across the bottom, in tidy serif letters: Point Judith Light, Rhode Island.

Elias's hands stilled. He turned it over.

E— They gave us our stations today. Mine's at the keeper's desk, the one facing east. The mornings here are silver—like the mountain fog before sunrise, but heavier, slower. I think about the way the light moved across the Inn's walls, how it changed everything it touched. I'm learning that's what good light does—it doesn't fix the shape of things; it just lets them be seen more clearly.

I'll write more soon.

—J.

For a long moment, he said nothing. Just stood there, the world folding quietly around him. The café hum, the slow drip of the espresso machine, the murmur of guests—it all moved like a distant river.

Alyssa leaned over his shoulder. "He wrote?"

He nodded, voice low. "He's there."

She smiled, eyes soft. "Then so are you."

Elias looked again at the lighthouse. The sea around it wasn't calm, but the beam from the tower cut through cleanly —unwavering. There was something steady in that image, something that mirrored the Inn itself: both watchful, both holding space for those who left.

He slipped the postcard into the corkboard behind the counter, pinning it beside the photograph from their winter Gingerbread Competition—Jacob mid-laugh, icing on his cheek, Alyssa making a mock salute in the background.

The bell above the door rang. New guests. The day began again.

By evening, a soft warmth had returned to the Inn. Lanterns glowed along the porch. The air smelled faintly of pine and rain. Elias stood at the piano, dusting the keys. He pressed one—the note rang out, faint but true.

Outside, the clouds had broken, and a single shaft of sunlight fell through the valley, cutting across the inn's windows like a benediction. He smiled, just barely, and whispered to no one:

"See you soon, lightkeeper."

The piano answered in silence, but somehow it was enough.

CHAPTER TWELVE

THE KEEPER'S STATION

———

G

THE FIRST THING JACOB NOTICED WAS THE SOUND.

Not the ocean itself—that endless, crashing rhythm—but the silence between each wave. The space that followed the break, the pause where the world seemed to inhale again. That was where he lived now: between the noise and the stillness.

The lighthouse stood at the edge of the cliff like something half-dreamed, half-built by the wind. Point Judith Light. His new post. His world for the next three months. He'd arrived two weeks ago, but it already felt older than that—like time here didn't move in days, but in tides.

Mornings began before dawn. He woke to the cry of gulls and the smell of salt-heavy air pressing through the open window. The floorboards were rough beneath his feet; the walls hummed faintly with history. Sometimes, when the fog rolled in thick and close, he swore he could hear the sea breathing through the cracks.

He liked it. The solitude, the ritual, the rhythm. But some mornings, he'd catch himself turning toward the empty chair across from him—half expecting Elias's laugh, the clink of his spoon against the demitasse.

The postcard he'd sent sat pinned above his desk, its twin to the one now resting on the Inn's corkboard. Beneath it, he'd scribbled a line on a notepad:

"If light reveals, what does distance do?"

He didn't have an answer yet. Maybe he wasn't supposed to.

That afternoon, he climbed the narrow spiral of the lighthouse, notebook in hand. The metal railing was cold against his palm, the air sharp with brine. From the top, the Atlantic stretched out in every direction—gray, infinite, alive. The beam rotated lazily, its reflection sweeping across the horizon like a pulse.

He sat against the glass, legs stretched out, journal open.

Friday, June 14th The sea has a way of listening. It doesn't answer, but it doesn't leave either. I think that's what Elias did for me—he didn't try to fix the storm, just stood with me through it. Maybe that's what love looks like after all the metaphors are gone.*

He paused, chewing the end of his pen. A storm was forming to the south, dark and slow-moving. He could smell it in the air. The kind of storm that changed the sound of everything.

He smiled faintly. "You'd like this one, Eli," he murmured. "All drama, no direction."

A wave crashed below, the spray lifting into the wind. The lighthouse groaned, ancient and solid.

At night, the isolation was heavier. The others had gone to the mainland for supplies, leaving him alone with the hum of the generator and the rhythm of the beacon. He poured a small glass of red wine and leaned against the window. The fog had swallowed the coastline. The beam cut through it like a steady heartbeat.

He thought of the Inn—the smell of cedar and lemon oil, the sound of Alyssa laughing in the kitchen, Elias's hands moving through the air when he talked. He thought of the way the mountain light used to catch the edges of Elias's hair, turning it gold for a moment before the world dimmed again.

He closed his eyes and let the memory play out like a film he didn't want to end.

The wind shifted, rattling the panes. He smiled.

"You still there, mountain boy?"

The question disappeared into the fog.

But in the quiet after, he could almost hear the answer—the soft sound of a coffee grinder, the whisper of pages turning, the echo of someone still tending the light from far away.

Chapter: The Other Keeper

The storm had passed sometime before dawn. Jacob woke to the sound of rainwater slipping from the eaves, soft as breath. The air smelled of salt and iron and wet rope. Down below, the sea was a pale sheet of pewter—restless still, but calmer now, as if apologizing for the night before.

He pulled on his sweater, still damp from yesterday, and made his way toward the keeper's quarters. The hallways were dim, lined with peeling maps and photographs of men who had stood watch long before him—faces sunburned and wind-bitten, eyes full of that same quiet endurance.

In the kitchen, a man sat at the small wooden table, sipping coffee and reading a newspaper that looked two weeks old. He looked up when Jacob entered.

"You're the new one," he said. His voice was gravelly but kind. "Jacob, right?"

Jacob nodded. "That's me. And you must be—"

"Henry," the man said, setting the cup down. "Been here long enough that the walls have started calling me by name. Hope you don't mind company."

"Not at all," Jacob said. "I was beginning to think the fog was my only friend."

Henry chuckled, folding the paper. "It'll do that to you, if you let it. Trick you into thinking silence means you're alone."

Jacob smiled, something easing in his chest. He poured himself a cup of coffee and sat across from him. The mugs clinked softly in the stillness.

"You from the mountains, right?" Henry asked after a while. "Heard the other guys mention it."

"Yeah. Frisco. Colorado."

Henry nodded. "So you traded snow for sea. Fair exchange."

"Maybe," Jacob said, staring out the small window. "Though I think I left something important behind."

Henry didn't press. He just nodded, the way people do when they recognize the kind of ache that doesn't need explaining.

The day passed in quiet labor. They scrubbed salt from the railings, checked the fuel lines, catalogued the incoming weather reports. Henry worked slowly, methodically, as if every task was a form of reverence. Jacob found comfort in that rhythm—it reminded him of Elias, of mornings at the Inn when the world still felt reachable.

During lunch, they sat outside on the cliff edge, sandwiches balanced on their knees. The wind tugged at their sleeves. Seabirds traced the horizon in looping arcs.

"You ever think about leaving?" Jacob asked.

Henry chewed, swallowed, then smiled faintly. "Leaving? Every damn day. And then I remember—I already did. Just didn't get far."

Jacob looked at him, puzzled.

"Spent thirty years running tugs out of New Bedford," Henry said. "Had a wife, two boys. One of 'em's in Boston now. The other's... somewhere. I came out here after she passed. Thought I'd find peace." He looked out over the water. "Turns out, peace just means learning to stay."

Jacob let the words settle between them. They landed somewhere deep.

He thought of Elias—his stillness, his patience, the way he could make an entire room feel held just by breathing in it. He thought of the Inn, glowing soft and golden in the early morning light, of how care there had never been stillness at all, but movement made gentle.

"Maybe peace isn't staying," Jacob said quietly. "Maybe it's knowing what's worth returning to."

Henry smiled, the lines around his eyes deepening. "Then you've got it better figured out than most."

That night, after Henry had gone to bed, Jacob climbed the stairs to the beacon room. The glass walls creaked as the wind picked up again, and below, the waves hurled themselves against the rocks like memory—relentless, familiar.

He wrote in his journal:

Saturday, June 15th Henry says silence isn't the same as loneliness. I think he's right. Today felt almost like forgiveness —not from anyone else, just from the world itself. Elias would've loved the way the light broke through the fog at noon. I swear it looked like home.*

He closed the journal and leaned his forehead against the glass. The rotating beam passed over him, warm for a second before it slipped away again.

The sea roared below, vast and unending, and for the first time since he'd arrived, Jacob didn't feel like a man adrift.

He felt—just for a moment—like a keeper.

─ ≈ ─

The Letter

─ ≈ ─

B Y JULY, THE MOUNTAINS HAD SHED THEIR LAST TRACES OF SNOW. The mornings came quicker now—light spilling through the tall aspens like liquid gold, birdsong trickling in through the cracked windowpanes. The Inn moved with its own summer rhythm: hikers trading boots for slippers, the smell of scones and lemon curd in the air, bicycles stacked neatly by the porch railings.

Elias had learned to move through the days without thinking too much about distance. He had his rituals: polishing the coffee counter before dawn, checking the linen closet before noon, lighting the terrace lanterns just before sunset. Each small act a thread holding the day together.

Still, every now and then—when the wind came down from Mount Royal and rattled the old windows—he thought of the sea. He wondered what Jacob saw when he looked out over that horizon, what he felt when he turned the light on.

It was a Tuesday when the letter came.

Alyssa found it in the small brass box by the front steps and handed it to him with a teasing grin. "No postcard this time," she said. "Looks serious."

The envelope was thick, cream-colored, the kind that felt deliberate. His name written in neat, steady cursive—Elias Warren. No return address. Just the faint scent of salt.

He took it upstairs to his small room above the lobby, sat at the old oak desk, and ran a thumb under the seal. The paper unfolded with a whisper.

Eli,

The ocean has moods the way you used to—soft one morning, impossible the next. I've learned to read it the way you read the Inn: by its sounds, its silences, the way it settles after the storm.

I thought I came here to start over. Turns out, I came here to remember what it feels like to care for something that doesn't owe you anything.

Henry—the older keeper—says peace is a long conversation with yourself. I think he's right. But some days, when the fog lifts, I swear I hear laughter carried on the wind. Alyssa's laugh. Yours. I hope you're still making the coffee too strong, still waking before the light trusts the room.

There's something I didn't say before I left. Maybe because it wasn't ready to be said. Maybe because I wasn't ready to believe it. You didn't fix me, Elias. You reminded me that I wasn't broken.

I keep the mountain light in mind when the nights get long. Tell it I said thank you.

—J.

Elias sat for a long time after reading it, his hand resting on the letter as if to keep it from floating away. Outside, thunder murmured faintly over the peaks, the sky just beginning to darken. He leaned back in the chair, eyes closed, and let the air move through the window—pine, rain, and that faint sweetness that always came before a storm.

Downstairs, the lobby filled with the soft clatter of teacups, the low hum of conversation. Someone laughed. It wasn't Alyssa's laugh—it was lighter, younger—but it rippled through the walls like a memory revived.

He stood, folded the letter, and slid it into the drawer beside the ledger. Then he went to the kitchen.

The espresso machine hissed as he pulled a double shot, the sound sharp and alive. He poured it into two cups.

Only one would be used. The other sat beside it—a small, waiting symbol. A conversation not yet finished.

The first raindrops struck the window. The scent of cinnamon and cream filled the air.

Elias smiled faintly.

"You're not broken either," he whispered.

And somewhere beyond the rain, across mountains and ocean, a light swept through the fog as if answering back.

—— ～ ——

The Run

—— ～ ——

THE MORNING CAME SILVER AND SLOW. A FAINT MIST CLUNG TO THE pine needles outside his window, the air cool and damp with promise. Elias sat at the edge of the bed, the letter still folded on the nightstand. He hadn't opened it again, but its presence was enough — an echo, not a weight.

He pulled on his running shoes, the same pair worn soft at the heels, and tied the laces with deliberate care. The old rhythm. The one that asked nothing but motion.

Downstairs, the Inn was still asleep. The scent of cedar polish lingered from the night before. He paused by the espresso machine, poured a small cup of the house roast, and stood by the front window as the sky lightened. The world outside was half-shadow, half-beginning.

He whispered, "One mile at a time."

Then he stepped out into the quiet.

The streets of Frisco were empty except for the faint hum of a delivery van somewhere down Main. The mountain loomed, soft-edged against a sky the color of pewter. Elias's breath came in slow draws — steady, practiced, honest.

He started down Galena, past the bakery where the ovens had just begun to warm. The smell of sugar and yeast curled through the air, mixing with the clean scent of thawing snow. His steps fell into rhythm: in for four, out for four. A language older than thinking.

By the time he reached the bike path that curved behind Tenmile Creek, the mist had begun to lift. The world was waking — birds stitching morning songs through the branches, water rushing against stone in a hymn of motion.

Elias ran harder. Not from anything. Toward something he couldn't quite name.

The first mile was always bargaining — body versus memory, lungs versus the echoes that still whispered from old versions of himself. By the second, something loosened. The thoughts stopped forming full sentences. They became texture — color, breath, sound.

At the bridge near the base of Mount Royal, he slowed, resting his hands on the cool metal rail. The mountain loomed above, vast and unbothered. A thin ray of sunlight broke through the clouds, touching the summit in gold.

He looked up, chest heaving, and laughed under his breath. "You never let me hide, do you?"

The wind answered with a low rustle through the trees. He stood there, breathing in the scent of pine and thawed earth, the steam of his breath curling into the cold.

He thought of Jacob's letter — the words You reminded me that I wasn't broken — and felt something twist softly inside him. Not pain. Recognition.

He closed his eyes.

I'm still learning who I am when I'm not healing, he thought. Still learning how to stand still and call it progress.

When he returned to the Inn, the front steps were damp with dew. Alyssa was sweeping the porch, earbuds in, humming off-key to something bright and summery. She smiled when she saw him. "Morning, mountain man. You look alive."

"Trying to be," he said, stretching his arms. "You open yet?"

She nodded toward the door. "Guests are up. Coffee's on."

He followed her inside. The warmth hit him like an embrace — roasted beans, cinnamon, and faint lavender rising from the vents. The playlist in the corner murmured softly, Ruel's "Say It Over" threading through the space.

Elias moved behind the counter without thinking. The espresso hissed, milk frothed, laughter drifted from the dining room. The morning rush was beginning.

For the first time in a long while, he didn't feel like he was performing the routine. He was inhabiting it.

Each gesture — setting cups, refilling sugar, greeting guests — was a quiet affirmation. The work, the rhythm, the small acts of care — they were his proof that he was still here. Not just surviving the morning, but belonging to it.

Later, when the guests had settled and the hum softened to background, Elias took a moment alone at the counter. He poured himself another cup, darker this time, and leaned against the marble.

Through the window, the mountains glowed with that peculiar mid-morning gold that only lasted a few minutes. Steam curled above the cup. Somewhere down the hall, Alyssa's laughter rang out again — pure, unguarded, alive.

He smiled.

"One mile at a time," he whispered again.

And for the first time since the letter had come, the phrase didn't sound like a promise. It sounded like peace.

— ~ —

The Afternoon Guests

— ~ —

B Y NOON, THE INN WAS ALIVE IN EVERY SENSE OF THE WORD. THE porch doors stood open to the sunlight, letting in a cross-breeze that carried the scent of espresso, mountain air, and freshly baked lemon scones. The old stereo in the lounge murmured with low music — LANY again, of course — soft enough to feel like memory rather than sound.

Elias stood behind the counter, sleeves rolled, towel tucked at his waist. His hands worked from muscle memory: refilling the pastry tray, polishing the brass, pouring another round of americanos for the couple by the window who couldn't stop smiling at each other.

It was the kind of day that felt balanced — everything in motion, everything belonging.

Alyssa flitted between the tables, a ribbon in her hair and an energy that filled the whole room. She'd been making small talk with a young family who'd just come in from Denver, laughing about how their little boy had mistaken the library nook for a "secret treasure room."

"You're not wrong," she said with a grin, handing him a cookie shaped like a snowflake. "There are some pretty magical things in there."

Elias watched from the bar, smiling to himself. She had his mother's warmth, that way of making people feel like they'd been here before — like the Inn wasn't a stop but a return.

The bell above the front door chimed.

Elias looked up.

A man stood in the doorway, framed by sunlight. He carried a small duffel bag, wind-tossed hair, and that unmistakable look of someone who'd just decided to stop running for a while. His eyes moved through the room slowly, taking in every detail — the books, the coffee, the laughter.

Then he smiled.

"Hi," he said, voice soft, uncertain. "I have a reservation. Under Moore."

Elias's hand stilled over the tray. "Of course," he said after a beat. "Welcome to the Frisco Inn on Galena." He gestured toward the desk, heart steady but alert. "You made it just in time for coffee."

The man laughed lightly. "Perfect. That's the only reason I travel, really."

"Then you'll fit right in," Elias said.

As he checked him in, their hands brushed — an accidental touch, brief but electric. Jacob's letter was still folded upstairs, but this was different. This wasn't nostalgia; it was curiosity. It was the kind of spark that didn't demand, only reminded. And what it reminded him of was already named. The men who passed through that winter and spring—Moore, and the ones after—were weather. Jacob was the mountain. You could be moved by the weather and still know which one the window faced.

By midafternoon, the Inn had found its rhythm again.

Someone was playing piano softly in the corner — an older guest who returned every summer and claimed that the mountain air made the keys "speak sweeter." A faint melody — Malibu Nights — drifted through the space, threading through conversations and laughter.

Elias arranged cups on the counter. Alyssa joined him, carrying a tray of empty glasses. "He's cute," she whispered, nodding toward the new arrival, who was now reading by the fireplace, legs folded, completely absorbed.

Elias rolled his eyes, smiling. "You say that about every guest under forty."

"Only the ones who look like trouble in nice sweaters," she said. "You should talk to him."

"I already did. It's called check-in."

She nudged him with her elbow. "You know what I mean."

He did. And that was precisely why he didn't. Still, he found his gaze returning to the man — to the way he traced the edge of his cup absentmindedly, the way he occasionally glanced up at the window as if memorizing the shape of the mountains.

It wasn't about attraction, not really. It was recognition — the quiet, wordless kind. Two people who'd both come to the same place looking for something unnamed.

Later, when the guests had dispersed — some off to the spa, others out exploring Main Street — Elias found himself in the kitchen, rinsing glasses that didn't need rinsing. The window above the sink framed Mount Royal in its golden hour glow. The mountain had a way of changing color depending on the hour: honey at dusk, silver at dawn, deep blue at night.

He heard footsteps behind him. "Beautiful view," the guest said. It was Moore — the man from earlier. His voice carried that soft steadiness of someone used to quiet.

"Always is," Elias said without turning. "The light never quite repeats itself."

Moore stepped closer, hands in his pockets. "I noticed that. It's like the mountain's performing, but only for people who pay attention."

Elias smiled faintly. "Most people don't."

"Then they miss the best part."

Elias turned then, meeting his gaze. The sunlight from the window caught the edges of Moore's face — brown eyes, tired but kind, the faintest scar at the corner of his jaw. Someone who'd seen too much, perhaps, but hadn't hardened because of it.

For a long moment, neither said anything.

Finally, Elias said softly, "Coffee?"

Moore nodded. "Always."

By evening, the Inn glowed with warmth — not the fevered kind of summer, but the deep, amber kind that clings to wood and laughter. Alyssa had lit candles along the windowsills; someone had opened a bottle of sparkling cider, its fizzing sound joining the chorus of clinking cups and soft jazz from the stereo.

Elias stood behind the bar, pouring. Moore sat nearby, listening as Alyssa told stories about the Gingerbread Competition they hosted each winter — her hands moving wildly as she described frosting disasters and candy catastrophes.

When she mimed a peppermint avalanche, Moore laughed so hard he nearly spilled his drink. Elias couldn't help but laugh too — that same bright, unguarded laugh he hadn't felt in months.

The night grew fuller. The light dimmed to gold. The Inn, once again, felt like a heart — open, imperfect, and alive.

After Hours at the Inn

T HE GUESTS HAD GONE QUIET BY NINE. THE LAST OF THE DINNER plates clinked faintly in the kitchen as Alyssa loaded the washer, humming some pop song off-key. The scent of lemon oil and pine cleaner hung in the air — proof of a day well spent. Outside, dusk wrapped the mountains in lavender light.

Elias sat alone at the corner table in the lounge, journal open beside a mug of chamomile tea gone cold. His handwriting, steady and slanted, ran down the page in ink the color of deep ocean:

Six whole months sober today. It's truly amazing. I am thankful for everything I've been given so far this year. Never before have I felt so focused — and more than content.

He stopped, letting the words linger. The Inn creaked softly — old wood settling into sleep.

He thought about the morning run, the letter, the guests who'd passed through. And about how, without even realizing it, he'd begun to measure his days differently. Not by what had gone wrong, but by what he'd managed to love despite it.

The door to the lounge opened. Alyssa peeked in, her hair loose now, face flushed from work. "You still up?"

He smiled. "Finishing the day."

"Don't finish it too hard," she teased, heading toward the stairs. "Tomorrow's a full house again. And you're opening."

"Wouldn't have it any other way."

"Night, Eli."

"Night, Lyss."

Her footsteps faded, leaving only the sound of the dishwasher and the steady tick of the grandfather clock by the piano. The stillness didn't feel empty tonight — it felt earned.

He flipped to a new page.

The pen hesitated, then began again:

I've learned that peace doesn't arrive all at once. It shows up in fragments — in laughter, in clean sheets, in a stranger's thank you. In forgiving yourself before the world does. I think I'm finally beginning to believe that I belong here.

He leaned back, eyes closing for a moment. The Inn's warmth hummed around him like a low, familiar chord. Outside, wind slipped through the pines, whispering against the windows.

Later, he walked through the halls, checking locks, dimming lamps. In each room: traces of stories. A scarf draped over a chair. An empty cup left by the window. A paperback folded open, waiting for morning.

He paused at the last door — the one belonging to Moore, the guest from earlier. The faint sound of a page turning drifted out. Elias smiled, then moved on.

In the lobby, he stopped by the front desk, touching the old brass bell. It gleamed faintly in the low light. A reminder: the world comes and goes, but some places — some people — stay.

He whispered, "Thank you," not sure whether to the Inn, the mountain, or himself.

When he finally turned in for the night, the moon had climbed high over Frisco. Through the attic window, he could see its light shimmering on the snowmelt creek behind the

Inn — that small ribbon of water running steady, constant, alive.

He thought of his morning mantra: One mile at a time.

Now, it felt truer than ever.

He closed the journal, the ink still drying, and whispered into the dark:

"Here's to the good things."

Coffee with Moore

B Y THE TIME ELIAS HAD SHOWERED AND CHANGED, THE FIRST golden light was slipping through the east windows, brushing the counter in warmth. The espresso machine hummed to life, the familiar hiss filling the silence like a soft sigh. The scent of freshly ground beans rose — chocolate, cedar, a hint of citrus — the same comfort he never tired of.

He was setting out two cups, as he always did — one for himself, one for whoever might wander in — when he heard footsteps from the stairs.

"Early bird," came a voice from behind him.

Elias turned. Moore stood there, tousled hair, a flannel half-buttoned, holding a book under one arm.

Elias smiled faintly. "Or just can't sleep."

"Guess that makes two of us," Moore said. He gestured to the espresso machine. "Is that offer from yesterday still open?"

"Always," Elias said, and reached for another demitasse cup — the same one he'd set out by habit earlier, without knowing why.

As the machine hissed, Moore leaned against the counter, watching the quiet ritual unfold — the measured tamp, the pull, the slow curl of steam.

"I used to work in a place like this," he said softly. "Years ago. Before I switched to... well, whatever I'm doing now."

"And what's that?" Elias asked, pouring the shot.

Moore smiled wryly. "Trying to figure that out, mostly."

Elias slid the cup toward him. "Then you came to the right place. The Inn's full of people doing that."

Moore took a sip, winced slightly, then grinned. "Strong."

"Good strong or bad strong?"

"The kind that wakes you up and tells you to stop lying to yourself."

Elias laughed, quiet but real. "Then it's working."

The morning eased on slowly. Guests trickled in — a couple asking for hiking recommendations, a family heading toward Breckenridge. Alyssa appeared, bright as ever, setting pastries into baskets and teasing Elias about his "new coffee buddy."

But between each small moment, conversation between the two men deepened.

They spoke about nothing and everything — favorite places, what silence meant, how cities sometimes made you forget to breathe. Elias told him about the mountain runs, about how the Inn had this way of demanding both care and surrender.

Moore listened like someone who'd forgotten how.

And when he finally spoke, his words came slow, careful. "I left a lot behind to get here," he said. "A job. Someone I loved. I thought distance would fix the ache." He met Elias's gaze. "It didn't. But maybe... maybe it changed what I'm supposed to want."

Elias didn't answer right away. He just looked out the window, where the light had shifted again — brighter now, spilling across the snow-capped roofs.

"I think that's what we're all figuring out," he said finally. "What to want when we stop running."

Moore nodded. "You sound like someone who's made peace with that."

Elias smiled faintly. "I'm still learning."

Alyssa interrupted the silence with a soft clatter of mugs. "You two look like you're solving the world's problems."

Moore chuckled. "Maybe just our own."

Elias grinned. "That's where all the big revolutions start."

They laughed, and for a moment, everything felt suspended — the scent of cinnamon, the sunlight through the windows, the murmur of conversation in the background.

Not a grand revelation. Just a quiet connection. The kind that stays.

Later, when Moore left to walk through town, Elias stayed behind, wiping the counter slowly. His reflection shimmered faintly in the steel of the espresso machine — steady, a little tired, but at peace.

He thought of what Moore had said. What to want when you stop running.

He didn't have the answer yet. But maybe, he thought, this was how you found it — cup by cup, morning by morning, word by word.

Outside, the sunlight caught on the porch railing like liquid gold. The day had fully begun.

Rainlight

—— ~ ——

BY LATE AFTERNOON, THE SKY HAD TURNED SOFT AND GRAY. THE mountains disappeared behind low-hanging clouds, and the first drops of rain traced slow, glistening paths down the Inn's tall windows.

Elias stood by the front desk, arms folded, watching the street below turn glossy with drizzle. The sound of the rain was steady, comforting — the kind that seemed to dissolve everything sharp around it.

A few guests had gathered in the lounge — one couple playing cards by the fireplace, a man reading near Plato's Corner, and two sisters from Denver sharing tea by the window, their laughter lilting and light. Alyssa flitted between them with that effortless warmth she carried, topping off mugs, adjusting the fire, humming something half-remembered from the radio.

The Inn felt alive — not busy, but present.

Elias exhaled. The air smelled like cedar and coffee and faint citrus from the potpourri bowl he'd set out that morning.

He hadn't realized how much he'd missed days like this — the ones that asked nothing of him except to be there.

The bell over the door jingled softly, and Moore stepped inside, shaking the rain from his jacket. His hair was damp, curls sticking to his forehead, eyes bright from the cold.

"Looks like you brought the weather back with you," Elias said, smiling.

"I'll take the blame for it," Moore replied. "But only if you make another one of those coffees."

Elias gestured toward the machine. "Already ahead of you."

They settled at the counter again, their quiet becoming part of the rain's rhythm. The steam curled upward, the smell rich and grounding.

Moore glanced toward the windows. "You ever think about leaving this place?"

Elias paused mid-motion, the tamper in his hand. "Leaving?"

"Yeah. Traveling. Starting over somewhere new."

Elias poured the shot, watching it bloom dark and slow. "I used to. A lot, actually." He handed him the cup. "But I think I was more interested in escaping than exploring."

Moore sipped thoughtfully. "And now?"

"Now I think..." He looked around the room — the flicker of the fire, the rainlight over the guests, the quiet hum of belonging. "I think I finally want to stay."

Moore nodded, eyes soft. "That's rare."

"Maybe," Elias said, "but it feels right."

The rain grew heavier. The roof gave a low, steady drumbeat, the kind that filled every room with its gentle insistence.

Alyssa passed by with a tray of pastries and paused, lowering her voice with a grin. "You two want one before the guests devour them all?"

Elias laughed. "What's left?"

"Cinnamon twists and one lemon scone that's somehow survived three rounds of tea."

"Twists," Moore said quickly.

Alyssa winked. "Good choice."

As she walked off, Moore leaned in slightly, elbows on the counter. "She's got good timing."

Elias smirked. "She's also my sister. So watch it."

Moore nearly choked on his coffee, laughing. "Noted."

The conversation drifted — travel stories, books they'd loved, memories that tasted of both warmth and regret. When Moore spoke of his last winter — how he'd left a life that no longer felt like his own — Elias didn't interrupt. He just listened. There was something in the way Moore's voice softened that reminded him of his own before sobriety — that searching tone, not broken, but unsure where to rest.

"Sometimes I wonder if I'll ever stop looking for peace," Moore said.

Elias tilted his head. "Maybe you already found it. Maybe it's not loud enough for you to recognize yet."

Moore smiled faintly. "You talk like someone who's been through the dark."

Elias met his gaze. "I have. But I also know the way back."

Outside, thunder rolled low in the distance, a heartbeat beneath the sound of rain.

Hours slipped by unnoticed. Guests ordered second cups of tea, the fire crackled louder, and the sky began to dim again — shifting from pewter to violet to that deep blue that only existed between day and night.

Elias stood to refill the pot, and when he turned, Moore was looking toward the rain-slicked window, expression unreadable.

"You ever think," Moore said quietly, "that places have souls?"

Elias followed his gaze. The Inn's reflection shimmered faintly in the glass — light and warmth surrounded by the dark.

"Yeah," he said. "And sometimes I think they find us when we need them most."

When the rain finally stopped, a faint mist hung in the air like memory. The last of the guests retreated to their rooms. The Inn exhaled, settling into its nighttime stillness.

Moore rose, slipping on his jacket. "Thanks for the company."

Elias smiled. "Anytime."

Moore hesitated at the door. "Tomorrow?"

Elias met his eyes. "Tomorrow."

The bell chimed softly as he left, and the sound lingered — fragile, beautiful, full of unspoken promise.

Elias looked out into the night. The cobblestones glistened, and the mountains loomed like guardians beyond. He whispered, "Here's to the good things," then turned off the lights.

— ~ —

The Stranger by the Creek

— ~ —

T HE MORNING BROKE OPEN CLEAR AND BRIGHT. THE STORM HAD scrubbed the sky clean, and sunlight spilled in honey-thick rays across the mountains. The peaks gleamed white against the blue, and the air held that sharp, crystalline chill that only follows a night of heavy rain.

Elias woke early — earlier than usual — and felt a pull he couldn't name. Maybe it was the light. Maybe it was restlessness. Maybe something in him already knew the day would shift.

He left the Inn quietly, shoes crunching over damp gravel, breath forming small clouds in the morning air. The world was all sound — the whisper of the stream, the soft coo of doves under the eaves, his own steady inhale.

The trail behind the Inn was slick, patched with puddles that mirrored the sky. He ran slow at first, easing into his rhythm, every stride loosening the remnants of yesterday's rain. His lungs burned, his heartbeat found its tempo.

Halfway along the creek, he stopped to stretch — palms on his knees, chest rising with the effort. Across the water, the world was glowing: pine needles jeweled with dew, the faint curl of mist lifting from the earth.

And that's when he saw him.

A stranger stood at the bend of the trail, near the wooden bridge — tall, lean, dressed in a black windbreaker and worn running shoes. His hair caught the light, a deep auburn with gold threads running through it. He was sketching something in a small notebook, head bent, wholly absorbed.

Elias hesitated — that private tug of curiosity. The kind that wasn't attraction, not yet, but recognition.

He started walking, slow and deliberate, the sound of his steps muffled by the damp earth. When he reached the bridge, the stranger looked up.

"Morning," Elias said, a little breathless.

The man smiled — a small, patient curve of the lips. "Morning. You caught the best light."

Elias glanced at the stream. "Yeah. Guess I did."

The stranger turned his sketchbook slightly. On the page, a loose watercolor wash — the Inn, framed by the mountain, a hint of dawn on the roofline. It was unfinished but alive, the kind of art that didn't try to impress, only see.

"That's—beautiful," Elias said.

The man nodded once, humbly. "Thanks. It's my first morning in Frisco. I try to paint wherever I land."

"You're visiting?"

"For a while," the man said. "Maybe longer. Depends how it feels." He extended his hand. "Julian."

"Elias."

Their palms met — a brief, grounded handshake. And something about it felt both startling and familiar, like déjà vu in daylight.

Julian's gaze flickered past him, toward the Inn down the slope. "You work there?"

"Yeah," Elias said. "I live there too. Helps to stay close to the coffee."

Julian smiled. "I might take you up on that. I booked a room for the week. Needed a place that looked..." He trailed off, searching for the word.

"Safe?" Elias offered.

Julian's eyes softened. "Yeah. Safe."

They stood there for a moment — the sound of the creek filling the space between them, sunlight dripping like gold through the trees.

Then Elias said, almost shyly, "You should come by the café later. First cup's on me."

Julian closed his sketchbook, tucking it into his satchel. "Careful. I might hold you to that."

"I'm counting on it."

By the time Elias returned to the Inn, the scent of fresh pastries drifted from the kitchen, and the front lobby glowed with the warmth of the morning. He moved through his routine as if nothing had changed — coffee, counters, music — but the rhythm felt slightly off, like a song played half a beat too slow.

When Alyssa came in, she noticed immediately. "You're humming," she said, eyebrows raised.

"Am I?"

"Yeah. That's usually a sign."

"Of what?"

She smiled. "Something's coming."

Elias laughed, but his heart flickered. Because maybe, just maybe, she was right.

Outside, the sunlight caught the windows in a flare of gold, and at the far edge of the street — barely visible through the glass — Julian crossed toward the Inn, sketchbook in hand.

And just like that, the air changed again.

CHAPTER THIRTEEN

THE CAFÉ BETWEEN
HEARTBEATS

———

G

L ATE MORNING. THE INN BREATHED IN SUNLIGHT.

The windows had dried from the rain, and streaks of gold slipped through the glass, warming the café in thin ribbons. Elias was behind the counter polishing a row of cups — a small ritual that grounded him when the world felt like it might shift. The playlist hummed softly in the background — Ruel's "Free Time" fading into the low thrum of LANY's "Malibu Nights."

He moved with intention, that same quiet rhythm he'd built his peace upon. Every sound, every scent was part of his composition: the crackle from the fireplace, the murmur of voices, cinnamon woven through the air.

The bell above the front door chimed.

Julian stepped inside.

He carried that same calm presence as before, though his eyes — green-gray, rainwater light — seemed sharper in the sun. He glanced around the room, taking in the fire, the shelves, the map of old Frisco on the wall, before his gaze landed on Elias.

"Hey," he said, approaching the counter. "I think you owe me a cup."

Elias smiled, a genuine one that reached his eyes. "I was hoping you'd call my bluff."

Julian set down his sketchbook. "I never pass up good coffee. Or good conversation."

"Then you've come to the right place."

He poured two espressos — the dark, rich scent rising between them. The hiss of steam filled the pause, soft but deliberate. Elias slid the cup across, fingers brushing briefly against Julian's — a spark disguised as happenstance.

Julian took a sip, eyes widening slightly. "That's incredible."

"House roast," Elias said. "We blend it here — a little Colombian, a little Ethiopian. Like opposites that insist on harmony."

Julian smiled. "Kind of like people."

Elias laughed, low and surprised. "Maybe exactly like people."

They fell into easy rhythm — talk of travel, light, and the way small towns breathe differently than cities. Julian had a quiet humor, the kind that drew you in instead of demanding attention. He spoke of places he'd painted — Hanoi, Lisbon, Kyoto — but each story circled back to the same undertone: searching.

Elias recognized it instantly.

"You run," Julian said at one point. "I can tell. The way you breathe between words."

Elias blinked. "You can tell that?"

"Yeah," Julian said, smiling, and let it go at that.

Before Elias could answer, the bell chimed again.

Moore stepped through the door.

It was the kind of coincidence the universe likes to arrange when it's feeling poetic — not cruel, just precise. Moore carried his familiar energy — worn leather jacket, hair slightly damp, the smell of mountain air trailing after him. He saw Elias first, then Julian.

For a fraction of a second, something unreadable passed over his face.

"Morning," Moore said, voice even.

Elias nodded. "Morning. Want your usual?"

"Please."

Moore took the seat two stools down, giving Julian a polite, measured glance. Julian, unaware of the quiet shift, turned back toward Elias, sketchbook open again.

"Mind if I?" he asked, gesturing with his pencil.

Elias tilted his head. "Sketch away."

The espresso machine hissed again, filling the pause between them. The sound was almost orchestral — pressure and release, breath and heat. Elias glanced between the two men — Moore's stillness, Julian's curiosity — and something in his chest began to ache, quietly, beautifully.

Julian spoke first. "You built this place to feel alive."

Elias smiled softly. "I didn't build it. I just... listen to it."

Moore looked up. "That's the trick, isn't it? Listening without trying to fix."

Elias met his gaze. "You'd know."

The air between them shimmered faintly — not sharp, not heavy, just charged with recognition.

Julian looked between them, sensing the undertow but not naming it. "You two go way back?"

Elias hesitated. Moore answered. "Long enough to know when he's pretending not to miss something."

Julian smiled, unaware of the history being quietly measured in the spaces between words. "That must make for good coffee."

Elias laughed softly, shaking his head. "Depends on the morning."

By early afternoon, the café had filled with the hum of guests — hikers trading stories, the clink of plates, Alyssa calling out from the kitchen that the scones were "too perfect to eat." The three men occupied the counter like points on a compass: Elias steady, Moore watchful, Julian bright.

And though the air carried warmth and laughter and cinnamon, something new had entered — the first flicker of uncertainty in Elias's once predictable rhythm.

It wasn't unwelcome. Just undeniable.

When Julian left, he placed a folded slip of watercolor paper by the register. On it — the Inn, rendered in quick, tender strokes. Beneath it, in looping script:

Stillness isn't the absence of movement. It's the grace inside it.

Moore watched him go, then looked at Elias. "You okay?"

Elias nodded. "Yeah. Just... feels like the air changed."

Moore smiled, faintly wistful. "It always does, right before something begins."

The Walk Back

The air outside carried that clean, rain-washed scent — pine and stone and a hint of espresso still clinging to his hands. The street gleamed with leftover puddles, small mirrors holding pieces of sky.

Elias slipped his hands into his jacket pockets, the collar turned up against the lingering chill. The sun hung low behind the ridge, spilling light through the bare aspens like scattered gold.

Frisco was quiet at this hour — that small-town hush before evening settles in. The bakery's sign creaked softly.

From somewhere down the block, a guitar played faintly, the melody threading through the air like memory.

He passed the storefronts — the bookshop with its dusty window display, the boutique with new spring scarves in the window. He slowed near the old post office, where a child had drawn a chalk heart on the step. It made him smile without realizing.

He should have felt content. He almost did.

But beneath the quiet satisfaction of the day — the laughter, the coffee, Julian's gentle ease, even Moore's familiar steadying presence — something deeper stirred. A tremor, small but insistent. The sense that his careful peace had been shifted a fraction of an inch, and the world no longer aligned quite the same way.

He could still feel the ghost of Julian's gaze — curious, calm, but alive with questions. And Moore's silence — not angry, not jealous, just knowing. The two sensations overlapped, creating a hum somewhere behind his ribs.

At the crosswalk, he stopped, glancing back toward the café. Through the window, Alyssa was wiping down the counter, her hair catching the golden light. She looked content — steady in the rhythm he'd helped build. He envied that ease, that belonging untouched by complication.

The wind picked up slightly, rustling the flags along Main Street. Elias crossed toward Galena, his shoes clicking softly on the wet pavement.

The Inn came into view — that familiar façade of wood and stone, the soft lamps glowing in the windows, smoke rising faintly from the chimney. It looked like a photograph of comfort. But even from here, it felt different tonight — alive in a new way. As if it, too, had sensed something shifting in the air.

He paused at the gate, hand resting on the worn brass latch. The light from the lobby window spilled onto the path, warm and golden.

Inside, he could see Alyssa lighting candles for the evening. Beyond her, the piano sat untouched, dust motes swirling in the air above it.

He thought about playing again. It had been months — maybe a year — since he'd last let himself touch those keys.

Maybe tomorrow.

He opened the door, and the familiar scent of cedar and cinnamon welcomed him like a memory that hadn't forgotten his name.

"Hey," Alyssa called from the counter. "I was just about to come find you. You left your journal again."

He smiled faintly, taking it from her. "Guess I had too much on my mind."

"Too much?" she teased. "Or someone?"

He laughed softly. "You really don't miss much, do you?"

"Not when it comes to you."

She leaned on the counter, studying him. "So, who's the new artist?"

"Julian," he said, flipping the journal open as a deflection. "He's staying for the week."

"Interesting," Alyssa said, stretching the word like a song. "He seemed... grounded."

Elias nodded. "Yeah. Grounded."

She waited, as if expecting him to say more. When he didn't, she just smiled knowingly and went back to arranging the tea set.

Later, after the lights dimmed and the last guest retired upstairs, Elias stood by the window of the library lounge. The mountain loomed against the stars, the town lights glittering below.

He opened his journal and began to write, pen scratching softly in the stillness:

There's a strange peace in uncertainty — like the moment between inhale and exhale. I used to run from that space. Now I think it's where all the truth hides.

He paused, looking at the words. Somewhere outside, a door closed. Footsteps on gravel.

He turned — just in time to see a figure passing the window, walking slow toward the back of the property. A coat, a flash of auburn hair in the lamplight.

Julian.

Elias watched him disappear into the shadowed garden, the faint sound of the creek rising again in the distance.

And he realized, not for the first time, that stillness was rarely still.

Morning in the Garden

THE INN WAS STILL WAKING WHEN ELIAS STEPPED OUTSIDE. THE AIR was crisp, the kind that stings lightly at first breath before softening into warmth. The mountains were haloed in pale gold, their snowcaps slowly surrendering to spring. Somewhere nearby, a raven cawed and was answered by the quiet hum of water from the creek.

Elias held a mug of his first coffee—half cinnamon, half cream, the scent rising like comfort—and followed the sound of the stream. The gravel crunched under his shoes, the world still unbothered by hurry. He liked this hour: everything new, but nothing yet asked of him.

The garden glistened, dew clinging to the blades of grass, and the wildflowers—tiny bursts of purple and yellow—looked as though someone had painted them just before dawn. He slowed at the sound of paper turning.

Julian was there.

He sat near the low stone wall, one leg folded under the other, sketchbook open across his lap. A cup of tea rested beside him, steam curling upward. He was drawing the view of the Inn reflected in the stream, capturing not its exact shape but the feeling of it—wobbled lines, soft color, living light.

Elias hesitated for a heartbeat, then stepped closer.

"Morning," he said quietly.

Julian looked up, that half-smile already waiting. "Morning. I was hoping you'd come by. You seem like a morning person who pretends not to be."

Elias laughed under his breath. "You can tell that too?"

"I notice people," Julian said simply. "It's part of the job."

"Artist?"

"Observer," Julian corrected. "Artist's just the title I put on my taxes."

Elias smiled and came to stand beside him. "May I?"

Julian handed him the sketchbook without hesitation. The page showed the Inn, yes, but through a lens Elias had never seen before—soft, luminous, warm. He looked at it longer than he meant to.

"You made it look kinder than it is."

Julian tilted his head. "I didn't make it kinder. I just drew it the way you look at it."

The words landed quietly but deep. Elias wasn't sure what to say, so he sipped his coffee instead, eyes dropping to the water.

After a long moment, Julian spoke again, softer this time. "I used to travel to forget where I'd been. Lately, I travel to remember what mattered."

Elias nodded. "I know that feeling. I used to run for the same reason."

"Do you still?"

"Not away," Elias said. "Not anymore."

Julian studied him, as though sketching with his eyes instead of a pencil. "You have the look of someone who rebuilt himself carefully."

Elias looked up. "And?"

"And maybe you left a few walls half-finished."

The honesty stung, but not cruelly. More like light finding its way through a window that hadn't been opened in a while.

Elias let the silence stretch. A breeze carried the smell of fresh bread from the kitchen window. Somewhere inside,

Alyssa's laughter rang out—bright, unguarded.

Julian closed the sketchbook and stood, brushing dew from his jeans. "You don't have to invite me in," he said, tone easy but eyes serious. "But I'd like to come by again. Maybe show you what I see when you're not looking."

Elias managed a small nod. "We're always open."

Julian smiled. "I wasn't talking about the Inn."

Elias stayed there long after Julian walked away, the mug cooling slowly in his hand.

The creek whispered its endless story, the kind that never ends, only shifts with the listener. He watched the reflection of the Inn in the water, fractured and soft, and thought of what Julian had said—the way you look at it.

Inside, he could hear the morning come alive—guests greeting each other, the clatter of dishes, Alyssa calling for more milk.

He turned back toward the Inn, toward the warmth, the scent, the rhythm of everything he'd built. But his heart—steady, careful—beat just a little faster than usual.

—～—

The Afternoon Light

—～—

B Y NOON, THE INN WAS ALIVE IN ITS GENTLE HUM — VOICES overlapping like soft melody, dishes clinking, the smell of sugar and cinnamon blooming from the kitchen. A breeze carried in through the open front door, pushing against the curtains and stirring the scent of pine from outside.

Elias moved through the space with quiet precision, his rhythm tuned to the life around him. He refilled the sugar bowls, replaced a vase of tulips on the corner table, adjusted the tilt of the framed Gingerbread Competition photo still hanging near the espresso bar. The photo caught the afternoon light — ribbons gleaming faintly, a frozen echo of laughter from months before.

From the speakers above, Taylor Swift's "Delicate" began to play. The song wrapped around the air like silk, her voice hushed and intimate — This ain't for the best / My reputation's never been worse, so / You must like me for me.

Elias smiled faintly, recognizing the irony of it — how the simplest lyrics could find their way to the deepest corners of the day.

He was wiping down the marble counter when Alyssa emerged from the kitchen, her apron dusted with flour and cinnamon. She placed a tray of lemon scones on the bar, still warm.

"You look lighter," she said, studying him.

Elias arched an eyebrow. "Do I?"

"You do," she said, grinning. "And I've known you long enough to know that means one of two things: either you finally slept through the night, or someone new has you thinking about what shirt you're wearing."

He laughed, shaking his head. "You really don't hold back."

She leaned against the counter. "You've been smiling at nothing for two days. That's either enlightenment or attraction. And between the two, I'd bet my best croissant it's the latter."

He didn't answer right away. The espresso machine hissed behind him, filling the space with its steady breath.

"I met someone," he said finally, voice even. "He's... different."

"Different's good," she said softly. "Different means you're still open."

Before he could respond, the bell over the door chimed.

Moore stepped inside.

He wore that familiar half-smile — the one that didn't give much away — and took his usual seat by the window. Alyssa's grin shifted into something knowing.

"Ah," she whispered. "Different just got complicated."

Elias shot her a look, but she only winked and disappeared back into the kitchen.

He walked to the counter, drying his hands on a towel. "Afternoon, Moore. The usual?"

"You know me too well."

Elias poured the shot, the air filling again with the rich, dark scent of roast. Taylor's voice floated between them — Is it cool that I said all that? Is it chill that you're in my head?

When Elias set the cup down, Moore looked up at him, steady. "So. The artist."

Elias blinked. "Word travels fast."

"Alyssa has a mouth and a big heart," Moore said, smiling faintly. "She means well."

"She always does."

Moore took a slow sip, then set the cup down. "You seem... different, Eli. Lighter. But maybe also like you're holding your breath."

Elias leaned against the counter, arms crossed. "Maybe I am. It's strange, isn't it? How someone can walk in and make you see the same light differently."

Moore nodded, eyes softening. "Sometimes that's how the world reminds us we're still alive."

The song shifted into its bridge — Sometimes I wonder when you sleep / Are you ever dreaming of me?

Neither spoke for a while. Outside, the wind picked up, scattering petals from the tulip planter across the porch. One drifted through the open door and landed beside Elias's shoe — soft pink against the polished floor.

He crouched, picked it up, turned it between his fingers. "Maybe this time I'm not running," he said quietly.

Moore looked at him a long moment before answering. "Then don't."

Later, when the crowd had thinned and the afternoon leaned toward gold, Elias stood by the window, watching the light move across the street. He could see Julian walking down the far sidewalk — sketchbook under his arm, scarf loose at his throat, the air shimmering faintly around him like some quiet promise.

Taylor's voice faded into the final refrain — This is delicate.

And Elias, heart beating steady but awake, whispered to the empty room, "Yeah. It is."

— ~ —

Dusk Run

— ~ —

THE LIGHT OUTSIDE THE INN HAD TURNED TO HONEY — THAT fleeting hour when everything felt suspended between what had been and what might be. The day's warmth lingered on the porch rails, the scent of baked sugar and cedar still holding in the air. Guests' laughter drifted through the lobby, soft and tired from a day in the sun.

Elias laced his shoes by the door, pulling his jacket close. The mountain always called a little louder at this hour.

He slipped outside, the gravel crunching underfoot, and started down Galena toward the lake. The rhythm came easily — the low thud of his steps, his breath syncing with the quiet pulse of the town. Above, the first stars pricked through the lavender sky, one by one.

Running wasn't escape anymore. It was sorting — sifting the noise from the knowing.

He passed the bakery, now dark except for a single lamp flickering inside. He could still smell the cinnamon, faint and ghostlike. A group of kids rode past on e-bikes, their laughter echoing off the storefronts. Somewhere down the street, someone was strumming a guitar — a tune that almost, but not quite, matched "Delicate."

The trail curved past the creek, and the mountain opened before him — vast, still, merciful. The snowmelt rushed like applause. He breathed it in, the clean sting of pine and cold air in his lungs, the sharp pull of gravity in his calves.

And then, as it always did, the quiet filled with memory.

Jacob's voice — low, amused — came back in fragments. The way he'd looked at him over coffee that morning months ago, teasing about the extra shot of espresso. The way he'd said You always overthink what's good for you. The way his presence once steadied the chaos, even when it shouldn't have.

They'd built something unspoken between them — part friendship, part habit, part history. He'd been sure it was over, but lately, the thought of Jacob lingered in odd places — in a song lyric, in the quiet between guests' check-ins, in the way light fell through the east windows just before dawn.

He slowed his pace, the gravel soft beneath his shoes.

Julian had stirred something else entirely — curiosity, maybe. Not the comfort of an old love, but the thrill of possibility, sharp as air at altitude. The two feelings collided somewhere under his ribs — not as rivals, but as reminders that his heart still had depth he hadn't mapped yet.

He reached the clearing by the overlook and stopped. Below, Frisco lay scattered in amber and blue — porch lights flickering on, the reflection of town lamps dancing on the lake. The mountains behind him caught the last edge of sunlight.

He pulled in a breath, slow and deliberate. The cold burned clean.

Then, faintly, he heard a voice.

"Didn't think you'd be up here this late."

Julian.

He turned, and there he was — sitting on the low fence, sketchbook open on his knee, pencil moving like breath. His hair caught the fading light; his expression was half shadow, half smile.

Elias managed a small laugh. "Didn't think anyone else would be either."

"I could say the same thing." Julian closed the book, resting it on his thigh. "You run to clear your head?"

"Most days," Elias said. "Some days I just hope the wind will do it for me."

Julian tilted his head. "And tonight?"

"Tonight..." Elias hesitated, looking out at the mountain. "Tonight it's just noise."

Julian didn't push. He just nodded, looking out at the same view. "You know, I sketch places to remember what they felt like. Maybe you run for the same reason — to remind yourself how it feels to move forward."

The line hung there — simple, but clean and true.

Elias exhaled, the tension easing. "You make it sound poetic."

Julian smiled. "I make it sound honest."

The wind shifted, carrying the smell of rain from somewhere higher up the slope. Elias felt it — that small hum of connection, quiet but insistent.

For a moment, neither spoke. The town lights blinked below them like a living constellation.

Elias turned slightly, studying Julian. "Do you ever stop searching for meaning in everything?"

Julian shrugged. "Only when it finds me first."

They walked back together in near silence, their steps syncing without effort. Somewhere behind them, thunder rolled softly across the ridge. The song still played in Elias's mind — Taylor's voice whispering the question he wouldn't say aloud: Is it cool that I said all that? Is it chill that you're in my head?

By the time they reached the Inn, the porch light glowed warm against the deepening blue. Julian paused at the gate.

"Good run?" he asked.

Elias smiled faintly. "Better ending."

Julian nodded. "Then maybe that's the point."

Elias watched him walk down the path toward town, the night closing around him like a slow breath. The world felt both smaller and larger all at once.

He looked back at the Inn, lights golden in the windows, the scent of cinnamon still faint in the air.

And for the first time in a long while, Elias didn't know whether he was standing still or falling forward.

We'll feel Elias's inner shift as Jacob's name appears again, uninvited and inevitable.

— ~ —

The Morning Rain

— ~ —

R AIN BEGAN SOMETIME BEFORE DAWN. BY THE TIME ELIAS STIRRED, IT had already settled into rhythm — a steady patter against the eaves, the slow drip from the gutters, the faint hum of tires on wet asphalt beyond the porch. It was the kind of morning that blurred edges, where even time seemed to move softer.

He sat up slowly, the sheets cool against his skin, the scent of rain-damp wood seeping through the open window. Downstairs, the first clink of mugs told him Alyssa was already awake. The espresso machine sighed, a long breath that belonged to the house more than to any person.

He moved through his small routine — pulling on a sweater, tying back his hair, making the bed with the same care he gave the lobby. The room was lit only by the silver wash of rainlight.

When he reached the kitchen, the smell of roasted beans and butter met him like memory. Alyssa was bent over a tray of pastries, her headphones in. Through the low hum he caught the familiar guitar of Taylor Swift's "Delicate."

She noticed him and grinned. "Rainy-day anthem. Figured it suits the mood."

"It does," he said, voice rough from sleep. He poured himself a cup of house roast — cinnamon and cream, exactly right — and leaned against the counter. "The guests still asleep?"

"For now," she said. "A couple's up in 205 — they're whispering loud enough for a movie."

Elias smiled into his mug. "Love doesn't keep quiet."

"Neither does coffee," she replied, sliding the tray into the oven. "What about you? Couldn't sleep?"

He shrugged. "The rain woke me." But that wasn't the truth. What woke him was a dream — a voice he hadn't heard in months.

Jacob's voice.

He carried his cup to the front desk where the old iPad glowed faintly with new messages. One from the delivery vendor. Another from a guest extending a stay. And then — the name.

Jacob R.

He stared at it for a moment before opening it.

"Hey, Eli. Passing through Denver for work next week. Thinking of coming up for a night — if it's not too strange. I know the season's changing, and so are you, but... I'd like to see the place again. And maybe you. —J."

He read it twice, the rain tapping insistently on the glass. Outside, the mountains were half-hidden by mist; even the trees seemed to be listening.

Alyssa's voice broke through from the kitchen. "Everything okay?"

"Yeah," he said automatically.

She leaned in the doorway, drying her hands on a towel. "You look like someone who just read a ghost story."

"Maybe I did."

"Jacob?" she guessed.

He didn't answer, but the silence told her everything. She walked over and placed a fresh croissant beside his cup. "Eat something before you start thinking too much."

He looked up. "I'm not—"

"You are," she said, smiling. "You always do."

The morning moved slowly. Guests trickled in, grateful for warm air and stronger coffee. The rain softened to drizzle, the world outside washed clean.

By ten, Julian appeared at the door, raincoat damp, sketchbook tucked beneath his arm. He smiled when he saw Elias. "Told you I'd bring you the finished piece."

He unrolled the page — the Inn again, but different this time. Painted in gray and gold, reflections shimmering across a rain-dark street.

"It's beautiful," Elias said, tracing the faint brushwork.

"It's honest," Julian replied. "Everything softens in rain. Even truth."

Elias set the painting on the counter, his pulse unsteady. Even truth.

Julian noticed, but didn't ask. He just smiled faintly. "You okay?"

"Just a busy morning."

Julian looked at him for a long moment. "If that's what you want to call it."

He left soon after, leaving behind the smell of wet pine and a question that hung in the air long after the door closed.

Elias carried the message from Jacob in his pocket all day, unopened again but not unread. The words pulsed quietly, like a heartbeat against his thigh — an invitation, or a warning, he couldn't yet decide.

That evening, when the rain finally stopped, he stood on the porch under a sky the color of steel and lavender. The air smelled of earth and cedar and something that might have been forgiveness.

He whispered, half to the mountain, half to himself, "Still, by design."

The wind lifted the words and carried them out toward the lake — soft, uncertain, alive.

—~—

The Return

—~—

T HE STORM HAD CLEARED BY MORNING, LEAVING THE WORLD GLAZED and golden. Raindrops clung to the windowpanes like tiny prisms, bending the sunlight into soft halos. The mountains looked impossibly near, their peaks still dusted white where the snow refused to melt.

Elias stood by the front desk, ledger open, pretending to check the week's reservations though he already knew each one by heart. The air smelled faintly of cardamom and rain-soaked pine. Someone upstairs was playing Ruel's "Suburb's" low enough that it sounded like memory leaking through the floorboards.

He'd told himself he wouldn't look for Jacob. That if Jacob came, he'd feel it — not because of logic, but because some part of him would always recognize that particular gravity.

And then, just after eleven, the front door opened.

The bell chimed once, soft and clean.

Jacob stood there — raincoat slung over one arm, hair still damp from the drive, that same unassuming steadiness he always carried, the kind that made chaos feel almost orderly.

He smiled, uncertain. "Hey, Eli."

For a heartbeat, Elias couldn't move. Every carefully folded morning unraveled all at once.

"Jacob," he said finally, voice too even. "You made it."

"Wasn't sure I would," Jacob admitted, stepping inside. "But I guess the mountains have a way of pulling people back."

Elias gestured toward the fire where fresh logs were still crackling. "They don't let go easily."

Jacob set his bag down near the bench. His eyes scanned the lobby — the polished wood, the soft light spilling through stained glass, the bowl of scones Alyssa had just placed out. He smiled faintly. "You've changed things."

"Some," Elias said. "The rest changed me."

Jacob looked at him then, really looked. "You look good, Eli."

"Good as in healthy or good as in different?"

"Both," Jacob said. "And better."

The words landed softly but deeply, like a note struck on the low end of a piano.

Alyssa appeared from the kitchen, her apron dusted with flour. When she saw Jacob, her brows lifted in quiet surprise. "Well. The ghost returns."

Jacob laughed. "Good to see you too, Alyssa."

She grinned, wiping her hands on a towel. "You're lucky it's check-in time. Otherwise, I'd make you sweep the porch just to prove you still belong here."

Jacob glanced toward Elias, a flicker of something — gratitude, nostalgia, maybe longing. "I wouldn't mind earning my stay."

Alyssa smiled, the kind that saw more than it said. "Coffee's fresh," she said, and disappeared back into the kitchen.

The silence she left behind felt delicate, balanced on the edge of something unnamed.

Elias gestured toward the espresso bar. "Still take it black?"

Jacob hesitated, then smiled. "You remember."

"Some things don't fade."

He busied himself with the machine, the hiss of steam filling the space between them. It was safer than silence, but not by much. The scent of cinnamon rose again, grounding, domestic, too gentle for what trembled under his ribs.

Jacob leaned against the counter, studying him. "So," he said, "how's life treating you in paradise?"

Elias gave a small, knowing smile. "Paradise takes work."

Jacob chuckled. "You always were better at the work than the rest of us."

"I had to be," Elias said quietly. "Some of us don't get to coast."

Their eyes met — just long enough for everything unsaid to flicker between them.

Later, when guests had come and gone and the fire burned low, they found themselves sitting in the small lounge by the window. The rain had left the air sharp and clean. Through the glass, the peaks glowed faintly under the rising moon.

Jacob held his cup loosely between his hands. "I've thought about this place more than I should admit."

Elias looked out at the mountains. "Places remember us, too."

"That why you came back?"

"I came back because I had to," Elias said. "Because it was the first place that didn't ask me to prove I deserved to be here."

Jacob nodded slowly. "I get that."

"Do you?"

Jacob looked at him — eyes tired, honest. "I didn't back then. But I do now."

Something in Elias softened, but not enough to let him fall. "And what are you looking for now, Jacob?"

Jacob smiled sadly. "Maybe the same thing you are. Maybe just proof that we didn't ruin everything by trying too hard to fix it."

Elias exhaled, the sound somewhere between a laugh and a sigh. "You always were better at saying the wrong thing beautifully."

"Maybe that's all I ever knew how to do."

The song changed upstairs — "Paper Rings." Light, messy, achingly happy. The sound drifted down like irony.

Jacob leaned back in his chair. "Do you ever miss it? The way things were?"

Elias looked at him for a long moment. "Sometimes. But I think I miss who I thought I was more than I miss who we were."

Jacob nodded, eyes down. "That's fair."

When Jacob finally went upstairs to his room, Elias stayed behind, listening to the fire settle into embers. The clock ticked softly. The mountain wind pressed against the windows.

He whispered into the quiet: "You came back too late, Jacob."

But even as he said it, he wasn't sure whether he meant too late or just in time.

When the House Holds Its Breath

—— ∼ ——

J ULIAN HAD LEARNED TO READ THE INN BY ITS SOUNDS. THE SCRAPE OF a chair meant someone had settled in with a book. The low hiss of the espresso machine meant Elias was nearby. The faint music spilling from the kitchen meant Alyssa was in one of her moods — baking when the world felt too large.

But that afternoon, something was off. The sounds didn't quite fit together.

He'd come in from a walk around noon, shoes damp, sketchbook tucked under his arm. The clouds had lifted, but the air still held that strange after-rain glow — the kind that makes every color look like it's been washed new. When he stepped into the lobby, though, he stopped.

The light was the same as always — golden, steady — but the air felt... interrupted. Not broken, just aware of itself.

Elias was behind the front desk, pretending to read a guest's note but his shoulders were tense. His voice, when he greeted Julian, was careful — polite in a way it hadn't been yesterday.

"Hey," Elias said, too casually. "Out sketching again?"

Julian nodded. "The sky wouldn't stop showing off." He smiled, but it didn't land.

That's when he saw the man standing by the fire. Jacob.

He didn't need to ask who he was — the weight of unspoken history gave it away. There was a pause between every glance, a softness in how Elias moved around him, like handling a photograph you're not sure you're ready to look at.

Julian smiled politely when Elias made the introduction. "Julian, this is Jacob — an old friend."

The word friend felt wrong — too small, too safe — but Julian nodded. "Good to meet you," he said.

Jacob extended a hand. "Likewise. I've seen your work around here. Elias talks about your sketches."

Julian smiled faintly. "He exaggerates."

"Not by much," Elias said, eyes flicking up, then away.

For a few beats, they all stood there — the hum of the heater filling the silence, the soft crackle of logs shifting in the fireplace.

Alyssa appeared from the back, holding a tray of lemon bars, her timing impeccable. "I thought I heard ghosts," she said, eyes darting between them with a knowing grin.

Elias shot her a look. "Alyssa."

"What? I'm just saying hi." She winked at Julian and retreated, leaving the sugar and tension behind.

Julian spent the afternoon sketching in the library, though he barely touched the page. He could hear them downstairs — Elias and Jacob — laughter, low and almost hesitant, like two people trying to remember how to speak a language they once knew fluently.

He told himself it didn't matter. That what he felt wasn't jealousy, just curiosity. But the pencil pressed too hard, the line broke, and when he finally looked down, all he'd drawn was a mess of cross-hatched gray.

The Inn felt different now — like a song that had changed key without warning.

Even the light had shifted. The soft amber that usually glowed through the lobby had deepened into something warmer, heavier — dusk creeping in early.

By the time he went downstairs, the music had changed too. Someone had queued Taylor Swift's "Delicate" again, low and looping. It filled the space like a question.

Elias was wiping down the counter, his sleeves rolled up, his focus deliberate. Jacob was sitting nearby, a book open but unread.

Julian hesitated in the doorway before saying softly, "You two make it look easy."

Elias looked up, almost startled. "What?"

"Being comfortable," Julian said. "Like time never moved."

Jacob smiled faintly. "Maybe it didn't."

Elias shot him a glance, then forced a laugh. "Or maybe it did, and we're just pretending not to notice."

Julian nodded, his own smile tight. "Pretending's an art form."

No one said anything for a moment. The song played through again, that delicate refrain — "Is it cool that I said all that?" — and the words seemed to hang in the air long after it ended.

That night, long after the guests had gone quiet, Julian went out onto the porch. The stars were faint, dimmed by low clouds. From somewhere inside, he could hear Elias's voice — soft, tired, the murmur of someone speaking to the past as if it might finally listen.

Julian didn't move. He didn't go back inside. He just stood there in the cool air, the boards creaking softly under his feet, and thought about how sometimes even the most beautiful places could make room for ghosts.

And how the hardest part of loving something steady is watching it tremble.

CHAPTER FOURTEEN

THE UNRAVELING HOUR

———

G

B Y THE TIME THE GUESTS HAD GONE TO BED, THE INN HAD FALLEN into its steady hum again — the sound of pipes breathing, the soft creak of floorboards settling under dreams. But Elias couldn't sleep.

He'd tried. He'd turned off the lights, stared at the ceiling, listened to the slow tick of the baseboard heater counting out seconds that didn't seem to move. Then he'd given up.

Outside, the night smelled like snowmelt and pine needles, that early-spring fragrance that felt like clean slate and ache all at once. The moon hung thin and silver above Mount Royal. He laced his running shoes without thinking — it had become instinct, the way he metabolized emotion.

The streets of Frisco were empty, quiet but not silent. His breath rose in soft bursts, rhythm syncing with his steps. The sound of his shoes against pavement echoed down Main Street — thup, thup, thup — steady, measured, controlled.

He passed the coffee shop that closed too early, the park where he and Jacob once sat with paper cups and nothing left to say, the alley where the first snow of winter had once fallen so perfectly he almost believed in grace.

He ran until the tightness in his chest softened into something else — not peace, not quite, but space.

When he returned, the Inn glowed like it always did — warm, amber, patient. The sign out front flickered once before settling steady. It felt like the building was exhaling, waiting.

Through the kitchen window, a light was still on. Of course it was.

August sat at the counter, reading glasses perched low, a cup of tea cooling beside him. He didn't look surprised when

Elias stepped in, flushed and breathless. He'd been gone a stretch of weeks—family down in the valley, a roof that needed him more than the Inn did—and the house had held the shape of him while he was away, the way a chair keeps the warmth of whoever just left it. Some keepers go, Elias thought, just so the place can prove it remembers them.

"Couldn't sleep?" August asked. His voice was soft enough not to startle the quiet.

Elias shook his head, wiping sweat from his temple. "Too much noise."

"Ah," August said, closing his book. "The kind that doesn't come from outside."

Elias gave a half-smile. "Something like that."

"Jacob's still here," August said, not as a question.

Elias leaned against the counter, arms folded. "You saw him?"

"Saw him, heard him, felt the air change the moment he walked through that door. Houses like this, they notice things before we do."

Elias laughed softly. "I should've known you'd say that."

August studied him for a moment, then said, "You've built a rhythm here, Elias. One that's taken root. But rhythms can't protect you from the past. They just give you a place to rest when it comes knocking."

Elias stared at the floor. "I thought I was past it."

"No one ever is," August said gently. "We just learn how to greet it differently."

Elias let out a slow breath. "He still has this... effect. Like time folds when he's near. I hate that I still feel it."

"That's not weakness," August said, standing to pour another cup of tea. "That's proof you've loved deeply enough for it to matter."

Elias looked up. "And if I can't go back?"

"Then you don't," August said simply. "You go forward — with what the love taught you, not what it took from you."

For a long while, they stood in companionable silence. The kettle hissed. Somewhere upstairs, a door clicked shut.

August slid the second cup toward him. "Chamomile. You need rest more than answers."

Elias smiled faintly. "You always did know what to prescribe."

"That's not wisdom," August said, grinning. "That's just age and insomnia."

They both laughed quietly, the kind of laughter that belongs only to the middle of the night — small, shared, and necessary.

Then August added, "You know, you remind me of this place more every day."

"How's that?"

"You both keep finding ways to forgive what comes through the door."

Elias didn't answer. He just looked at the rising steam from the cup, then past August to the window where the mountain loomed in the dark — steady, indifferent, eternal.

When he finally spoke, it was almost a whisper. "Do you ever get tired of being the one who knows?"

August smiled, eyes kind. "Every day. But then someone like you walks in at midnight, and I remember why I stay awake."

That night, when Elias finally climbed the stairs, the house seemed to breathe easier. He paused halfway up, glancing toward the hall where Jacob's door was closed and still.

For the first time since the morning, he didn't feel haunted. Just human.

He whispered into the quiet, "I'm still here."

And the Inn, faithful as ever, seemed to answer — a small sigh through the vent, a soft crack from the beam, a promise in its own quiet language: Yes. You are.

Morning Light Knows
Everything

T HE INN WOKE EARLY THAT DAY, AS IF THE NIGHT HAD LEFT something half-finished.

The air carried that clean, post-storm hush — the smell of pine sap and coffee grounds, wood smoke from a nearby chimney curling into the blue. Light gathered slowly through the dining room windows, catching on the steam rising from freshly brewed espresso. The floors creaked, but softly, like the house itself was stretching after a long dream.

Elias stood behind the counter, already moving in rhythm. Mug. Milk. Steam. Pour. The small choreography that had become his grounding ritual. His sleeves were rolled, his hair still damp from a quick shower, and the faint sound of "Delicate" hummed from the speaker — quiet, unassuming, just enough to fill the air.

Across the room, August was reading the paper with his usual calm that made chaos feel optional. Alyssa whisked batter in the kitchen, humming along, her voice blending with the soft rhythm of utensils.

And then Jacob appeared.

No footsteps this time — just the door opening, a rush of cold mountain air, and him — in a dark sweater, coffee-colored eyes steady, a tired smile that still somehow worked like gravity.

Elias felt his chest tighten, just slightly. "Morning," he said, too lightly.

"Morning," Jacob replied, pausing just long enough to watch the espresso pour. "You still make it look like an art form."

"Or a coping mechanism," Elias said with a faint smile.

Jacob smiled back. "Maybe both."

August looked up from his paper, eyes twinkling. "Coffee's a language around here, not a beverage. You'll learn the dialect again soon enough."

Jacob chuckled. "I remember."

"Good," August said, folding his paper neatly. "Because some languages don't forgive grammar mistakes."

He rose, leaving the two of them alone. The door closed softly behind him, as if even the hinges understood boundaries.

The silence stretched, but not awkwardly. Just full.

Elias handed Jacob a cup. Their fingers brushed for the briefest moment, and it was enough to send a quiet tremor through the morning's stillness.

Jacob exhaled. "You look... lighter."

"Recovery has a way of forcing that," Elias said. "It doesn't let you carry what isn't yours anymore."

Jacob nodded, eyes soft. "I didn't know how heavy I'd made things."

"You didn't," Elias said. "Life did. We just kept trying to outpace it."

Outside, the snowmelt ran fast through the gutters, the sound crisp and alive. The air was thin enough to taste.

Jacob leaned against the counter, watching him work. "Do you ever think about what might've been if we hadn't—"

Elias cut him off gently. "All the time. But that's not where peace lives anymore."

Jacob looked at him, then down at his cup. "You really found it here."

Elias followed his gaze toward the window. "I think it found me."

Julian entered then — hair tousled, sketchbook under one arm, a quiet observer of worlds he never quite belonged to but always understood. He took in the scene — Elias behind the counter, Jacob in soft focus, the morning light cutting between them — and said, "You two look like a film I'd watch twice just to catch what I missed the first time."

Elias laughed, tension breaking. "That's because you'd color-grade the pain out of it."

Julian smiled. "Maybe. But not the hope."

Alyssa appeared, holding a tray of scones dusted with powdered sugar. "Breakfast for the emotionally fragile," she said cheerfully, setting it down.

Jacob raised a brow. "You always this gentle?"

"Only before nine a.m.," she said. "After that, I'm brutal."

The table filled with warmth — laughter, clinking mugs, the scent of cinnamon and lemon zest. The kind of domestic symphony that made even ghosts feel welcome.

When the guests began to trickle in, August returned, setting his paper aside. He caught Elias's eye and nodded once — the kind of nod that said you did it right, even if it still hurts.

As the morning carried on, Julian sat by the window, sketching — his pencil tracing three figures and the light between them. He wasn't drawing likenesses; he was capturing gravity. The way the room seemed to hold everyone just slightly closer than usual.

He titled the sketch quietly at the bottom: The Inn Breathes Easier Today.

Later, when Elias stepped outside to breathe in the thin mountain air, he saw Jacob sitting on the porch steps, head tilted toward the light.

For a long moment, neither spoke. The snow on Mount Royal shimmered in the distance.

Finally, Jacob said softly, "You were right, you know. This place forgives what people can't."

Elias nodded. "That's why I stayed."

The wind shifted, carrying the scent of cedar and coffee, the faint echo of Delicate drifting from the open door.

Jacob smiled — small, sincere, resigned. "Then maybe it's my turn to listen."

And for the first time in years, Elias didn't feel the need to fill the silence. The Inn did that for him — steady, golden, and alive.

*The Edges of Someone Else's
Story*

J ULIAN ALWAYS DREW BETTER WHEN THE WORLD WAS HALF-ASLEEP.
Morning light did something to the air at the Inn — it softened it, made every surface gentler. Coffee steam caught the sun like it was rehearsing for a halo. The scent of lemon zest and cinnamon from Alyssa's kitchen seemed to slow the heart rate of anyone who entered. It was the kind of peace that never announced itself; it just unfolded when you stopped trying to deserve it.

He sat in the corner of the library, sketchbook open, pencil hovering. From here, he could see the entire rhythm of the house: Elias behind the counter, sleeves rolled and eyes quiet; August at the table, annotating his newspaper margins with thoughts too kind to ever be published; Alyssa humming along to something only she could hear.

And Jacob — always half in shadow, like he hadn't quite decided if he belonged here or not.

Julian wasn't jealous, not exactly. It was something more complicated — admiration tangled with longing. Watching Elias move through the day was like watching someone repair a cathedral using light and forgiveness instead of tools. Every motion deliberate, sacred, unfinished.

He thought of how Elias smiled differently depending on who was near. With August — gentle reverence. With Alyssa — the easy warmth of family. With Jacob — something more fragile, almost reverent, like a page he didn't want to turn but couldn't stop reading.

Julian wrote a note in the corner of his sketchbook:

Some people live as if they're building places where love can rest when it gets tired.

That's what Elias was doing here, he realized. Not performing. Not escaping. Building.

That afternoon, he followed the familiar sounds — the hum of the espresso machine, Alyssa's soft laughter from the kitchen, the porch chime ringing once as wind moved through. The day outside was blinding — the kind of blue that made you feel both small and infinite.

He stepped onto the porch and saw Elias kneeling beside a planter box, hands dusted with soil. The air smelled like cedar, clean and ancient.

"You're early for summer," Julian said.

Elias smiled without looking up. "Spring's about patience. I'm just practicing."

Julian leaned against the railing. "Does patience hurt?"

Elias finally looked up, eyes full of that quiet light. "Only until you remember what it's for."

Later, Julian returned to his sketchbook and added another line:

Maybe peace isn't found. Maybe it's grown — like thyme and trust.

He drew them all — Elias by the planter, August with his tea, Alyssa mid-laughter, Jacob in soft focus near the window. Together, they looked like something he didn't have a word for yet — maybe family, maybe forgiveness, maybe home.

That evening, he left the sketchbook open on the library table. The fire burned low, shadows stretching long. He didn't notice when Elias came by later and paused to read the words.

Elias's fingers lingered over the page, tracing the pencil line beneath Maybe peace is grown. He smiled, quiet and full, and whispered, "Maybe it is."

And for once, the house didn't answer back. It didn't need to.

— ~ —

Where the Light Lands

— ~ —

T HE LETTER WASN'T ADDRESSED TO ANYONE, AT LEAST NOT IN INK. Just left on the front desk, folded twice, edges soft from the press of fingertips.

Elias found it after the breakfast rush, tucked between the guest ledger and a vase of tulips Alyssa had brought down from the attic window box. The handwriting was slanted and elegant — the kind that belonged to someone who'd written more apologies than love notes.

He turned it over once before opening it.

I don't know if you remember me. I stayed here two winters ago. I came broken, and I left lighter. I still think about the way you said good morning like it meant something. Please keep doing that. The world needs more mornings like yours. — No name.

Elias read it twice. Once with his eyes, once with his breath.

He didn't remember the guest exactly — just a faint image, maybe a woman in a navy scarf who always asked for honey in her tea. But the note was enough. Proof that the small things — a clean counter, a cup set down gently, a word offered instead of withheld — mattered.

He tucked the letter beneath the register. Not as a trophy. As a reminder.

Outside, the snowmelt was running fast, the creek behind the Inn glinting in the sunlight like veins of glass. Elias stepped onto the porch, mug in hand, and exhaled.

Frisco was alive again. Bicycles leaned against storefronts. The air buzzed faintly with the murmur of spring travelers and locals with dogs. The sky was wide, unpunctuated blue.

He felt the familiar pull to run — that private ritual that had become his heartbeat. So he did. Down Galena Street, past the bakery with the open windows, past the bridge where couples carved initials into the wood. His strides matched the rhythm of the town's waking pulse.

The scent of pine. The taste of air cold enough to sting. The sound of Ruel's "Suburbia" bleeding through his earbuds — a song about youth and wanting, about the ache of beauty.

By the time he looped back toward the Inn, his chest ached in the best way. Breathless but clear.

And there — sitting on the porch rail, sketchbook open — was Julian. He was drawing the mountain again, though Elias suspected the sketches were never really about the mountain.

"Morning," Elias said.

Julian looked up, smiling. "You run like you're trying to outrun the sunrise."

"Maybe I am."

"Did it catch you?"

Elias laughed softly. "It always does."

Julian turned the sketchbook so he could see. "You ever notice how the light always finds this place differently? Never the same angle twice."

Elias looked — the sketch wasn't perfect, but it was honest. The Inn glowed like it was alive. "Maybe it's trying to remind us to keep noticing."

Julian nodded. "Seems to be working."

Back inside, Alyssa was setting out cookies for the afternoon guests, humming off-key. August was at the piano, coaxing something tender from its uneven keys — a melody that sounded half like memory, half like forgiveness.

Jacob wasn't there. Not yet. But Elias felt his absence differently now — not as a wound, but as space.

He carried a new calm through the day, unhurried. Guests came and went; laughter threaded through the halls. Someone played Taylor Swift's "Delicate" softly through a portable speaker upstairs, and the sound seemed to ripple through the old wood like light on water.

And by evening, when the lamps were lit and the porch chime sang its one clear note, Elias finally understood what August meant when he said that rhythm wasn't peace — it was participation.

He didn't need to fix anything. He just needed to stay in tempo.

CHAPTER FIFTEEN

THE ROAD TO ASPEN

———

G

T HE ROAD WOUND OUT OF FRISCO LIKE A RIBBON PULLED THROUGH light. The morning was still pale when Elias locked the front door of the Inn, leaving Alyssa in charge. She stood at the porch rail, coffee in hand, the hem of her sweater catching the soft mountain breeze.

"Bring back stories," she said, smiling.

"I'll bring back peace, if I find any," Elias replied.

She waved him off. "You're taking the long way, then."

He laughed, slipped his overnight bag into the passenger seat, and started the drive east.

The mountains opened around him — endless, solemn, and impossible to look away from. The sun climbed slow, bleeding gold through the tree line. He rolled the windows down, letting the cool air slap against his face, the scent of pine and melting snow heavy in the wind. Ruel's "As Long as You Care" played quietly through the car speakers, his voice blending into the hum of tires on asphalt.

Every mile felt like a conversation between who he'd been and who he was trying to be.

Aspen appeared around a bend, the valley spilling open like a secret kept too long. Redbrick buildings, art galleries, a farmer's market just setting up — all dusted with early spring light. People moved differently here, as if they were practiced at beauty.

Elias checked into a small inn just off Main Street — charming, but not quite home. Nothing could replicate the Frisco Inn's heartbeat. He dropped his bag on the bed, exhaled, and sat at the edge for a long minute, listening to the quiet pulse of an unfamiliar room.

He didn't realize how much he'd missed the sounds of his own house — the creak of the third stair, August's soft footsteps in the hall, the smell of cinnamon and coffee that clung to everything.

Still, there was something freeing about distance.

He walked through town. The streets were alive with motion — painters setting up easels, cyclists passing with bursts of laughter, the metallic chatter of shop doors opening and closing. He bought a coffee from a café with plants spilling over its windowsills and sat outside, notebook open, pen in hand.

The page stayed blank longer than usual.

A voice broke his focus. "You again."

He looked up. Jacob. Standing there, hair tousled from wind, a paper bag tucked under one arm, eyes half-smiling, half-sincere.

Elias's chest tightened, but not in panic. More like recognition.

"You following me now?" he asked.

"Maybe the coffee," Jacob said. "Maybe you."

"Either way, you found both."

Jacob pulled out the chair across from him. "There's a farmer's market down the street. Come on. You look like someone who needs something sweet."

The market was small but alive — the smell of honey, roasted almonds, and mountain lavender filling the air. Musicians played a slow cover of "Delicate", and Elias almost laughed at the coincidence.

They wandered without hurry. Jacob bought two peaches even though they weren't quite ripe. Elias sampled homemade marmalade, orange and bitter, and thought about how flavor mirrored emotion — you never got the sweet without the sting.

"You okay?" Jacob asked, catching the flicker in his eyes.

Elias nodded. "I'm just remembering what beauty costs sometimes."

Jacob's gaze softened. "You don't have to pay for it alone."

That evening, they sat by the Roaring Fork River, legs dangling over the bank, the water a shifting mosaic of gold and gray. The air had that late-spring chill that made every breath feel earned.

"I keep thinking about the Inn," Elias said. "How it's more than a place now. It's like... it's breathing through me."

Jacob looked out at the water. "Then maybe this is its way of reminding you to exhale."

For a long moment, neither spoke. The sky deepened into violet, the first stars trembling awake.

When Elias finally did speak, it was softer than the river. "You ever feel like you're getting close to something real, but you're scared to hold it?"

Jacob smiled faintly. "Only when I'm looking at it."

— ∼ —

The Night Between

— ∼ —

ASPEN'S EVENING LIGHT FELL LIKE HONEY ACROSS THE BRICK streets. The air hummed with the aftertaste of laughter, music, and soft conversation — strangers who felt, for a moment, like friends. Elias and Jacob walked side by side, no agenda, no performance. Just motion.

Shop windows glowed with warm lamplight, each one a tiny world. An antique bookstore smelled of cedar and dust. A couple danced barefoot in front of a wine bar, swaying to a jazz trio whose trumpet spilled gold into the night air.

Elias stopped for a second, drawn to the scene. Jacob noticed. "You used to hate crowds."

"I still do," Elias said. "But sometimes they remind me that people are trying. That's enough."

Jacob smiled. "You always did have a poetic way of avoiding direct answers."

"And you always wanted the truth before it was ready," Elias said, meeting his gaze.

The words hung between them, alive and electric.

They walked until the noise faded behind them, ending up near the old bridge at the edge of town — wooden planks, faintly damp, river whispering below. Aspen trees leaned over the water, their leaves like coins catching the wind.

Jacob leaned against the railing, shoulders relaxed, face half in shadow. "You know what's strange?" he said. "This town looks like it's always waiting for someone to fall in love."

Elias laughed softly. "Maybe that's what makes it so dangerous."

"Dangerous?"

He nodded. "It tricks you into believing time's on your side."

Jacob studied him for a long moment. "And do you believe it?"

Elias looked toward the mountains — dark now, rimmed in silver moonlight. "I believe some moments deserve to last longer. Even if they don't."

The quiet that followed wasn't empty; it pulsed with everything they didn't need to name. Somewhere in the distance, a bar's door opened and spilled out Taylor Swift's "Delicate." The lyrics carried faintly across the water, almost too perfect.

Is it cool that I said all that? Is it chill that you're in my head?

Elias closed his eyes, the sound threading through him like a confession he hadn't spoken yet.

Jacob's hand brushed his — barely, like testing a theory. Elias didn't move away.

For a moment, it wasn't about the past or the things they'd broken. It was about this: two people standing still while the river kept moving, both aware that stillness could be a kind of surrender.

When he finally opened his eyes again, Jacob was looking at him — not asking, not expecting. Just seeing.

Elias smiled. Small. Real. "You always find me in the quiet."

Jacob's voice was low, almost a whisper. "That's the only place you ever really exist."

They stayed there until the wind shifted, colder now, carrying the scent of rain and something green. Elias shivered.

Jacob handed him his jacket without a word.

Back at the inn, the hallway light hummed softly. Their rooms were across from each other, doors half-closed. Elias paused at his threshold, looking back.

"Goodnight," he said.

Jacob's eyes caught the dim glow. "You mean that?"

"I'm trying to."

Jacob nodded, a faint smile tugging at the edge of his mouth. "Then that's enough."

The doors shut with twin, soft clicks.

Elias couldn't sleep. The storm came just after midnight — gentle, rhythmic, tapping against the glass like a second pulse. He lay awake, listening to it. The room smelled of rain and cedar, of unfamiliar peace.

He thought of the note he'd read that morning — "Please keep doing that. The world needs more mornings like yours."

Maybe peace wasn't in staying still. Maybe it was in learning how to carry light with you wherever you went.

He fell asleep with the window cracked open, letting the mountain air wander through.

—~—

Home

—~—

B Y THE TIME THEY LEFT ASPEN THE NEXT DAY, THE STORM HAD
cleared. The mountains were washed clean, blue and
endless. Jacob drove this time, one hand on the wheel, the
other drumming lightly to the rhythm of LANY's "Good Guys."

Elias watched the road unwind — tunnels of pine, flashes
of river, the occasional elk grazing like a dream against the
horizon.

"You know," Jacob said, not looking over, "you smile more
now."

Elias turned to the window. "I think I just stopped
apologizing for joy."

Jacob nodded, his own smile small and knowing. "That's a
good start."

When they reached Frisco, the Inn came into view —
familiar, welcoming, alive. Alyssa was sweeping the porch,
August adjusting the sign out front. The sight of it all made
Elias's chest tighten in the best way.

"Home," Jacob said quietly.

"Still," Elias replied, "by design."

— ~ —

The Shapes of Home

— ~ —

THE ROAD CURVED BACK INTO FRISCO JUST AS THE FIRST REAL warmth of spring began to press its hand against the valley. The mountains still held their ribbons of snow, but the air was softer now — scented with thawed earth and pine.

Elias could see the Inn from half a mile out: the roofline sharp against the morning light, the porch chimes stirring, the faint glint of the brass sign that read Frisco Inn on Galena.

He felt it before he parked — that small, impossible pull. The house didn't just wait for him. It recognized him.

Alyssa was already on the porch, hair tied up, broom in hand. "You're late," she said, grinning.

Elias laughed, stepping out of the car. "I didn't know I was expected."

"You always are," she said. "August said the plants looked lonely."

He carried his bag up the steps, breathing in the smell of cinnamon and cedar that seemed to pour from the door. It hit him like memory — the way scent could undo time.

Inside, the Inn was alive. The espresso machine hissed in greeting, a kettle whistled somewhere in the kitchen, and the floors hummed under his step, as if the old wood had been waiting to feel his weight again.

August appeared from the hallway, polishing a copper tray. "You went away, and yet somehow I still had to make coffee," he said dryly.

Elias grinned. "You survived?"

"Barely."

They hugged — brief, unspoken, the kind of embrace that happens between two people who have built something together. When they pulled apart, August gave him that look — the one that wasn't quite a question but waited for an answer anyway.

"It was good," Elias said simply. "I remembered how to breathe somewhere else."

"Then bring that back in with you," August said. "The guests are teaching a yoga class in the lounge. God help us."

The day unfolded in its old rhythm, but every small thing felt rewired. The morning light over the counter. The clean pull of espresso — crema gold and steady. The faint sound of LANY's "Thick and Thin" humming low through the speakers.

Jacob had gone for a hike before sunrise, leaving a note on the counter that said only:

"See you in the still parts."

Elias folded the paper into his pocket.

By noon, guests drifted through the lounge, voices low and content. Alyssa passed through with a tray of shortbread, the kind she only made when the weather was changing. The Traveler — who'd returned for another stay — sat by the window with their notebook, occasionally glancing up as if the light itself might inspire something.

Elias moved quietly among them all, a current of calm motion — wiping the marble counter, adjusting the flowers, refilling cups. He caught fragments of conversation: plans for hikes, laughter over postcards, someone reading aloud from The Alchemist in the library.

And through it all, he felt the slow, golden ache of gratitude.

He didn't think about leaving. He didn't need to. This was the part of life that stayed.

When Jacob returned that afternoon, sun-tired and wind-dusted, he stood just inside the doorway, the light framing him in a way that made the whole room pause.

"Missed your shift," Elias said, trying to sound disapproving.

Jacob smiled. "You would've done it better anyway."

Elias set down a cloth, half-smiling. "Maybe. But it's good to have you back."

Something unspoken moved through the air — soft, unfinished, necessary.

Later, when the guests had gone to dinner and the Inn exhaled into its evening rhythm, Elias stood on the porch with a mug in hand. The sky was painted in bruised lavender and orange. Somewhere down the street, wind chimes played the wrong song and somehow made it right.

Jacob joined him quietly, holding two small paper bags. "Bakery was closing. Thought I'd bring dessert."

"What'd you get?"

Jacob held one out. "Guess."

Elias opened it. Inside — a single ginger cookie, dusted with sugar. The kind August used to make for guests in December.

"Christmas in April?" Elias asked.

Jacob shrugged. "Some things shouldn't have seasons."

Elias smiled at that — really smiled. "You're not wrong."

They stood there in companionable silence, the town settling around them, the Inn glowing softly through the windows behind them.

The chime rang once, clear and sweet, before the wind fell still.

—~—

Later

—~—

T HAT NIGHT, ELIAS SAT BY THE FIRE, A NOTEBOOK OPEN BUT untouched. The house hummed with small, living sounds — the creak of settling beams, a kettle cooling, a page turning somewhere upstairs.

He thought of Aspen — the bridge, the rain, the way Jacob had said you smile more now. He thought of the letter left on the desk — The world needs more mornings like yours.

He thought of how the Inn wasn't just a place to stay anymore. It was a place to begin again.

Elias looked toward the staircase, where a faint shadow moved — August heading to bed, or maybe just checking the locks one last time. He smiled and whispered into the quiet:

"Still, by design."

And the house, as always, answered with warmth.

The Sound of Summer Light

B Y June, the mountains had turned green again. The last threads of snow clung stubbornly to the north-facing slopes, but down in Frisco, the air was thick with lilac and sun-warmed pine. The lake glimmered like a held breath, and every street hummed with bicycles, dogs, and the soft clatter of open windows.

The Inn, too, shifted with the season. Doors stayed open longer. Music drifted freely — Ruel's "Growing Up Is___" spilling gently through the speakers one minute, LANY's "You!" the next. Guests filled the lounge with maps, laughter, and the comforting chaos of people trying to make memories.

Elias moved among them easily, but something in him was quieter now — observant in a way that came from peace rather than caution. He'd begun to notice things again: the way morning light gathered on the copper French press, the sound of August humming while rearranging wildflowers in a vase, the faint echo of Alyssa's laughter from the hallway.

Still, there was a current under the calm — not worry exactly, but awareness.

That afternoon, he set up the café terrace for aperitivo hour. The tables were polished, the glassware gleaming in their ordered lines. He'd just finished labeling a tray of honey and rosemary almonds for the boutique when Jacob appeared beside him, carrying a bucket of ice and that smile that seemed designed to undo small pieces of restraint.

"You're humming," Jacob said.

"I am not."

"You are," Jacob insisted, grinning. "That's Ruel, right?"

Elias laughed. "You're impossible."

"And you're happy," Jacob said, lowering his voice just enough to make it true.

Elias didn't answer. He reached for a tray of glasses — delicate, thin-stemmed, sparkling — and began to polish them one by one. His hands moved slowly, carefully, tracing the edge of each flute as if blessing it.

Jacob leaned against the counter, watching. "You treat everything like it's alive."

"It is," Elias said, eyes still on his work. "If you touch it with enough care."

The words landed heavier than he meant. For a moment, the air between them felt charged — sunlight catching the motes of dust, turning them to gold.

Then the chime over the door rang, and Alyssa's voice cut through the tension like music. "Delivery! Two crates of lavender syrup and one of optimism!"

Jacob snorted. "Saved by the sister."

"Always," Elias said, smiling.

Evening gathered like honey — slow, golden, and deliberate. The terrace filled with soft laughter, clinking glasses, and the scent of orange peel. Elias lit the candles, one by one, their flames catching in the copper lanterns. LANY's "Heart Won't Let Me" hummed low in the background, and the air felt almost too perfect — the kind of moment that made him nervous in its stillness.

Alyssa joined them, balancing a tray of lemon spritzers. "Full house tonight," she said. "Two couples from Boulder, one writer from Denver, and a family that can't stop taking pictures of the scones."

Elias smiled. "We've become our own kind of postcard."

"And you," she said, narrowing her eyes, "you look... lighter."

"Must be the altitude," he teased.

She wasn't fooled. "Or the company."

Her glance toward Jacob was obvious enough that even August, who had just emerged from the kitchen, raised an eyebrow.

"Are we gossiping again?" August asked. "Because I can get the good china."

Laughter rippled through the group. Elias rolled his eyes but couldn't hide the warmth that crept into his chest.

Later, when the last guests had gone and the candles burned low, the four of them sat outside — Elias, Jacob, Alyssa, August — surrounded by the scent of rosemary and late-summer air. The stars above Frisco shone with the kind of clarity that only altitude allowed.

Jacob poured coffee instead of wine, and Elias found himself grateful for that — for the ritual, the simplicity, the way conversation stretched easily between them.

Alyssa leaned back in her chair, half-asleep. "You know," she murmured, "the Inn feels different this year. Like it's older, but happier."

August nodded. "Houses grow, same as people. Just quieter."

Elias looked up at the dark windows of the Inn. "It's breathing easier," he said. "Like it's finally exhaling."

Jacob smiled faintly. "Maybe because you are."

Inside, later, Elias wiped down the counters one last time. The air smelled of citrus and clean wood. Through the open door, he could hear the faint murmur of Taylor Swift's "Daylight" drifting from the stereo in the lounge.

I once believed love would be burning red...

He looked at his reflection in the espresso machine — tired, sun-warmed, content. The kind of face that didn't belong to someone running anymore.

Outside, the chime rang once in the wind.

He whispered, almost without thinking, "Still."

Then he smiled. "Still, by design."

And the Inn, alive and listening, seemed to hum back in agreement.

— ~ —

The Weight of Light

— ~ —

THE MORNING AIR WAS CRISP ENOUGH TO STING, BUT THAT WAS PART of why he loved it. Frisco in early summer was all reflection — light bouncing off the mountains, dew clinging to the porch rail, clouds caught in the lake like memories too soft to let go.

Elias laced up his blue On Clouds, the same pair that had carried him through the slow thaw of spring. The rubber met gravel with a faint crunch, steady and sure. Running wasn't about escape anymore — it was the closest thing he had to prayer. Each stride loosened something inside him; each breath was a reminder that he could still move forward, still choose what to carry.

The ring on his right hand — a mine cut diamond signet, smooth with time — flashed briefly as he reached down to tighten his laces. It was heavy in all the right ways. One hand made for motion, the other for memory.

He started up the hill behind the Inn, where the air thinned and the town opened beneath him — rooftops like scattered postcards, Mount Royal still crowned in light frost. The rhythm came easily now: inhale, exhale, step, release. The kind of motion that makes you remember you're alive.

By the time he returned, sweat dampened his collar, and the world smelled of wet pine and espresso drifting from the kitchen. The front windows glowed amber. Alyssa was refilling pastry stands; August was lecturing the espresso machine like it could hear him.

Jacob leaned against the counter, holding two mugs. "You ran," he said.

Elias smiled, breath still shallow. "Habit."

"Or faith," Jacob offered.

Elias laughed softly. "Same thing these days."

Jacob's gaze dropped briefly to the ring. "You still wear that old thing?"

"It fits now," Elias said simply.

Jacob smiled — slow, knowing. "So do you."

Outside, the clouds moved fast across the ridge, blue on blue. The shoes waited by the door, mud-splashed and honest. The ring caught the light one more time before Elias took it off to wash his hands.

There was something poetic in that — movement and stillness, both belonging to him.

Morning, In Motion

H E LACED HIS BLUE ON CLOUDS ON THE PORCH, THE BOARDS COOL under his arches. Breath in four, out four. The sky was a pale wash, the kind that promised heat later but offered hush now. He tugged once at the laces, and the mine-cut diamond signet on his right hand flashed—small dawn caught in old stone. Motion and memory. Both his.

He set off toward the lake.

Frisco breathed with him—sprinklers ticking behind picket fences, a raven scolding from the power line, the bakery's first sweetness spilling into the street. The shoes found their rhythm fast: thup, thup, thup, each stride a quiet zeroing-out. He took the hill by the school, felt the soft pull in his calves, lengthened into it. The air tasted like pine and thawed earth. He listened for the noise that used to crowd this hour and didn't find it. Only a clear metronome of breath.

At the switchback, he glanced over town. The Inn's roofline cut a clean shape against the pale blue, porch chime motionless, windows holding the first light like a blessing not yet spoken. He smiled without meaning to and ran on.

By the creek, the melt water stitched silver through willows. He hopped the narrow board, let a bead of cold flick up his ankle, welcomed it. A cyclist nodded; a dog tugged its sleepy owner; the mountain shouldered sky like it had all the time in the world. He counted thirty strides easy, ten strong, twenty easy, ten strong—then stopped counting. The day had its own count.

When he turned back, the wind lifted just enough to make his shirt cling and cool. He slowed at the corner of Galena, wiped a thumb under his eye, and felt the gritty salt of work well done. His chest thrummed, but the thrum was clean. He touched the ring, a quick tap against his knuckle. "Still," he said, not to anyone, and crossed the street.

The Inn welcomed him with the warm, living smell he trusted—cedar polish, brown sugar, house roast already ground. He toed off the On Clouds at the mat and stood for a second in socked feet to feel the cool of the slate. The lobby held the blue of early light; dust curled lazy in it.

"Athlete," Alyssa called from the kitchen, voice bright, metal bowls chiming. "Did you outrun your thoughts or just ask them to walk beside you nicely?"

"Second one," he said, heading for the sink. He slid the signet free, set it on the sill, and let cold water run over his wrists until the pulse in them slowed. The mirror offered a flushed face and clear eyes. He approved of both.

August appeared with a dish towel flung over one shoulder and the solemn expression he reserved for sticky bun glaze. "We made it to morning again," he said. "Heroic work, team."

"Speak for yourself," Alyssa said, swiping flour off her cheek. "Some of us are making art."

Elias dried his hands, slipped the ring back on. "Coffee?" he asked, already tamping.

"Language," August said, and folded himself into his preferred chair with the morning paper.

The first pull sang like it always did—hiss, bloom, ribbon of dark with a tiger-striped crema crowning it. The sound settled into his bones, a familiar chord. He poured an americano for himself—half cinnamon, half cream—set two espressos at August's elbow without asking, and slid a mug across to Alyssa. She drank without looking, eyes closed in theatrical gratitude.

From upstairs, a door clicked. Footsteps, hushed and hopeful. The day began to populate.

He carried his cup toward the front, checked the porch plants—lavender thriving, thyme shy—and propped the door so the coolness could wander in. The playlist whispered awake: Ruel's "Free Time," then a hush, then the soft synth of LANY's "Malibu Nights" like someone remembering without permission. He turned it down to the volume that asked you to lean in.

"Good morning," said a voice from the stairs. The Traveler—back again—hair damp, notebook under their arm. They lingered on the landing as if gauging the angle of light.

"It's a good one," Elias said. "You want the corner by the window?"

"That's where the day tells me the truth," they said, and smiled.

He set a cup there with a small plate and a napkin folded into an off-hand tulip. On the way back, he adjusted a frame that had tilted overnight, centered the bowl of lemons, wiped a crescent from the marble that wasn't there.

Jacob arrived with trail dust at his cuffs and air in his grin. He stopped in the doorway, eyes finding Elias like they had a map no one else could read.

"You were out early," Jacob said.

"Had to remind my legs we're friends," Elias replied.

Jacob's gaze flicked to the ring. "We're all fitting better these days."

"Seems so," Elias said, and set an americano to cool beside him.

By eight, the murmurs stacked gently: a couple murmuring over maps, a kid counting blueberries into a bowl with exaggerated precision, someone laughing softly at a page from The Alchemist left open on the library arm. Alyssa ferried lemon scones and quiet jokes; August refolded the paper into improbable geometries and offered two-sentence philosophies to anyone brave enough to ask.

Julian appeared last, hair wind-mussed, sketchbook under his arm. He paused in the doorway, squinted as if the room were too bright, then crossed to the counter.

"How's your morning?" Elias asked.

"Arrived in pieces," Julian said, "then found rhythm here." He tapped the espresso machine. "You conducting?"

"Just keeping time," Elias said, handing him a macchiato. "The house writes the melody."

Julian's smile was all edge softened. "Then I'm just drawing the notes."

The Inn thickened into itself. Small kindnesses passed— chairs pulled, doors held, new pours offered with a nod. Elias moved through it with the littlest corrections that kept it all humming: a napkin before the need, a hand to steady a wobbly table, a pitcher swapped before it ran dry. When he felt the old lift of wanting to do too much, he breathed, let the moment meet him halfway, and did only what belonged to him.

By nine, sunlight had picked up warmth and hazard. It flooded the counter, turned the spoons into slender mirrors, caught the diamond's facet and scattered a bright fleck onto Jacob's cheek. Jacob blinked at the surprise and left it there on purpose.

"Your ring's flirting with me," he said.

"It has excellent taste," Alyssa called, passing with a tray.

They all laughed, the kind that releases rather than binds. Elias wiped his hands on a linen towel that had once been part of a tablecloth, repurposed and appreciated. He loved how the place carried its own afterlives—the piano with one honest sour note, the chandelier that hummed a little when the mountain wind pressed its palm to the windows. Perfection had never helped anyone feel welcome. Honesty had.

He carried pastries to 205—anniversary, a note in his ledger, a habit in his heart. At the door he knocked softly, congratulated softly, left two flutes that would hold sparkling cider, not wine—no alcohol for him, none for the room if his hands were on the tray. He tucked in a sprig of rosemary because ritual could smell like something, too.

On the way back down, he paused at the landing and listened. The house made its layered choir: water through pipes like a muted drumroll, a page turning, silverware chiming, the low confidence of August humming a melody older than the piano. Under it, the faintest scuff of Julian's pencil. And through all of it, the creek, steady and indifferent, stitching sound to sound.

He returned to the bar, pulled three shots in a row without looking, muscle memory singing. Jacob took one without asking. Julian took the second, held the cup like it contained weather. Elias let the third ride to a long, soft pour and cut it clean.

"Tell me," August said, materializing as if the line had summoned him. "What did this morning give you that you didn't ask for?"

Elias looked past him to the window, where the day had taken on a color he couldn't name. He thought of the shoes drying by the mat, the ring's quick bright, the runner who waved, the child's methodical blueberry mathematics, the page of The Alchemist whispering its old certainty to a new set of ears.

"Permission," he said.

August nodded as if he'd been waiting all morning for that word. "Use it well."

By ten, the room tilted toward its daylit ease. He refilled creams, relabeled jars in the boutique with handwriting that had finally learned to trust its own loops, and slid two mini-cards into the brass clip on the desk. Still, by design. On the second, smaller: Pay attention; that's the prayer.

The bell over the door chimed. Two hikers came in with cheeks wind-clean, eyes bright, boots dusted. Elias set water on the counter before they spoke and another plate between them for sharing because it always went that way. One pointed at the sign above the espresso machine.

"What's that mean?" she asked.

August answered from a chair he hadn't been sitting in a second ago. "It means we believe small things can save a day."

Elias watched the words land. He didn't need to add anything. He simply adjusted the flame under the kettle, shifted a candle one inch, and felt the whole room balance around the smallest change.

His heart—stubborn, practiced—kept impeccable time. Not racing. Not lagging. Present. He caught Jacob's look and held it for two beats longer than habit, then let it go without losing anything. He caught Julian's half-smile and returned only the part of it that belonged to this hour. He glanced up the stairs where the Traveler had left their notebook open to a line he could not read from here and decided it was better that way.

At the sink, he washed his hands again, cool water, quick rinse, a habit that honored every task by beginning and ending clean. The ring shone wet then dried; he turned it once with his thumb and felt the weight say stay.

He lifted his cup, now only warm, and finished the last swallow. Cinnamon, cream, the good dark underneath.

"Alright," he said, to no one in particular and to everyone. "Let's open the next breath."

And the Inn—obliging, grateful—did.

The Space Between Notes

T HE INN WAS WIDE AWAKE BY NOON. THE SCENT OF ROASTED COFFEE beans and sugared almonds curled through the hallway like music, catching in the sunbeams that pooled across the floors. Elias had just finished labeling a row of new items for the boutique—hand-poured candles, linen sachets, jars of mountain honey that caught the light like amber.

He liked the rhythm of it: the scratch of pen on paper, the tiny clink as the glass lids met the jars, the murmurs of guests wandering through the shop with soft voices and slower feet.

It was the kind of afternoon that lived between moments. The kind where the world didn't ask for anything.

From the open door, he could hear August talking with a couple who had just checked in. Alyssa was restocking soaps near the spa staircase, humming something low and bright—Ruel's "Suburbs." Elias smiled at the sound.

He loved how music carried through the Inn like water through stone—quiet but persistent.

He turned to hang a sign on the shelf, and through the reflection in the glass, he saw someone standing in the doorway. Not a guest he recognized.

A stranger—tall, mid-thirties maybe, wind-flushed from travel. He had that look mountain people often wore: part exhaustion, part awe. A canvas bag slung over his shoulder, eyes scanning the space like he wasn't sure whether he'd arrived or stumbled into something private.

"Welcome," Elias said, the word easy, practiced. "You've found us."

The man smiled, hesitant. "I hope so. I was told there's a room—if not for tonight, then soon. I'm not great at planning."

Elias tilted his head. "Then you're in good company."

The man laughed, a quiet, honest sound. He stepped closer, taking in the shelves, the soft light, the framed sketches on the wall. "This place... it's not what I expected."

"It rarely is," Elias said. "That's the point."

Their eyes met then—one of those split-second things that don't ask permission. Elias felt something shift, subtle but certain. Not longing exactly. More like recognition.

"Let me see what I can find," Elias said, reaching for the ledger. His fingers brushed the spine of the old book, and for a moment, he thought of Jacob.

Jacob, who hadn't called since Aspen. Jacob, whose absence had settled into the Inn like a silence that didn't hurt, but didn't heal either.

The stranger's voice brought him back. "Do you always write by hand?"

"Always," Elias said, smiling faintly. "Some things deserve to be remembered slowly."

The Guest Who Stayed Too Quietly

THE MAN'S NAME WAS CALLUM. HE SAID IT SOFTLY, LIKE IT WAS something borrowed.

He arrived with only one bag and a look that said he'd been walking longer than planned. Elias noticed that first — the red of his knuckles, the fine dust along the hem of his jeans, the way his breath lingered between sentences, as if still catching up with itself.

"I was driving through," Callum said, setting his bag down carefully, "and then I saw your porch light." "That light saves more people than we'll ever know," Elias said. "Or it finds them," Callum offered.

Elias wrote his name into the ledger, looping each letter deliberately. Ink pooled in the grain of the paper. C-a-l-l-u-m. The kind of name that sounded unfinished — waiting for something to follow.

He led him upstairs, past the photographs lining the hall. Snow in one frame, wildflowers in another, faces of guests who'd sent postcards after leaving. Callum paused at one — the Gingerbread House competition, last winter. Elias laughed under his breath. "That was chaos in sugar form." "You won?" "Depends on your definition of winning," Elias said. "Ours collapsed under the weight of ambition. Still tasted good, though."

They stopped outside Room 7. Elias pushed open the door — clean linens, the faintest hint of cedar, the mountain framed by the window like a painting that changed hourly. "This'll do," Callum said, stepping inside. Elias nodded. "It usually does."

For a moment, Callum didn't unpack. He stood at the window, shoulders rising and falling with the altitude. "You ever get used to that view?" Elias leaned against the frame. "You learn to listen to it instead of just looking."

That night, after the last plates had been stacked and August had retreated with his notebook, Elias found himself replaying small things: the way Callum's gaze lingered on the light fixtures, the quiet gratitude when he accepted his key, the absence of any rush to leave.

He made himself a cup of Vietnamese coffee — condensed milk, vanilla, dark roast — and took it to the porch. The wind carried the low hum of Taylor Swift's "Delicate" from the speakers near the door. The song drifted like a confession neither of them had yet made.

He thought about Jacob then. The way they had built something not quite a future, not quite a past. How silence had followed where plans used to be.

Then, a sound — the door behind him creaking open. "Didn't mean to intrude," Callum said. Elias turned, gestured with his cup. "There's no such thing here. Only timing."

Callum sat, not too close. "You run this place?" "I try to let it run me less than I used to." "That sounds like surrender." "It's practice," Elias said.

The porch light flickered once. Somewhere down the street, a train groaned low and faded. Callum's eyes followed the sound until it disappeared. "I used to chase things," he said quietly. "Now I just let them pass." Elias studied him — the way weariness clung like an unbuttoned collar. "Does it help?" "Sometimes," Callum said. "Other times, I miss the noise."

The air shifted — the kind of quiet that means something new is beginning but no one wants to name it yet.

The next morning, Elias woke before dawn. The Inn was still — the same sacred hush that had greeted every day since his return. He went through the ritual: grind, tamp, pour. The smell of coffee spread like memory.

He set two demitasse cups on the counter, out of habit. But this time, when the second one steamed, a voice behind him said, "Smells like forgiveness." Callum stood there, barefoot, hair disheveled, eyes bright from sleep. Elias handed him the cup. "It's house roast." Callum smiled. "You mean penance." Elias chuckled. "Same difference."

They drank in silence, both watching the light edge over Mount Royal.

"You make it look easy," Callum said. "What?" "Belonging."

The words landed heavy, then soft. Elias turned the ring on his finger — the mine-cut diamond catching the new gold of morning. "It's not," he said. "But it's honest."

By noon, the staff had adjusted to the new rhythm without realizing it. August asked Callum to help carry a crate of wine glasses to storage. Alyssa offered him scones that hadn't even cooled. Guests began to nod hello like he was part of the place.

Elias watched all of it — a stranger folding into the rhythm he'd worked so hard to protect — and felt something he couldn't name. Not jealousy. Not threat. Just the tremor that comes when something in you recognizes it's time to change again.

Outside, the mountain held its steady silence. Inside, the Inn exhaled. Still, by design.

CHAPTER SIXTEEN

YOUR HOME, TOO

G

C ALLUM DIDN'T SO MUCH CHECK IN AS SLIP INTO THE HOUSE'S rhythm. By the second morning he was up before most guests, standing near the east windows with a cup Elias had set down without asking. He traced the grain in the oak rail with a thumb like he was reading braille, then watched light climb Mount Royal the way people watch prayer take shape.

"You always catch the first color," he said.

Elias nodded, tamping a fresh puck. "It's when the house chooses its mood."

"What's today?"

"Merciful," Elias said, and let the shot bloom.

Alyssa passed through, ponytail swishing, a sheet pan balanced on one hip. "Stranger," she said, eyeing Callum with mock suspicion, "you look like someone who can lift without complaining."

"I can," Callum said.

"Good," she grinned. "You're family until noon."

He took the heat-proof gloves like ritual items and followed her into the kitchen. The door swung, then stilled. Elias felt the room shift half a degree toward welcome.

August arrived late, in his careful way—blue cardigan, reading glasses, the calm of a man who trusts morning to do its job. He clocked the second cup at the bar, the way the demitasse saucer had been turned slightly—Elias's unspoken invitation.

"Guest, or gravity?" August asked.

"Both," Elias said. "Name's Callum."

"Mm," August hummed. "Word means 'dove.' Or 'column.' Depending which root you choose."

"Which would you choose?" Elias asked.

"We don't choose names," August said, taking his seat. "We grow into their better meanings."

2) The House Learns a New Footstep

By lunch, the Inn had already memorized Callum's cadence —quiet, even, the pause he took before entering a room as if asking the air permission. He browsed the boutique without buying, read the placard under the framed sketch Julian had gifted, and asked if the thyme on the porch needed water. (It did. He watered it twice.)

Julian showed up wind-flushed, sketchbook open to a loose study of the morning—lavender strips of cloud, the Inn rendered as a series of soft edges. He saw Callum through the doorway and offered the patient half-smile he gives strangers who feel more like furniture than threat.

"New?" Julian asked Elias at the bar.

"Passing through," Elias said. "Or that's how it began."

Julian glanced toward the porch. "Some people arrive like commas. Others arrive like ellipses."

"And him?"

"Parenthesis," Julian said, mouth tilting. "He changes how the sentence reads without altering a word."

They stood in companionable quiet as LANY's "you!" threaded the room at low volume. When Julian reached for his macchiato, Elias saw the smudge of graphite along his index finger and thought: belonging is a material you can hold. When Callum re-entered, the music seemed to lean toward him and then recover—like even the song was making room.

3) Small Work, New Hands

The afternoon unfolded in tasks that looked too small to matter and somehow mattered most. Callum re-labeled two jars with a neat, square hand. He volunteered to carry a crate to storage and didn't argue when August said, "Watch the third stair; it tells the truth loud." He sat in the library and finished half a chapter of The Alchemist, underlining twice —"And, when you want something, all the universe conspires in helping you to achieve it." He left the book open for the next person, underline showing, a breadcrumb of witness.

Near three, Alyssa brought out rosemary shortbread, lemon zest bright in the air. "Staff tax," she declared, placing a plate by the espresso machine. Callum reached, then stopped, eyes flicking to Elias.

"Eat," Elias said. "Then tell me if the rosemary's bossy."

"It's polite," Callum answered after the first bite. "It knows the room it's in."

"Look at him," Alyssa said, delighted. "He speaks flavor."

August, without looking up from his paper, added, "He speaks listening."

Elias smiled despite himself. He busied his hands—wipe, align, polish—but his chest carried that faint, unsettled tuning you get when the key signature shifts and your ear hasn't caught up.

4) Run, Return, Repeat

Late afternoon, Elias laced his blue On Clouds and tilted into the thin air toward the lake. The rhythm arrived quick— thup, thup, thup—the kind of gait you get from miles of not giving up. He ran the boardwalk, the creek line, the small rise behind the church where the sky opens like a clean page.

Breath counted itself. The ring tapped once against his knuckle when he tightened lace; sunlight snagged on the old cut and scattered into the weeds. Proof, he thought, that some lights are earned.

On the return he saw them through the lobby glass—Alyssa laughing big, August pretending to scowl, Julian half-turned with pencil raised, Callum listening like a student to a language he already knew. The sight landed somewhere low and tender. Love, he realized, was not a triangle but a room. You kept making more space or you started closing doors.

He stepped inside to the smell of cinnamon and cedar. Someone had queued Ruel's "Face to Face," and the chorus brushed along the ceiling like chalk dust. He peeled off the shoes at the mat, rinsed wrists, turned the ring, found his pulse steady.

"You run to decide," August said, not looking up.

"To remember," Elias answered. "Deciding comes later."

5) A Letter Finds Its Way

The message arrived just after sunset, when the blue hour made the lobby glass a mirror. The iPad blinked—new reservation inquiry—and then another alert from the contact form with a name he'd told himself not to wait for.

Jacob R. Passing back through in two weeks. If the porch light's still there, I'd like to see it. If it's better that I don't, tell me plainly, and I'll understand.

Elias read it twice, once for sense, once for breath. He didn't answer. Not yet. He set the iPad face-down like a too-bright star and went to light the terrace candles, one by one. Flame, wick, breath. The work steadied him.

Alyssa found him with a stack of linen napkins. "News?"

"Weather," he said.

"Storm or clearing?"

"High thin clouds," he said, almost smiling.

She bumped his shoulder with hers. "You don't have to narrate it alone."

"I know."

"Good," she said, then softer, "You're allowed to be chosen, you know. Not just choosing."

He tied the last ribbon around the napkins more slowly than the task required.

6) The Porch, Four Chairs, One Truth

After service, they sat where they always landed: four chairs on the porch, mugs instead of wine, the street a soft river of quiet. Taylor Swift's "Delicate" shimmered out of the speaker low enough to belong to no one. August tapped his cup with a forefinger in lazy time. Alyssa cocooned in a knit throw. Julian's sketchbook stayed closed, as if the evening asked to exist without evidence.

Callum turned his cup once in his hands. "I used to think calm meant nothing was happening," he said. "Now I think it means I can hear what's happening."

"What do you hear?" Elias asked.

"You," Callum said, without flourish. "Deciding whether your peace is portable."

Elias looked down at the ring, the old cut holding porch light like a small moon. "Maybe peace is a language. Some days I'm fluent."

"And some days you stutter," August said, kind. "Both are speech."

Julian finally opened his book and wrote a single line: A room becomes a home when it can hold more than one story at a time.

Alyssa yawned. "Put that on a card and sell ten for twelve."

They laughed, the shared, relieved kind. The chime gave one clear note in a wind that wasn't there.

7) Rooms at Capacity

The next two days showed how quickly a house can adopt a person. Guests greeted Callum by name. He learned the third stair's complaint and the piano key to avoid. He refilled waters without ceremony, held the door for a stroller without performance, and listened to the Traveler read a paragraph aloud like it mattered. In the kitchen, he asked Alyssa where the sugar lived and then remembered.

"Danger," August told Elias in the doorway, half-smiling. "He knows where the sugar lives."

"Do we...?" Elias started, then didn't finish.

"Let it be what it is," August said. "Don't name a weather system before it crosses the ridge."

That afternoon, Julian hung a small, framed sketch by the boutique mirror—ink and wash, the Inn's facade in rain. He titled it, in the smallest hand: House With a Second Heart. No one commented. They didn't need to.

8) The Ask Inside the Silence

At closing, Callum lingered at the counter while Elias dried the last glass. The speaker clicked through to LANY's "If This Is the Last Time," guitar gentle as breath.

"I wasn't planning to stay," Callum said. "But my plans haven't been good to me lately."

"How long do you need?" Elias asked.

"Enough to remember how to be new somewhere."

"We can do that," Elias said. "We do it all the time."

"For everyone else," Callum said. "Will you let it be for you, too?"

The question landed like a weight he recognized and had avoided lifting. Elias set the towel down, looked over Callum's shoulder to the window where the Inn's reflection trembled in the glass and then steadied.

"I'm trying," he said. "Some days that looks like staying. Some days, like letting people arrive."

"Then I'll arrive slowly," Callum said. The smile didn't ask; it promised.

9) Reply

Later—after chairs on tables, lights in their low positions, the house reduced to its essential hum—Elias flipped the iPad over and typed without dragging it out of poetry:

Porch light's on. Come for one night. We'll see how the air sits.

He hovered over send, then didn't. He closed his eyes, found his breath, found the clean space between past and habit, then pressed his thumb to glass. The message went, small and bright in the dark.

He slipped the On Clouds beside the mat and turned the signet once. Motion. Memory. Both his.

The beam over the door clicked, wood answered with a soft settling sound, and the house took the word as instruction.

Chapter: Morning Pages (Before the Storm)

The world was still folded in blue when Elias woke. No sound but the hum of the heater, the steady exhale of the building that had learned to breathe with him. The clock on the nightstand read 4:36 A.M., but he was already halfway into his shoes—On Clouds, worn smooth along the sole. He didn't need light; the path from room to lobby was muscle memory.

Outside, frost whispered against the porch rail. The mountains were outlines, shy of color. The air, sharp as truth.

He started slow, the rhythm of his shoes syncing with his pulse. thup-thup-thup.

Half a mile in, the chatter began—the kind that didn't need another voice.

With everything that I do have... it truly is amazing, the life that I'm starting to build here.

The sentence had come to him before, written in his notebook weeks ago, and it rose now like breath made visible. He smiled through it, chest tight, because believing it took work.

One day, I'll have my little family. Could you imagine having someone like Nathan as their husband?

He winced at the memory—Nathan had been a name he'd scribbled, but what it meant was hope dressed in someone else's clothes. Still, he couldn't shake the picture: sunlight on a porch, laughter from another room, a quiet cup of coffee and no ache in the ribs.

He ran faster, maybe to outrun that vision, maybe to chase it.

The boardwalk curved, ice giving way to packed snow, and the creek beside him sounded like applause. His breath steamed in rhythm with the morning, the mountain watching without judgment.

He would for sure be a good father, a loyal partner. If this is all a daydream life, I don't see how I could ever let that go once I was attached.

A crow lifted from a pine, dark against the half-light, and he thought of Jacob—his almosts and not yets. There was always that single word between them: timing.

Back at the Inn, the sky was beginning to blush gold. He slowed near the porch steps, hands braced on his knees, laughter escaping like a cough.

Inside, he brewed a small pot, the kind that made one perfect cup and no apologies. He journaled as he cooled down, handwriting uneven, still shaking from the run.

I'm thankful for my family, for the ones who love me unconditionally. Maybe I'm lonely—but that's okay. It means I'm ready for something honest.

He stared at the words, letting them sting and soothe. Then, softer, wrote—

Let's make one goal for sure: to be mindful of what I get every day.

He tapped the pen twice, set it aside. Outside, tires crushed fresh gravel.

He didn't turn immediately. Just listened—the car door, the hesitant pause, then footsteps. That rhythm. That weight.

He looked up in time to see the silhouette through the window glass, haloed by dawn. Jacob.

The pen rolled off the desk and hit the floor, but Elias didn't move to catch it.

Some mornings rewrite the day before they even begin, he thought. This might be one of them.

Chapter: The Space Between

Elias didn't move at first. He just watched. The windowpane fogged slightly as he breathed, blurring Jacob into something spectral—half memory, half man. Then, with a slow exhale, he straightened his shoulders, brushed a hand through his damp hair, and opened the door.

Cold air swept in, scented with pine and the faint smoke of someone's fireplace down the street. Jacob stood there with his duffel bag slung over one shoulder, a hesitant smile tugging at his mouth. His eyes—still that soft, sunlit brown—met Elias's for the first time in months.

"Morning," Jacob said quietly.

It wasn't enough. It was everything.

Elias nodded, voice catching somewhere behind his sternum. "Morning. You—you're early."

Jacob glanced toward the mountains as if they might answer for him. "Didn't sleep much. Figured I'd just drive."

The silence after was gentle, but not comfortable. The kind of silence you step around.

Inside, the Inn was glowing awake: cinnamon-scented air drifting from the kitchen, the hum of the espresso machine. A vase of tulips Alyssa had arranged last night leaned toward the sunlight, petals half-open as if eavesdropping.

"Come in," Elias said finally. "You look cold."

Jacob stepped over the threshold, boots leaving a faint print of melted snow. His gaze traveled across the lobby—the bookshelf corner with Plato's Republic splayed open on a side table, the fire that hadn't quite caught yet. Everything familiar, yet rearranged by time.

"This place still smells the same," Jacob murmured. "Coffee and something... like cedar and soap."

Elias smiled. "I like to think it's the smell of trying again."

Jacob laughed—softly, almost gratefully. "Still poetic."

That laugh landed somewhere deep. It reminded Elias of why he'd once memorized the sound.

They stood near the reception desk, words orbiting but not landing. The espresso machine hissed again. Finally, Elias broke first.

"You want a cup?"

Jacob nodded. "Please."

He busied himself with the coffee, hands steady but heart a riot. Jacob moved closer, standing just beside him now, their reflections caught in the chrome of the machine—two men looking like they'd aged differently from the same year.

Elias handed him the mug. Jacob's fingers brushed his—briefly, deliberately.

"I wasn't sure you'd still be here," Jacob said.

"I wasn't sure you'd come back."

Silence. Then the faintest smile from Jacob.

"Guess we're both full of surprises."

The front door chimed—August, in his worn fleece and knit cap, stepped in carrying a box of pastries. He froze for half a beat, sensing the weight in the room.

"Morning, gents," he said, breaking the spell with practiced ease. "Looks like I walked into a Hallmark reunion."

Elias shot him a glare, but Jacob laughed—real laughter this time. The kind that made the air warmer.

August winked at Elias. "I'll put these in the kitchen. Don't mind me."

When he was gone, Jacob leaned against the counter, sipping his coffee. "I missed this place," he said. Then, quieter, "I missed you."

Elias didn't respond right away. He let the sentence hang, suspended like the morning light on steam. His throat ached from the effort of calm.

"Let's see if the Inn still feels the same after a few days," he said finally. Jacob smiled knowingly. "Fair enough."

Outside, the snow began to fall again—light, almost invisible, but steady. Elias felt it: that strange, beautiful ache of something thawing too soon.

G

CHAPTER SEVENTEEN

SMALL THINGS THAT STAY

G

BY LATE MORNING, THE INN HAD SETTLED INTO ITS GENTLE RHYTHM — cups clinking, floorboards sighing, the faint whisper of someone's laughter from the breakfast nook. Sunlight spilled through the front windows and laid itself over the wooden banister like it belonged there.

Jacob had taken a room upstairs, one of the corner suites overlooking Mount Royal. Elias had offered the key without comment, though his pulse tripped when their fingers brushed again.

Now, as Elias moved through the lobby — straightening a stack of local brochures, refolding a throw on the couch — the quiet felt alive. The kind of quiet that listens.

The espresso machine hissed in the background, filling the room with the scent of cinnamon and cream. From the kitchen came the soft percussion of Alyssa's playlist — Ruel this morning, "Growing Up Is_____" fading into "Face to Face." She was humming along, off-key and perfect.

He smiled. Alyssa brought her own rhythm to the place. It was in the way she arranged tulips to face the window, or how she left hand-written notes for guests — "Remember: everything feels better after tea."

From the stairwell, Jacob's footsteps came slow. Careful. He'd changed — the kind of change time forces on you when life's quiet enough to make you look at yourself. His hair was a little shorter, his smile slower to appear. He paused halfway down, fingers tracing the old wooden railing.

"You refinished this," he said.

Elias glanced up. "Last spring. I couldn't stand how dry it looked."

Jacob smiled faintly. "Still can't leave anything half-finished."

Elias shrugged. "Some things deserve to be kept."

The words landed between them, soft and deliberate. Jacob didn't reply, just nodded and continued down.

They passed through the lounge — Plato's Corner, as guests had started calling it — where morning light caught the dust motes midair. A half-read copy of The Alchemist rested on the armchair, open to the same page as months ago. Someone had underlined: "When you possess great treasures within you, and try to tell others of them, seldom are you believed."

Jacob stopped, thumb brushing the line. "You still read this?"

"Guests do," Elias said. "I just make sure it stays where it belongs."

Jacob chuckled. "Still sounds like you."

From the kitchen, the smell of orange zest and baked scones drifted in. The laughter grew louder — Alyssa teasing August about his ancient sweater again. A door closed softly upstairs. The Inn moved with its small, lovely life.

Jacob turned toward the windows, where snow had begun to fall again — tiny flurries swirling like memory.

"It feels smaller," he said after a moment. "Not in a bad way. Just... cozier. Like the world outside stopped running and you didn't."

Elias followed his gaze. "It's not smaller," he said quietly. "I just stopped needing it to be bigger."

For a while, they stood in silence, the kind that meant something. The fire crackled faintly. The espresso machine clicked off. Somewhere, a guest laughed down the hall.

Jacob finally broke the quiet. "You've built something good here, Elias."

He looked down at his hands — the faint coffee stains on his knuckles, the soft tremor of fatigue that never really left. "Yeah," he said. "I think I finally did."

A gust of wind rattled the glass, scattering the snow in sudden, frantic spirals. Jacob reached instinctively to steady the window latch — and Elias's hand went with his.

For a heartbeat, neither moved. Just the hum of the heater, the whisper of snow, and the weight of everything unspoken.

Then, a knock on the side door — August again, interrupting fate with impeccable timing.

"Hey boss," he called, half-grinning as he pushed through with a crate of coffee beans. "We're running low on the dark roast. You wanna do the order, or should I?"

Elias exhaled, stepping back. "I'll take care of it."

Jacob smiled into his cup, hiding the flicker of something in his eyes. "I'll, uh... grab my bag," he said softly, retreating toward the stairs.

Elias nodded. "Breakfast's still warm if you're hungry."

He didn't look back until the footsteps faded.

Outside, the snow thickened. Inside, the Inn breathed, alive with its quiet, beautiful chaos. And for the first time in months, Elias didn't feel like he was waiting for anything. He was already inside it — the life he was building, one small sacred detail at a time.

CHAPTER EIGHTEEN

EVENING LIGHT AT GALENA

———

G

B Y SIX O'CLOCK, THE INN HAD TURNED GOLDEN. THE LAST OF THE daylight pressed through the dining-room windows, scattering itself across the wood floors and the framed black-and-white photos of Frisco winters long past. The kitchen carried the smell of rosemary, butter, and something sweet that Alyssa refused to name until it was plated.

Elias stood by the counter, rolling the sleeves of his chambray shirt, watching steam curl from the kettle. Outside, snow fell steady now—thick enough to blur the streetlamps, soft enough to quiet the town.

Jacob appeared again, fresh from a shower, hair damp, sweater clean, eyes brighter. He hesitated in the doorway like someone walking back into a dream they weren't sure they still belonged to.

"Smells incredible," he said.

"It's Alyssa," Elias replied, nodding toward the kitchen. "She's in her culinary-witch era."

"Am not!" came Alyssa's voice from behind the stove. "I'm just following vibes."

She appeared with a grin, cheeks flushed from the heat. "You must be Jacob."

Jacob smiled. "Guilty."

"Thought so. You've been mentioned."

Elias shot her a look that said careful. Alyssa only smirked. "Dinner's ready. Hope you like lemon risotto and roasted vegetables."

They gathered around the small pine table near the windows. A candle flickered in the center—one of those locally made soy blends that smelled faintly of spruce and vanilla. Plates clinked, forks touched ceramic, and for a while the only sound was the comfortable rhythm of eating.

Alyssa talked about the couple in Room Four who'd gotten engaged that afternoon, about August's failed attempt at fixing the back-door latch, about the snow forecast. She was a master of keeping conversation moving just enough to disguise what everyone wasn't saying.

At one point, Jacob looked up at Elias and said quietly, "You really did it. You made this place into something alive."

Elias took a sip of water, buying time. "It was already alive," he said. "I just stopped running from it."

Jacob smiled—small, proud, almost tender. "Still poetic," he murmured, and Alyssa's knowing glance caught the flicker that passed between them.

When dessert came—something citrus and warm—Alyssa excused herself with a grin. "I'll check on Room Two. You two can handle dishes."

Elias rolled his eyes. "Subtle."

She winked. "Always."

The kitchen fell quiet once she left. Snow tapped the windowpanes. The candle flame leaned and recovered.

Jacob rinsed plates at the sink while Elias dried them, a quiet choreography that felt both foreign and familiar. The hum of the dishwasher filled the pauses.

"I forgot how peaceful this place feels," Jacob said after a while.

"It's deceptive," Elias replied. "By morning, it's chaos again. Coffee, check-ins, lost mittens..."

"I like that kind of chaos."

Elias looked at him. "You always did."

Jacob turned off the tap. "Elias..."

The word hung there—unfinished, trembling.

Elias waited.

Jacob shook his head and smiled instead. "Never mind. I'm just glad to be here."

Elias nodded slowly. "Me too."

The room stilled, save for the snow outside. In that moment, there was no past tense, no unsaid apology—just two people standing in a kitchen, surrounded by warmth and the faint smell of lemon and coffee.

Upstairs, a floorboard creaked. Somewhere, the fire crackled back to life.

And for the first time in a long while, Elias didn't feel like he was waiting for closure. He was standing right in the middle of something beginning.

The Weight of Quiet

J ACOB LAY AWAKE LISTENING TO THE INN BREATHE.
The old radiator hummed in the corner like a memory trying to finish its thought. Downstairs, a log shifted in the fireplace; the faint scent of cedar drifted through the air vents. He could hear the mountain wind moving against the windows, gentle but insistent—the same rhythm that had filled this valley long before he ever knew Elias.

He turned onto his side. The lamp on the nightstand cast a soft pool of amber over the room—old pine paneling, a single framed photo of Lake Dillon in summer, the corner chair draped with an extra blanket. The kind of room that asked nothing of you but presence.

His duffel sat half-unpacked on the floor. A pair of running shoes. A worn copy of Letters to a Young Poet. A folded map of trails he hadn't hiked in years. He reached for the book, thumbed through it until a line caught him: "Perhaps everything terrible is in its deepest being something helpless that wants help from us."

He closed it again, exhaling. That line used to feel like an answer. Tonight it just felt like truth.

He hadn't planned on coming back—not really. The drive had been impulsive, the kind of decision you only recognize as necessary once you're already halfway through the canyon. He told himself he just needed air, a pause, a weekend. But he knew better.

Elias's voice still lived somewhere in his head, the way certain songs do—unexpected, familiar, impossible to ignore.

He sat up, pulled the blanket tighter around his shoulders, and stared at the faint glow under the door. Somewhere below, a light was still on. Elias never slept early; he said nights were when the Inn felt most honest.

Jacob smiled faintly at the thought.

He swung his legs over the side of the bed, bare feet brushing the cool wood floor, and padded toward the window. Outside, snow blurred the street into watercolor. The lamppost across the way threw long shadows over the porch railing, the icicles gleaming like tiny glass prayers.

He pressed his palm to the cold glass—same gesture Elias used to make. It felt like touch, like memory.

A laugh drifted faintly from downstairs—August's, probably, carrying through the vents—and Jacob felt the old ache of belonging press against his ribs.

He'd left for good reasons once. They all felt smaller now.

There were things he wanted to say, things he'd rehearsed on the drive up, but language had never quite been enough for them. Elias understood things better through motion—the way he folded napkins, the care he gave a coffee cup, the pause before he spoke. Jacob had loved that. Still did.

He sat back on the bed, listening to the creak of the Inn settling into night. Every sound had its place here—the plumbing sigh, the whisper of snow, the heartbeat of something steady beneath it all.

"Still poetic," he murmured to the empty room, smiling at his own words.

He turned off the lamp, letting the dark fold over him.

Below, a single light still burned in the lobby—soft, gold, waiting.

CHAPTER NINETEEN

THE HOURS THAT STAY AWAKE

———

G

THE FIRE HAD BURNED LOW, JUST EMBERS NOW — ORANGE, PULSING, breathing like something alive. Elias sat in the leather chair by the hearth, journal open on his knees, pen paused mid-sentence. The page glowed faintly in the lamplight, words slanting where his hand had grown tired.

Outside, snow kept falling — a slow, silent theater. The glass panes shimmered faintly from the wind. He could smell cinnamon still, clinging to his sleeves from dinner, and the faint trace of cedar smoke that seemed to live in everything here.

The Inn was quiet except for the hum of the heater and the soft crack of settling wood. He liked this time — when the house exhaled, when even its ghosts seemed to rest.

He wrote: I am learning how to stay.

The words looked fragile on the page, as if they might melt under the weight of their own truth. He stared at them for a long time.

He thought of Jacob's laugh at dinner, of the way Alyssa had hidden her grin behind her mug, of how August had left a note on the kitchen counter before bed: "You deserve rest, boss. Don't out-think the stars."

Elias smiled at that. He rarely took advice, but the note felt like permission.

Upstairs, a floorboard creaked. Softly. Then quiet again. He looked up, instinctively. He didn't need to see to know who it was.

He imagined Jacob awake — the sound of him turning a page, the shadow moving against lamplight, maybe the same restless ache that was keeping him here too.

He turned back to his journal and wrote: The Inn listens. It holds what we can't say out loud. Maybe that's what I've been doing too — listening for what's still alive.

He leaned back in the chair, closing his eyes for a moment. The hum of the refrigerator. The ticking of the old clock near the desk. The low groan of the wind pushing against the eaves.

Everything had a pulse tonight.

When he opened his eyes again, the reflection in the front window caught him off guard — his own face softened by the glow, the mountains barely visible beyond the snow. He lifted his mug, still half-full of cooling coffee, and whispered, "You're still here."

The words weren't for anyone in particular. Maybe for himself. Maybe for the man upstairs.

He closed the journal, set the pen inside the crease, and stood. The fire crackled weakly, asking to be tended. He added a log, then another, and watched the sparks lift, orange and gold, disappearing into the chimney.

The air felt warmer now. Alive.

He turned off the lamp, letting the fire's glow take over, and stood there for a while — listening, breathing, belonging.

The Quiet Between

T HERE ARE HOURS THAT NEVER FULLY BELONG TO NIGHT OR DAY. They hover — a breath caught between one truth and the next.

In those hours, the Inn becomes something else. The hum of the baseboards sounds like a heartbeat. The walls remember the weight of laughter. The floorboards creak as if to say: You're not alone.

Elias feels it all. He walks the corridors barefoot, careful not to wake anyone, fingertips tracing the banister polished by a hundred other hands. The air smells of ash and lavender, of something half-finished and sacred.

He doesn't think of time here. He thinks in sensations — warmth, breath, the way the world exhales when it's finally unobserved.

He passes the front windows. The snow outside glows pale blue beneath the streetlamps, a dream laid out like linen. For a moment, he presses his palm to the glass again — the same way he did that morning, the same way Jacob might be doing now upstairs — and he feels the mountain pulse beneath his skin.

There's a rhythm to belonging, he realizes. It doesn't start loud. It hums. Quiet. Patient. It builds like light creeping through the seam of a door.

He returns to the chair, opens his journal once more, and writes without thinking:

The miracle was never the mountain. It was waking up and wanting to stay.

He underlines stay. The ink catches in the paper grain.

Outside, a snowplow moves down Galena with its slow, steady roar, clearing what has fallen, making space for what comes next.

Elias smiles faintly. Sometimes healing looks like that — not grand, just consistent.

He closes the journal and lets the room breathe. The fire shifts. The first birds stir. Somewhere above, a door opens quietly — soft footsteps crossing a floor.

Morning is coming. And for once, he doesn't dread it.

CHAPTER TWENTY

MORNING LIGHT

G

THE FIRST COLOR WAS GOLD.

It slid over Mount Royal and broke across the Inn's front windows, turning the dust in the lobby into slow-moving constellations. Elias stood behind the counter with two cups already warm in his hands—one for him, one set just to the right, the way habit and hope had taught him.

He'd ground the beans finer this morning. He wasn't sure why. Maybe clarity wanted a tighter pull.

Footsteps on the stairs—unhurried, careful. Jacob's shadow arrived on the wall before he did, long and soft across the framed photos. He paused at the newel post, palm brushing the worn groove that a hundred travelers had made without meaning to.

"Morning," Jacob said.

"Morning," Elias answered, and pushed the second cup forward. "House roast. Cinnamon. Cream."

Jacob smiled with his eyes first. "You remembered."

"I write things down."

"You always did," Jacob said, and took the first sip like you take good news—slow, grateful, a little surprised it's true.

The Inn's sounds gathered around them: the whisper of the heater's exhale, the faint rattle of the side door, Alyssa humming two rooms away, already in motion. Outside, a shovel skated along the walk. The porch chime gave one clear note and fell still.

They stood there a moment without filling the quiet. It didn't ask them to.

"How was your night?" Elias asked.

"I listened to the house breathe," Jacob said. "It's louder than I remember."

"It's steadier," Elias said, and then, gently, "So am I."

Jacob glanced at the small ledger open on the desk. "You still do this by hand?"

"Some things deserve to be remembered slowly," Elias said, and because honesty had to start somewhere, added: "I didn't know if you'd come."

"I didn't know if you wanted me to," Jacob said, thumb circling the rim of his cup once. "I said I'd understand either way."

"I know," Elias said. "I read it twice."

They both let that hang. Truth doesn't like to be rushed.

From the kitchen, Alyssa called, "If you two are going to have a second-chance montage, at least let me put scones in the shot."

Jacob laughed. Elias didn't try not to.

She swept in with a tray—lemon and rosemary, sugar catching the light—as August followed, carrying a bowl of winter fruit like an offering.

"Peace in the middle," August said, setting it down between them without comment, eyes taking their measure and moving on. "Congratulations on the weather."

"What's the forecast?" Jacob asked, playing along.

"High thin clouds," August said. "Good for decisions."

Alyssa slid napkins across the counter. "He means: don't say too much before the second cup."

Elias cut a scone, steam rising like a small proof of warmth. Jacob took half, fingers grazing Elias's—a brief static, an old code.

"I'm not here to make a mess," Jacob said softly.

"This place can hold more than one story," Elias answered. "It was built for it."

A silence settled, lighter now. The song on the speaker shifted—LANY's "you!" at a mercy-volume, the melody so gentle you had to lean toward it to catch the words. Sunlight climbed the banister. The floorboards gave their honest sigh.

Elias's blue On Clouds waited by the door, flecked with yesterday's salt. On his right hand, the mine-cut diamond signet turned once in the morning light and threw a bright, brief fleck onto Jacob's sweater. Jacob didn't brush it away.

"What do you need today?" Elias asked, not as a host but as himself.

Jacob met his eyes. "A walk. A room that's allowed to be quiet. A chance to be useful, if you'll let me."

Elias nodded. "Dish rack's to the left. Third stair tells the truth loud. The thyme on the porch needs water twice."

"Twice," Jacob repeated, as if committing a vow.

Alyssa leaned an elbow on the counter, smiling like the sun had just been upgraded. "I'm taking that as a yes, then."

"It's a yes to today," Elias said. "We'll let tomorrow ask its own question."

August lifted the bowl, made space for the ledger, and tapped the page with a forefinger. "Write down what you're keeping," he said. "Even if it's only a sentence."

Jacob looked at Elias. Elias uncapped the pen, wrote one line, and did not hide it.

Still, by design.

The bell over the door chimed; two guests stepped in, cheeks bright with cold, the kind of joy that makes a room larger. Elias moved to greet them, Jacob to hold the door. Alyssa disappeared into the kitchen, already singing something from Ruel. August pretended to scowl and failed.

The day opened like a window.

Elias felt it—how the Inn absorbed change and stayed itself, how his breath matched the building's, how everything important could be both fragile and certain in the same light.

"Ready?" Jacob asked, low, beside him.

"For the next breath," Elias said.

They took it together.

CHAPTER TWENTY-ONE

THE LIGHT THAT STAYS

———

G

ELIAS AND JACOB WAKE TO THE LATE-SPRING MORNING AT THE INN, the snow nearly gone from the peaks. The town hums below — bikes, wind chimes, laughter from the coffee shop down the street. Inside, Elias tends to the morning fire, the scent of cedar and citrus floating through the hall. Jacob helps Alyssa with guests, August hums an old tune while setting fresh herbs in the windowsills. There's peace — but also the quiet awareness that life, in its rhythm, never stops asking what comes next.

Jacob tells Elias he's thinking of leaving for a short time — a workshop in Oregon, something about restoration and design. Elias listens, nods, not with fear but with the calm of someone who's finally learned how to stay even when someone else must go. The day unfolds with unspoken tenderness: the way their hands meet briefly over the counter, the soft joke August pretends not to hear, the way the Inn seems to breathe differently when they're both in the room.

That night, Elias stands by the window. The mountain glows under moonlight. He whispers, "Still, by design." The house, as always, answers in its quiet way — a single creak, a settling sigh, a reminder that belonging doesn't need to hold tight to endure.

———～———

Notes on Stillness

———～———

T HE NEXT MORNING, BEFORE THE GUESTS STIR, ELIAS FINDS THE notebook Jacob left behind — the one with its spine nearly worn through. Inside, between sketches and unfinished sentences, he finds one page written to him.

Stillness is not silence, Eli. It's the sound of what keeps loving you, even when you forget to listen.

Elias closes the notebook, carries it to the kitchen, and sets it beside the espresso machine. He pulls two cups again out of habit. The crema blooms gold in the early light. A car hums down Galena Street. Somewhere, someone laughs.

The Inn exhales. So does he.

Summer, Later

B Y JULY, THE TOWN SMELLS LIKE RAIN AND WILD MINT. THE INN ON Galena is full again — travelers, families, artists, strangers who will leave a little more known than they arrived. Elias's hair has grown longer, his ring catches the light when he writes in the ledger. Alyssa teases him for humming too much. August's sketches now line the hallway — blueprints turned to memory.

One afternoon, a letter arrives from Oregon. The return address is written in Jacob's unmistakable hand. Elias doesn't open it right away. He sets it on the counter, finishes pouring coffee for a guest, adjusts the flowers near the window. Then he sits, opens the letter slowly.

Inside, one line:

The house you built keeps finding me.

Elias smiles — that quiet, knowing kind of smile. He looks toward the mountain, where the light folds itself across the ridge.

And for the first time, he doesn't wonder what comes next. He just lets the day begin.

G

Galena House

Stories for the spaces we return to.

———

FRISCO, COLORADO

Galena House Publishing is an independent imprint inspired by the Frisco Inn on Galena—an intimate fifteen-room inn at the base of Mount Royal. Our work is rooted in small places, quiet moments, and stories that remember where they came from.